Blood Money

Maureen Carter

D1373158

CREME DE LA CRIME

DEER PARK PUBLIC LIBRARY
44 LAKE AVENUE
DEER PARK, NY 11729

Also by Maureen Carter from Crème de la Crime:

Working Girls

Dead Old

Baby Love

Hard Time *

Bad Press

* also available in unabridged audio

Praise for Maureen Carter's gritty Bev Morriss series:

Many writers would sell their first born for the ability to create such a distinctive voice in a main character.
- Sharon Wheeler, Reviewing the Evidence

… a cracking story that zips along…
- Sarah Rayne, author of *Tower of Silence*

British hard-boiled crime at its best.
- *Deadly Pleasures* Year's Best Mysteries (USA)

… a first-rate book… Carter did an excellent job of showing the pressures… I have ordered the first books in this series!
- Maddy Van Hertbruggen, *I Love a Mystery* Newsletter

Though it's a grim story-line, there is also plenty of humour… The authentic… setting was a bonus, there are few books set in Birmingham
- Karen Meek, Eurocrime

… shows us another side of the hero and encourages us to connect with her on a deeper personal level than ever before.
- David Pitt, Booklist (USA)

… it is good to see a publisher investing in fresh work that, although definitely contemporary in mood and content, falls four-square within the genre's traditions.
- Martin Edwards, author of the highly acclaimed Harry Devlin Mysteries

Crème de la Crime… so far have not put a foot wrong.
- Reviewing the Evidence

First published in 2009
by Crème de la Crime
P O Box 523, Chesterfield, S40 9AT

Copyright © 2009 Maureen Carter

The moral right of Maureen Carter to be identified as the author of
this work has been asserted by her in accordance with the Copyright,
Designs and Patents Act, 1988.

All rights reserved. No part of this publication may be reproduced
or transmitted in any form by any means, electronic or mechanical,
including photocopying, recording or any information storage
and retrieval system, without prior permission in writing from the
publisher nor be otherwise circulated in any form of binding or
cover other than that in which it is published.

*All the characters in this book are fictitious and any resemblance to
actual persons, living or dead, is purely coincidental.*

Typesetting by Yvette Warren
Cover design by Yvette Warren
Front cover image by Peter Roman

ISBN 978-0-9557078-7-2
A CIP catalogue reference for this book is available
from the British Library

Printed and bound in the UK by CPI Cox & Wyman, Reading, Berks

www.cremedelacrime.com

About the author:
Maureen Carter has worked extensively in the media. A journalist and writer, she lives in Birmingham with her family.

www.maureencarter.co.uk

It's a great pleasure and privilege to work with Lynne Patrick and her inspirational and gifted team at Crème de la Crime. Huge thanks to everyone there – as always. I'm grateful, too, for the knowledge and expertise given so generously by Detective Sergeant Chris Elliott and Lead Forensic Manager Robin Slater. Their contribution to *Blood Money* is immense and goes far beyond answering my numerous questions. I thank both for their valuable time and expertise. Any error of interpretation is mine.

Writing – as I've noted before – would be a lonelier place without the support of some special people. For 'being there' even when they're sometimes miles away, my love and affection goes to: Peter Shannon, Veronique Shannon, Corby and Stephen Young, Paula and Charles Morris, Suzanne Lee, Helen and Alan Mackay, Frances Lally, Jane Howell, Henrietta Lockhart, Anne Hamilton and Bridget Wood.

Finally, my thanks to readers everywhere – as always, this is for you.

For Sophie and Dan

1

The woman is a bad sleeper at the best of times. Now it is the dead of night. She's drifting off when she's convinced she hears a faint sound on the landing. Her scalp crawls as she shoots upright, trying to identify the noise. After thirty, forty seconds hearing only her heartbeat, she sinks back under the duvet, chides herself. Without Rod's reassuring presence, it's easy to let the mind play tricks. She hates being a widow, vows to stop watching the news, reading the papers, always full of scare stories.

Then the door inches open.

Rigid with fear, she hardly dares breathe. Silhouetted in the threshold is an intruder, moonlight glinting off what she's sure is a knife in his right hand. She feigns sleep, desperately hopes it's a figment of her imagination, knows the dark figure will still be there when she opens her eyes. Another sound. She strains her ears. Footsteps pad closer. A smell wafts towards her. Lemon? Lime? Not sure.

Grab the phone. Call the police. Thoughts instantly dismissed. Reaching out would be futile. She fights an almost overwhelming urge to scream, to flee. Alone and afraid, she prays. Harder than she's prayed in her life. Sweet Lord, please make him go… sweet Lord…

"Turn over." The whisper is soft in her ear, his minty breath warms her cheek. The sweat feels clammy on her spine. Paralysed with fear, her pathetic whimper escapes involuntarily.

"On your back." It's an order. Barked. Spittle hits her face. "Now."

In slow terrified motion she obeys, then gasps in shock,

confusion. A grinning clown face looms over her, thick scarlet lips silvered by the full moon, shaggy ginger curls either side of a smooth pale pate. Dark eyes glitter through slits in latex.

"Please… don't… hurt me," she pleads. "Take whatever…"

"Shut it." With a gloved hand he switches on the bedside lamp, the other strokes her jaw with the knife. Their glances lock: prey and predator. It's no contest. She has neither will nor means to protect herself let alone counter-attack. Who is he? What does he want? The voice is muffled slightly, but the cadence suggests a young man: twenties, thirties, perhaps. The woman swallows hard; she's old enough to be his grandmother.

The clown's inane grin is fixed as the intruder ogles the contours of her trembling body. Despite her long white nightdress she feels naked, acutely aware how the flimsy cotton flutters in pace with her wildly pumping heart. Her breaths are short, shallow. She cuts a glance to the bedside table, a glass. He reaches for it. "Drink?"

"P… p… please." She parts dry lips, forces a wary smile. Maybe if she talks to him? Makes him see her as a human being? When she struggles to sit up, he flings the water in her face.

"I said don't move, dumb ass. What did I say?"

The tepid liquid runs down her cheeks, drips from her chin, her hair. "Don't m…"

"Including that." He taps the blade against her mouth. She shrinks back. "We do things my way or my way. Get it? Faith?"

Hearing her name from those mocking lips stings like a slap. She stiffens as the implication sinks in. "How…?"

He whacks her face with the back of his hand. "What part of 'shut it' don't you understand?" He hurls the duvet to the floor, hitches up her nightdress with the knife. With the tip of the blade, he strokes her naked breasts, the spread of her belly. She crosses her legs, tries to cover her chest; hot tears cool and pool under her ears. Mind-numbing fear? Would that it were. The woman's only too aware she's at the mercy of a callous thug in her own home. She knows she won't be able to live here after this – assuming she lives.

"Make a sound – you're dead. Clear?" Wide-eyed, she nods. He reaches a hand over his shoulder, and for the first time she notices the rucksack. She watches as he removes four lengths of thin cord which he places beside her, then a small velvet pouch which he slips into his jacket pocket.

Dark eyes still glittering, he flexes theatrical fingers, bounces on the balls of his feet. "Coming, dear… ready or not…" The sing-song taunt's more menacing than the snapped directions. When he straddles her, she loses control of her bladder.

"You should be so lucky," he sneers, shuffles forward, pins her arms with his knees, leers for what seems a lifetime. "'Kay, listen up. This is what's gonna happen." He wants cash and jewellery, keys to drawers and cabinets. If she co-operates he'll leave her in peace. If she doesn't… he thrusts his crotch in her face. Through racking sobs, she tells him what he wants to know.

"Good girl." He pats her head before snatching the rings from her fingers and the crucifix around her neck. He crams these in another pocket before reaching for the first length of cord. She's spread-eagled to the bed where she lies shivering on a urine-soaked sheet.

Prowling the room, he opens cupboards, rifles drawers. She watches as her favourite brooch and earrings are jammed into the rucksack followed by a silver jewellery box where she keeps Rod's watch and cufflinks. She likes to take them out each day; look, touch, remember. Unwittingly perhaps, her glance falls on a gilt-framed photograph on the dressing table. So does the intruder's.

She steels herself as he picks it up. "This the old man, love?" She imagines his sly smirk under the grinning mask. Closing her eyes, she pictures instead her good and gentle husband. The sound of cracking glass startles her. Suspecting what will happen next makes it no easier. Her heart hurts as he tears the wedding photograph, scatters tiny pieces confetti-like across the bed.

"Crap host, aren't you? Where's my drink?" She recoils as he reaches towards her but he only checks the knots. At the door, he lifts a hand. "Nah, don't get up." Sniggering, he sneaks downstairs. Ears strained, she traces his movements as he further invades, infests her home: floorboards creak, door handles click, drawers are yanked open. She imagines him fingering her possessions, thieving anything he can sell, anything he can get a good price for. What he's already taken can't be bought: dignity, confidence, self-esteem.

Slowly she turns her head, gazes out of the picture window where the sallow moon's now skulking behind the oak tree's bare branches. Rod often teased her about not drawing the curtains, but she used to love watching her tiny slice of world go by, the slow changes wrought by the seasons. Now she screws her eyes tight, bites her lip, tastes blood.

Then she feels it again: a tiny spark of defiance. She sensed the first flicker when he ripped the photograph – a needless spiteful act. Tears well but she blinks hard, urges herself to get a grip. White knights charge to the rescue in fairy stories – not a waking nightmare.

"I'll be off now, love." The clown face appears round the

4

door. "Nice seeing you." He touches finger to temple in mock salute, bows out. Faith jerks her hands; the cords bite tighter into her wrists.

"Whoops." Back again, he saunters towards her. "Almost forgot." She watches terrified as he takes the velvet pouch from his pocket, opens the drawstrings, tips the contents into his gloved palm. "Close your eyes, love."

"Please…"

"Close your fucking eyes."

She hears the lamp switch click, feels a sprinkle of sand, dust, something light settle on her eyelids. There's a draught as he leans across, lifts something from the bed. She smells fabric conditioner, knows where from, even before the pillow's placed on her face. Please, God. No! The pulse whooshes in her ears and through her own muffled moans, she hears his final words. "Said I'd leave you in peace, didn't I?"

Though barely conscious, Faith feels the blade's cold steel rake her belly… then all is silent as well as dark.

MONDAY

2

Detective Sergeant Bev Morriss opened one strikingly blue eye and glanced warily round before snapping it shut and stifling a groan. Next to this, death warmed up would feel good. The quick scan had registered empty wine bottles, overflowing ashtrays, foil tins with lurid leftovers from an Indian takeaway and twin trails of cast off clothes that ended at the bed. Big question: whose bed? She'd need to open the other eye to answer that. And remember the guy's name.

Gingerly turning her throbbing head, she took a peek at the naked bloke snoring slack-jawed gently beside her: blue-black hair, Jagger lips, long eyelashes. Rick, was it? Dick? Mick? Whatever. Nose wrinkled, she peered closer. Last night's healthy tan now held a tell-tale pale streak or two, and a saliva trail weaved through dark stubble. This time Bev's groan escaped. She closed her eyes, breathed deeply to try to quell the gut-wrenching nausea. Not that it was entirely down to lover boy.

To be fair, when she'd spotted him in the pub he'd fitted the bill OK. Unintended pun. Mental eye roll. Then she cast her mind back to the crowded bar. As per, she'd not revealed the Fighting Cocks was her local, or told him her real name. Who'd she been this time? Laura? Lorna? Something beginning with L. No matter. She'd come on to him because he was fit, well fancy-able and she could give him a good ten years. More to the point, there wasn't a string or ring in sight. These days she didn't do relationships, lost enough already; close was a no-go area. If tempted down that path again she'd buy a budgie. And staple its beak.

As for last night, they'd both known the score, and the condom on the shag pile indicated the result. Dead funny, Bev. Not. Come to think of it, hadn't he asked to see her again? Or was that a dream? Hard to tell after a vat of Pinot. Either way, it wasn't going to happen. Emotional baggage? She had more than Relate.

Her sigh lifted a Guinness-coloured fringe; her heart took its well-worn sinking path. Last night had just been another escape bid. Away from the flashbacks of the stabbing that killed her unborn twins, away from nightmare images of the bitch responsible, the so-called Black Widow. Away from herself? You bet. The casual sex and copious booze was meant to blunt edges. So how come reality always kicked in even before the hangover got a grip? Five months she'd tried blanking it all out – and nothing worked.

Work! Shit. Daylight through curtain. It was past late-o'clock. The mother of all bollockings beckoned. Swallowing a Balti-laced burp, she slipped soundlessly out of bed, struggled into last night's gear, scrabbled round for her bag. Turning at the door, she blew Sleeping Beauty a goodbye kiss. He was out for the count; he'd smoked several joints when they got back last night. As a cop, she'd probably not have hit on him if she'd known he went in for the wacky baccy. Wasn't the greatest career move. Even Bev knew the line had to be drawn somewhere. Still, live and learn…

As she came down the stairs, a mirror caught her un-awares; her reflection unavoidable and barely recognisable: mussed hair, panda eyes, pasty complexion. Flashing a too bright smile, she gave a mock salute. "Nice one, Bev." Her aim had been upbeat. It hit brittle.

3

The pretty smiling woman in the photograph bore little resemblance to the cowed individual Bill Byford had seen in the flesh. Diminished would be the detective superintendent's verdict on Donna Kennedy. He took a final look before dropping the print on his cluttered desk, then swivelled the black leather chair a hundred and eighty degrees towards the window. The big man raised an ironic eyebrow: the forecasters' promise of a white Christmas was only three weeks late.

He watched as skittish flakes flounced across a sober red-brick backdrop. The scene reminded him vaguely of the glass snowballs he collected when he was a kid, bought them on holidays mostly. He gave a wry smile. Highgate-nick-snowball-souvenir? Somehow, he couldn't see it catching on. Most people who spent time here couldn't wait to get away.

Like the Kennedy woman.

Sighing he swung back to his desk, tugged a pensive top lip as he recalled the only time he'd met her. He visualised lank fair hair, haggard features and eyes shot through with fear. It had been within hours of her ordeal and – of all the victims – Byford thought she'd been worst hit, psychologically as well as physically.

He reached for her file, flicked through the police interviews again, then closed his eyes, tried to imagine himself in the place of a small slight female. Not easy given he was six-five, well-covered and more than capable of fighting back, barring the odd bodily scar. Even so, when the door was flung open, a startled Byford scowled and snapped a peremptory, "Do you ever knock?"

"Got another, guv. It's just come in. Moseley this time. A Mrs Faith Winters." DC Mac Tyler, oblivious to – or ignoring – Byford's glower strode towards the desk brandishing a printout. Fifty-something and slightly flushed Mac stood across the desk, paunch straining at least three buttons on one of the red-checked shirts he generally wore. The Monty-Python-lumberjack look was deliberate. It fooled many a villain into a false sense of superiority. Though Mac did stand-up comedy in his spare time he was nobody's fool – as Byford was keenly aware.

The superintendent's gut tightened as he took the sheet of paper without comment. Questions were superfluous. Mac's body language and verbal shorthand must mean there'd been a development in Operation Magpie. That morning's brief – like several others over the last three weeks – had been dominated by the ongoing inquiry: a series of increasingly callous burglaries in which three, now possibly four, already vulnerable women had been left tethered and traumatised in their own beds. Every member of the squad had known it was only a question of time before the perp struck again.

Byford stroked his chin as he read. Without lifting his glance, he raised a hand to still Mac's fidgeting. The toe-tapping was getting on the big man's nerves. It was one of several habits Mac had picked up from his sergeant, the spiky Bev Morriss. Byford looked up half expecting to see her. "Bev not back yet?"

Mac kept his gaze on Byford's reading matter. "Identical MO. Has to be the same guy. What you reckon, guv?"

Byford reckoned Mac had ducked the question. He let it go for the moment, handed back the printout. "Certainly fits the pattern." A pattern he'd been re-tracing before

9

Mac's entry. He'd re-read every report and victim statement, replayed video interviews and studied crime scene
stills – hoping to establish a link between the women. Other
than suffering humiliation and abject terror at the hands
of a vicious sadist.

"There is a difference this time, guv…" Pausing, Mac
rubbed the back of his neck. The gesture was his usual
precursor to breaking bad news.

"Go on." Byford had a feeling he wasn't going to like it.

"The vic wants the press in on it."

"Oh, what joy." Realistically, he'd known it was bound to
happen sooner or later. Until now, media coverage had
been reasonable, restrained even, but only because the
police had withheld privileged information, and the
victims hadn't wanted their identity released. The papers
had run stories, but even local reporters – generally more
inquisitive and tenacious than national hacks – had failed
to dig out the more sensational details: the mask, the sand,
the £ sign carved in the victims' flesh. "Where is Mrs
Winters?"

"Still at the house, wouldn't go to hospital."

"And Bev?" The interview would need particularly
sensitive handling: Bev could still tease intimate details
from a Trappist nun. When she set her mind to it.

Mac's hesitation was barely detectable. "Said I'd hook up
with her there, guv."

Byford detected both the delay and the divided loyalty.
"Sure about that?" He suspected Mac Tyler was a lifeguard
when it came to hauling Bev out of professional deep water.
And he was pretty sure the DC had dipped a toe already
this morning. She'd not shown at the early brief, chasing a
lead – according to Mac. The big man watched and waited
in silence, observed beads of sweat appear above the DC's

top lip.

Mac lifted a palm, started backing towards the door. "I'd best make tracks, guv. I'll get it in the neck if I'm late."

He watched Mac lumber down the corridor, jabbing numbers into a mobile's keypad as he went. Byford sighed, got up to close the door. Clearly, Tyler's skills only extended to opening the damn things. He'd no doubt who Mac was trying to call. He clenched his jaw, hoped if Bev needed saving the water wasn't too hot or too deep.

4

"Took your time, didn't you?" Detective Sergeant Bev Morriss pushed herself up from the bonnet of a black MG Midget, and flicked a butt in the gutter where it joined another also ringed with crimson lipstick. Riled, Mac bit back a barb, then stared open-jawed as she hoisted a bag the size of Surrey on her shoulder and strode off casting a caustic, "Come on, mate, we ain't got all day," in her wake.

Her five-six-size-12-ish frame was encased in ankle-length leather coat and knee high boots. The gear wasn't black, or Mac reckoned he'd be goose-stepping to keep up. The coat, he noted, was dark blue. Her entire work wardrobe was blue, every shade in the solar system, though none matched the vibrancy of her eyes, even when she was well knackered, like now. Dark circles and drawn features were easily discernible under the warpaint. And Bev had clearly daubed it on. Talk about heavy. It was like a bloody mask these days.

Mac switched focus as they strutted down the damp pavement. The snow had melted and though the wide tree-lined road wasn't exactly bathed in light, a watery sun was doing its best. Blenheim Avenue, like much of Moseley, was neat verges, clipped hedges, manicured lawns. Imposing double-fronted redbrick Victorian properties were detached – and then some. Milton House had company: three police motors were parked outside, though only one was marked.

Bev reached the metal gates first, bowed ostentatiously as she ushered him in. "So what kept you?"

He tightened his lips. "I was on the job, boss. How about you?"

"You could say that."

It was her wink that did it. The proverbial straw on Mac's already buckling back. "Grow up," he hissed. "I'm telling you, sarge, I'm not happy."

"Get over it."

"I had to lie to the guv this morning to cover your back."

"What d'you want? A gold star?" Childish, churlish. She didn't need telling she was in the wrong.

He kept pace as she headed towards the door. "A bit of communication would do. I hadn't a clue where you were. I called the house, left voice mail, tried your mobile a million…"

"Yeah, sorry 'bout that, mate. Phone's gone AWOL."

As if. He stayed her hand as she made to ring the bell, forced her to make eye contact. "Don't Bev. Not that. Please." The 'Bev' was a rare enough personal touch to know he meant business.

"What?" The defiant glint in her eye was a warning. Maybe he couldn't read it.

"Lie to me." His pause was deliberately long. "We're partners. I have to know you tell me the truth."

"Moral high ground?" she snapped. "Get off your sodding stilts, mate."

"Shall I leave it on the latch – or are you coming in?" The young officer who'd opened the door looked like a member of a boy band wearing the uniform for a bet: dark-haired, smooth-skinned, clean-cut, PC Danny Rees was only a couple of years out of Hendon, but fancied himself as son of Morse. Given Danny's decidedly un-cool blush when his gaze met Bev's, Mac fancied the lad harboured the hots for more than promotion.

"Ta, Danny." Bev wiped her boots on the mat, dodged a couple of bulging bin liners, handed the rookie her coat.

"How is she now?"

He smiled. "Don't know what you said to her, sarge, but she seems calmer."

"I listened, Danny. Showed her a bit of respect." Mac's mouth could have garaged a bus. Double-decker. "Ask DC Tyler. He knows all about that don't you, mate?" She paused at the end of the hall. "You coming or what?"

A woman in her mid-fifties sat stiff-backed on a squashy three-seater sofa in a spacious L-shaped lounge. Not everything around her was beige, it just seemed that way. Soft furnishings the shade of weak tea, washed-out sepia walls, dried flowers in butter-coloured vases book-ending a marble fireplace. The woman herself was no shrinking violet. Faith Winters appeared to be into purple in a big way, from patent leather kitten heels to casually-draped pashmina. Even close-cropped grey hair was dusted with lilac. She was leafing through the local rag, laid it to one side when Bev – rehearsed smile fixed in place – entered.

"Me again, Mrs Winters." She jabbed a thumb over her shoulder. "This is my partner, DC Mac Tyler. Think you can tell him what you told me? Two heads and all that?" Bev cocked hers in hope.

"Of course." If there were qualms, the woman hid them well. She crossed slim legs at thin ankles, smoothed slightly trembling fingers over an already crease-free velvet dress, blackcurrant. Whether the moves were to skirt Mac's proffered handshake was anyone's guess.

"Appreciate it." Bev resumed her place alongside the victim. She'd motored straight here after catching breaking reports of the incident on her police radio. In a toss-up between late arrival at the Highgate brief ball and heads up at a breaking crime scene it was a no-brainer. Bev needed

14

the brownie points, and could get by without colleagues' questioning looks. Again.

When she'd first arrived the woman had been in a state of shock. Now Bev had the shakes. The tremor, she knew, was DC- as much as DT-induced. That Mac had accused her of lying about the phone was so far below the belt, it was ground-breaking. She might come out with the occasional white one to oil the wheels, but whites-of-the-eyes whopper? No way. Not to a professional partner.

"Whenever you're ready, Mrs Winters?" Mac was in gentle-coax mode. He'd opted for a chunky armchair facing the woman, adopted a non-threatening stance and wasn't overdoing the eye contact. He was pretty good at the victim-interview stuff. Bev had seen him in action; it was Mrs Winters she observed closely now.

Asking the victim to run through the story again wouldn't just bring Mac up to speed. Few witnesses have total recall when they first relate an incident – if ever. This time round, the woman might dredge up a nugget or two, a little extra detail. Bev took a metaphorical back seat, clocking body language, listening for discrepancies, contradictions, nuances, ready to pounce on anything that needed elaboration and/or follow up.

Mrs Winters fidgeted incessantly but the story emerged fluently and coherently. A man wearing dark clothes and a clown mask had entered her room, tethered her to the bed, subjected her to verbal abuse and physical attack. He'd ransacked the house, stolen property, left his mark. Bev had seen it: a £ sign traced on the woman's belly with a knife. Not deep, not life-threatening. Just because he could. And like he'd done before. Three times.

At previous crime scenes, he'd not shed so much as a skin cell. The cops hoped for bigger things here. Uniforms were on the streets, others were finger-tipping grounds at the back of the house. The odd muffled bump overhead signalled the presence of forensic scene investigators: FSI. The name change from SOCOs was still fairly recent. Why the West Midlands service hadn't adopted the more common initials, CSI, Bev hadn't a clue. Hopefully they did by now – they were upstairs videoing, dusting, lifting, fine-tooth combing, bagging and tagging anything with potential.

"I lay there for hours." Mrs Winters picked loose skin at the side of her thumb. "I was… it was…" She swallowed. "Then June found me… called you people." The cleaner. Bev had spoken briefly. June Mason had been adamant the back door was locked. There'd been no sign of forced entry anywhere. Begged the question did the intruder have a key? The alarm hadn't needed deactivating. It hadn't been switched on.

The sequence of events was easy to picture, Bev had witnessed some of the aftermath: the shredded wedding photograph, the shattered glass, four thin cords still dangling from bed posts. Imagining what the woman had gone through was more difficult. Mrs Winters had her voice under tight control, but the twitching and fiddling told a different story. The upper lip was starched but Bev reckoned Faith Winters was a quivering wreck inside. Took one to know one. As for the woman's attitude – there was a slight shift, something Bev couldn't quite pin down. It was more the way she spoke, rather than what was said.

The narrative – though not word-for-word – was close enough to the original for Bev to know the woman wasn't making it up as she went along, adding spice, aggrandising her ego, or even just pleasing the cops. Amazing how many punters did, fantasists getting off on their own fiction.

People lied all the time. Lied. Bugger Mac. Bev balled a fist. Her mobile *was* missing. Only doubt was whether she'd lost it for good or it would turn up where she least expected it. Sodding nuisance either way.

"Any questions, sarge?" Mac's snide tone suggested he thought she'd tuned out.

Finger still on the button though. "How many keys are there to this place, Mrs Winters?"

It looked as if she was totting them up in her head. "Six." The cleaner, a neighbour and the gardener had copies, which left Mrs Winters's plus two spares.

"And they're still around?" Nonchalant query from Bev.

"Of course."

"Check recently?"

"Well, no…" It didn't take long. She was back in a couple of minutes. "I keep them in the kitchen drawer normally." Normally. "Maybe I moved them?"

"P'raps you could have a search round later, Mrs Winters?" Mac urged gently.

The missing keys added to Bev's growing doubts that the burglary was random. "You say the intruder knew your name, Mrs Winters. Any chance you'd come across him before?"

She drifted back to the sofa, shaking her head. "I've thought about it but can't see how or where. I don't know many young men."

The woman and the burglar didn't have to be bosom buddies. Their paths could have crossed casually in any number of places: supermarket, garage, restaurant, coffee shop. Mrs Winters wasn't an agoraphobic hermit. On the other hand, the letter rack in the hall contained household bills, correspondence – all addressed to Mrs Faith Winters. Bev had spotted it, likely Coco the frigging clown had as well. Best keep an open mind for the mo.

"What makes you say young man, Mrs Winters?" Mac asked.

"His clothes." The description boiled down to man-in-black. "The swagger. What he said, how he said it." She traced an eyebrow with an aubergine fingernail.

"Tell us about the voice," Bev prompted. "Did he have an accent?"

"He may have…" Hesitating, she circled the finger where her wedding ring had been. Bev spotted the slight indentation in the flesh. "I had the feeling he was disguising the way he speaks. He sounded just a little different every time he opened his mouth." She shuddered, closed her eyes. The word must have revived an image of the gross red lips. Bev was freaked and she'd only heard about them.

"So you'd not recognise the voice again?" Bev asked.

"That's not what I said." Tad sharp. "At the moment I can't get the damn thing out of my head."

"Anything else you can think of, Mrs Winters?" Soothing interception from Mac.

"The worst thing was when he ordered me to close my eyes… the sand… then the pillow over my face… I thought… I was afraid… I…"

"It's OK now, Mrs Winters." Bev's outstretched hand was rebuffed.

"But it's not, is it? I was utterly humiliated. He made me feel worthless, insignificant. And I was so very afraid. If Rod were alive…" She closed her eyes, visibly trying to compose herself. Bev mouthed, husband, at Mac. The uneasy silence was shattered when the widow whacked the arm of the sofa. "And he's still out there. He could come back." The attitude shift was more pronounced, the growing hostility unmistakeable.

18

"We'll put a police guard on the house, Mrs Winters," Bev said. "There's no way he'll…"

"And how do you stop him attacking someone else? I'm not the first, am I?" She grabbed the paper she'd been reading, thrust it at Bev. "Page thirteen, sergeant." The headline in the week-old copy of the local rag read POLICE SEEK BURGLAR.

It wouldn't set Wolverhampton alight let alone the world. Nor the bland bog-standard story that appeared below the fold. The guv had wanted it down-played. That it was.

Mrs Winters rose, paced the carpet, arms folded. "I vaguely remembered reading the article before. When you went out, I retrieved that from the recycling box." The finger pointing at the paper was none too steady. "It's him isn't it?" She didn't sound certain, there wasn't much to go on in the story, but her conjecture was smack on. Bev reckoned she deserved the truth.

"Yes. It could be."

"Why no mention of the mask? The torment he puts his victims through?" She flapped a dismissive hand. "That's no warning to vulnerable women. Any woman. If I'd known…"

Bev stood, met the woman head-on, tried peacemaking. "It's a fine line, Mrs Winters: alerting people, alarming them, causing unnecessary panic." Fine line and the guv's official line, another one Bev didn't much care about toeing.

"Unnecessary panic?" she sneered. "What a great comfort, sergeant."

"We'll catch him, Mrs Winters."

"Then what?" She threw her head back. "A few months in jail? Time off for good behaviour? And me? I'll be looking over my shoulder every day, too scared to sleep at night. The man who did this should go to prison for life – and it still wouldn't be long enough."

Big Ben chimes broke the silence. There were muffled voices in the hall. PC Rees popped his head round. "It's the television people, Mrs Winters. Do you want to speak to them?"

"What do you think?" Defiant glare. "I asked them here."

"And, sarge?" Rees cocked an eyebrow. "Something you need to see."

Bev and Mac trailed Rees to a large detached white house just round the corner. One of the uniforms had spotted it: a small black-handled knife under a hedge. Crime scene manager Chris Baxter was just about to bag it.

"Hold on a min, Chris." Bev got down on one knee, gently nudged the knife with the tip of a Bic to turn it over. Except for blood on the blade, there was nothing to distinguish it from a zillion others. Nada. Worth a look before it entered the black hole of the labs though. She rose, brushed a dead leaf and damp grit from her Levis. "All yours, Chris." The sigh she'd tried stifling escaped.

"What's up, Bev?" Baxter joshed. "Hoping there'd be a name on it?" Sandy-haired, freckle-faced Baxter fancied himself as a bit of a wit.

Tad distracted, Bev's quip was on auto-pilot. "Address, phone number, inside leg. Y'know me. I'm easy."

"I'd heard that, babe."

Easy or babe? Nerves. Raw. Touched. "Don't friggin' babe me. Savvy?"

"Joke? Hello?" Was that a flush of embarrassment or anger? Baxter wasn't a bloke to get on the wrong side of. He mirrored her glare with one of his own. She broke eye contact first, raised a palm in token appeasement-stroke-apology, headed back up the road, coat-wings flapping. Mac kept pace. If not peace.

"How to win friends and influence people. Nice one, boss." The tuneless whistling of *Happy Days Are Here Again* didn't help: she'd got the message.

"I'm sorry, OK?" Arms splayed. "Got a splitting head." Not to mention the hangover, and multiple post-attack hang-ups. Her verbal strikes were defensive, but they were a pain in the butt for anyone in the firing line. She knew they needed curbing. Easier said than...

"Sarge?" She turned to see PC Rees jogging towards them. "Pretty damn good, eh, sarge? Think the perp dropped it running away?"

She reckoned Danny was from the Labrador puppy school of policing: boundless enthusiasm, not much nous. DC Darren New was a founder member. "Makes you say that, Danny?"

Frowny face. "He cut her, didn't he?"

Given the number of blades on the street, so what? With a knife crime every four minutes in the UK, Danny's assumption was a tad premature. "We'll see."

"Come on, sarge. So close to the scene?"

Dead convenient that. It bugged her. Coco hadn't put a foot wrong so far. Now they find a bloodstained weapon within spitting distance of the latest burglary. Seemed to Bev the only thing missing was the gift wrap. Course, she could be wrong. And there was no sense ruffling more feathers. "You're prob'ly right." She gave a lopsided smile, buttoned her coat, brought out a card from the pocket. "Give this to Mrs Winters, Danny. Tell her she can call me any time." She crossed out one of the numbers. "Say I'll get back to her soon as there's news."

Mac tilted his head towards the crime scene. "Vultures moving in, boss."

A lanky guy clad in denim and toting a camera was just

21

entering the Winters place, a big-haired blonde in killer heels brought up the rear. Remainder of the colony would doubtless be on the flight path, though a few would be circling Highgate nick.

Bev pursed her lips. The guv wouldn't like that. Byford loathed having his back against the wall, 'specially when it had been pinned there by the media. Tough. Though Bev hadn't warmed to Faith Winters, the woman had a point. If she'd been better informed, she might have been better protected. Now they were all in spilt milk mode. Pass the Kleenex.

They were alongside the MG when Mac reached into a back pocket. "Here y'go, boss." She frowned. He'd dropped a blister pack in her palm. Fact it was still warm was not a thought to hold. "What's this?"

"Paracetemol." Blank look from Bev. "Splitting headache?" he reminded her.

"Top man." She peered closer at the pack, felt her lip curve as she fumbled in her bag for car keys. "Sort the door-to-doors for us, Mac?" Police teams needed briefing, pointing in the right direction. Blenheim Avenue being a well-known insomnia hot-spot whose residents had nothing better to do at four in the morning than gaze through windows, note car numbers, video neighbourhood thugs. Yeah right. She unlocked the Midget.

"No prob," Mac said. "Where you off?"

"Carphone Warehouse." Casual. "Need a new mobile." Throwaway remark.

Mac caught it, reddened slightly. "'bout that, boss…"

"'s OK, mate."

"Yeah, but…"

"No sweat." She gave a mock salute. "And no worries – the lips are sealed."

Mac's brow was plough-able, the lines deepened as she slipped him the blister pack. He clocked the word, Viagra, and screwed his eyes. "Shit!"

"Makes you come – and go?" Her mouth developed a speculative pout. "Well I never."

5

The big man was running late. Half a dozen squad members were gathered in the Magpie incident room at Highgate nick waiting for him to show. The extra curricular brief was supposed to kick off at midday. Wall clock showed 12.10. Weak sunlight glinting on smeared glass suggested the window cleaners were overdue as well. At least the snow hadn't put in another appearance.

DC Darren New leant against a side wall, nose buried in the local paper. "Hey, sarge, seen what the *News* is calling the perp?"

Seated at one of a dozen cluttered desks, Bev squinted as she glanced up from her new toy. The latest high-tech Nokia had Hangman installed. She'd lost three times so far. Given the extent of the phone's menu, she was only surprised it didn't do espresso. Shame. With the guv imminent, nipping to the canteen was a non-starter and she was well parched. "Don't tell me, Daz…" Index fingers pressed to temples, she feigned profound thought. "Is it… the… Sandman?"

"That's a swiz. You'd seen it." He was miffed. A truculent frown marred what he referred to as his Tom Cruise looks. Daz was in a minority of one there.

"Piece of piss, mate. To a comic like that, sand plus man equals Sandman. The stuff's hacked out. It's not exactly Hemingway."

Puzzled face. "Hemingway?"

"Google it, Einstein." Head down, she missed Darren's dagger look. DC Carol Pemberton clocked it, which was why her snigger rapidly morphed into a coughing fit.

"Nice recovery, Caz," Bev murmured, focus back on her

phone. Bastard Hangman. Stuffed again. She shoved the sodding thing in her bag.

"Anyway Little Miss Smart-Butt, that's not all they're saying." Daz being enigmatic. He was about to close the paper.

"Gissa look." She reached out a hand.

"Buy your own." The lopsided smile was down to the tongue in his cheek. He sauntered over, dropped the rag on her desk, added: "Front page. A pop at Byford. They reckon he should've issued a police warning."

Nothing new there then – or news, Bev mused. She skimmed the lead: same old same old. Cops can't put a boot right. On the other hand…

"I think they've got a point." Carol who was tapping a keyboard next desk along, took the words out of Bev's mouth. At thirty-six, she had five years on Bev who frequently wished she looked as fit. Pembers bore a fleeting resemblance to Victoria Beckham during her Posh years. Except Carol was a head taller and had class. "As a punter, I'd want to know if some nutter was out there."

"Guv's call," Bev countered. "Think yourself lucky he's the one making 'em." Where did that come from? A second ago she was with Carol, now she was batting on Byford's side. Loyalty? Or lust? Don't, Beverley. She and the guv had been there – not done that, not bought the T-shirt. For years, they'd pussy-footed around then, after the attack, he'd asked her to live with him. Timing could've been better. They'd given it a go, but she'd been in no shape for intimacy – physical or emotional. She'd left just before Christmas. Ho sodding ho.

"Lowly DC me, sarge," Carol drawled. "We don't get to do decisions."

Bev arched a knowing eyebrow. She was well aware Carol

could walk the sergeant's exams, but it was academic, her kids came first. Come to think of it, Carol never mentioned the kids nowadays. Another verbal no-go area. Bev sighed, saw barbed wire, broken egg-shells.

Mac almost broke the desk; she felt it tip when he parked his butt. "Feeling peaky, sarge?"

"Peachy's the word, mate." His scrutiny was a tad too close for comfort. She reversed the chair, crashed into a tub containing what could've been a baby triffid. Some Monty Don manqué had donated a load of greenery recently, thinking it'd brighten up the wall-to-wall greys. She sniffed, strolled blithely to one of four whiteboards. "Damn peachy."

Unlike these poor sods. Eyes narrowed, Bev ran her gaze along the Sandman's expanding hit list: Beth Fowler, Sheila Isaac, Donna Kennedy and the latest pin-up Faith Winters. Their ages ranged from thirty-nine to fifty-five. All lived alone in posh houses: one in Edgbaston, one in Harborne, now two in Moseley. The pictures' high profile in the incident room was supposed to keep the team focused, allow them to put faces to names, see the victims as people not crime numbers. Guv's call again. Good one, given most of the squad hadn't even met the women, let alone interviewed them. Bev had. So why wasn't it helping? Where was the famed Morriss insight? The lauded empathy? Down the pan probably, with a load of other shit. Arms folded, she paced up and down, studied the victims' faces. Come on, Beverley, think. What was the link? Apart from the haunted look? And a pound sign carved in their flesh?

"I'm late. Sorry." Byford ferrying a steaming mug strode to the top of the room. Thank God he was on coffee. Peppermint tea and it meant his IBS was playing up.

Bev caught a whiff of Calvin Klein aftershave too. He'd converted after she told him Old Spice was for wrinklies. Why he had a thing about his age when he had a George Clooney smile was beyond her.

Grabbing a pew, she watched the big man shift a pile of files, before perching on the corner of a desk. He paused briefly while Mac finished a phone call, then with no preamble: "We need fresh impetus. The inquiry's not moving fast enough." Rocket up rectum time, then. Bev wondered if the guv was in the firing line as well. "It's three weeks since the first burglary," he said. "Each attack's more violent than the last and we're up to four. My big fear is he's losing control and if we don't stop him we'll have a murder inquiry on our hands. All this Sandman stuff in the papers isn't helping. As for the blow-by-blow account..." Deep sigh. No need to spell it out. Villains loved column inches; assuming they could read. Byford ran both hands through his hair. "We need a result, pretty damn quick."

Bev wouldn't mind betting the brass was on his back as well as the media. A top-floor bollocking could explain the tardy arrival, Byford was fanatically punctual. "Hate to say it, guv." She was counting on her fingers. "January fifteenth today, right? First burglary was Beth Fowler's place, Moseley, Christmas Eve." The bastard had nicked presents from under the tree as well as every piece of jewellery she owned. "Ten days between that and the break-in at the Isaac place, in Edgbaston. Seven days after that he turns over Donna Kennedy's pad in Harborne." She raised splayed fingers. "Latest gap's five."

They got the picture. Attack frequency as well as ferocity was increasing.

"What if it's not a bloke?" Daz speculating, hesitant.

"You having a laugh?"

"Sergeant." Soft warning from the guv. "Go on, Darren."

"No one's seen a face," he argued. "Voice is easy enough to disguise. Plenty of women wear dark gear."

"Like it, Daz." Bev nodded. "Why didn't I think of that? And what with rape threats being a girl thing... case closed. Let's all sod off down The Prince."

New reddened, looked as if he'd been out in the sun without protection. But no one laughed, the silence was uneasy and Byford took his time before breaking it. Bev stared straight ahead, arms tightly crossed. She might've said sorry but her mouth was full of feet.

"Keep the thoughts coming, Darren." Byford in face saving mode. "He may have a female accomplice. Who knows? There's no evidence either way, so no one rules out anything. Clear?" Bev sensed the guv's glare. It was eight seconds before he spoke again. "The knife found near the scene could be our best bet, but there's no sense pinning all our hopes on it." You can say that again, guv. Bev sniffed. She still felt the discovery was either coincidence or overly convenient. "Either way," Byford continued, "it'll take several days for the lab to come up with anything. That's time we can't waste. Right now, we need to go back to the beginning, look for what we've missed. There have to be connections we're not seeing." Pause to let that sink in then, "Bev, I want you to re-interview the victims. They may have come across each other without realising it. If need be bring the women together here. Get them talking. See what comes out." She nodded, opened her mouth to speak, but he'd moved on. "Remind me – who was checking stolen property?"

Carol and DC Sumitra Gosh had been trawling jewellers and pawn shops with photos of some of the items. Sumi wasn't at the brief, but Carol had a list in front of her. Not all the names had ticks. "We've still got a few to get to, sir, but…" She held out empty palms. Not so much as a nibble.

Odd that. Bev mulled it over while Mac reported progress on mask shops. Suppliers were ten a penny, he reckoned. There'd be better odds tracing the invisible man in Ikea. But the more Bev thought about the stolen goodies…

"Guv? What if he's not doing it for the money?" Her question drew dubious frowns all round, but she'd had longer to toy with the idea.

Byford slipped a hand in his pocket. "Go on."

She sat up, tucked an errant strand of hair behind an ear. "How much stuff's he nicked? Gotta be getting on for a hundred items, yeah? Sixty, seventy grands' worth?"

"At least," Carol confirmed.

"He's had some of it three weeks. We've not had so much as a sniff. Even Marty can't give us a steer." Marty Skelton, otherwise known as Boney M, was a veteran snout, or CHIS as cops were supposed to call them these days: covert human intelligence source. If a load of hot stuff was on the streets, Marty would've heard a whisper.

"Where are you going with this, Bev?" The key jangling suggested she'd best get on with it.

"What if it's a power trip? Not the cash. The control. The rape threat scares them shitless. Creams his jeans."

"The assaults haven't been sexual," Byford said.

"Yeah, well, maybe he can't get it up." Mac wasn't the only guy on Viagra. Pursed lips suggested Byford wasn't on board. "Come on, guv. He loves it. It's why the attacks are getting worse." Faith Winters had been stripped, the knife run over her body, and he'd whacked her in the face. He'd not gone that far before. "As for the mask, the sand, the pound sign? He's a clown. It's a game. A mind fuck. Cos he can't…"

"Thank you." Byford raised a hand: point taken. He gave it some thought, then: "If you're on the right track it moves things on, means more digging."

A new motive – if that's what it was – widened the operation's remit. Continuing checks on known thieves and burglars would have to be extended to cover convicted and suspected sex offenders: flashers to full blown pervs. Squad members would examine MOs looking for patterns, similarities, however vague, however small. It was a mammoth ask. It meant raking over scores of cold cases as well as looking again at God knew how many current inquiries. And it meant cross-checks with forces all over the UK. Coco could well be with a travelling circus.

Byford delegated the bulk of the work, made it clear he wanted Bev to concentrate on the victim interviews. "OK, let's get on with it. See you back here this evening." He stopped by her desk on the way out. "Press conference. Three o'clock. I'd like you there."

She curled a lip, it was news to her. The big man swirled his mug, glanced round for a tub, tipped the dregs. "Need more than a drop of Nescaff, that, guv. It's plastic."

The Pound Shop was in a one-size-fits-all Black Country high street: Warley, Walsall, Wednesbury – they were indistinguishable to the man in black. He was after a new knife and he rather liked the irony of pound signs plastered over the grubby windows. Not that they were a patch on the ones he left behind. He gave a sly grin. Bitches ought to be grateful. Body art was a skill. Looked at one way, he was throwing in a free tattoo. Last night was the best yet. The grin turned into a smirk as he recalled events at the Moseley pad, fancy the old biddy pissing herself then passing out. Before the fun had even begun.

He smoothed his hair in the glass, batted away smoke from a couple of fag-ash Lils hogging the doorway and entered the store. When he spotted the display, his dark eyes gleamed. He gave a quick glance round before approaching it. Place was full of lard-arse cheapskates stinking of chips and stale sweat. No way would he run into anyone he knew. He'd driven out of town just in case though, better safe than sorry. Like as if the plod were going to trace the sale. "Bleeding pigmies," he muttered.

Shoot. For one moment this morning, he thought they'd never find the knife. He'd sat in the back of the van watching the search team, wondering if he'd have to point the silly sods in the right direction. He'd killed a cat to get the blood. Not that they'd come across the carcass; he'd buried it well.

And planted the knife. What a hoot. It was part of the joke, wasn't it? And worth the risk. Nothing better than seeing woodentops race round like headless chickens. That reminded him. He took out his phone, replayed the action. Pics weren't brilliant, but it looked as if the bird in blue was calling the shots. He ran his tongue over his teeth. For a cop she wasn't in bad nick. He wondered what her name was; easy enough to find out. If he wanted to. He zoomed in on the face, took a final appraising look, nice eyes, shame about the job. He shoved the mobile back in his pocket. Duty called.

There wasn't a lot of choice. He selected a similar one to before, balanced it in his palm: good feel, excellent fit. He ran the blade lightly over his thumb, watched a thin pale line appear. Yep. It'd do. He'd sharpen it at home.

6

It was DI Mike Powell who'd dubbed the smokers' patch at the back of Highgate nick Death Row. Bev was out there now taking a well-earned breather. The last three hours had been non-stop, the next three would be all-go. Leaning against the wall, she pictured Powell as she lit up, a lazy smile spreading across her face. The DI was a tall, sarky blond who fired from the lips. They'd worked together for nearly ten years, had more run-ins than Ford motors. She missed the pops and verbal sparring. Still, his three-month stint at Hendon would soon be over, she'd probably feel like swinging for him before he'd been back a day.

Silk Cut midway to mouth, Bev paused, eyes creased. Sumitra Gosh. What was she doing here? Life member of ASH was the delectable DC. "Slumming it, are we, Goshie?" She realised her mistake the instant the woman turned. Though tall and willowy, with waist-length blue-black hair, she wasn't Sumi: close but no cigar. Should've realised. The DC usually kept her luscious locks under wraps at work, this girl's small delicate face was framed by sleek black curtains.

"Beg pardon?" The voice was similar, too, though not the nervy grin. Goshie wasn't short on confidence.

"My mistake, love. You've got a double." Bev glared as a traffic cop gunned an Astra, shot off in a cloud of spewed fumes and sprayed gravel. Petrol dick. "They all think they're Jeremy Clarkson round here," she quipped.

Diffident smile from the young woman. Bev watched her pull the collar of her sheepskin coat tighter. It was nippy out here. "I'm just waiting for someone." Hesitant,

32

wary. "Is that OK?"

Bev waved a magnanimous hand. "Feel free." Then flapped furiously at the resultant clouds of smoke. "Whoops."

Nervy giggle this time. "No worries. It doesn't bother me."

"Kushti." Bev took a few covert glances; shame about that chipped tooth. Other than that she was the spit of Sumi: high altitude cheek bones, dark chocolate eyes. They could almost be twins. The gene pool penny dropped. Stunning detection powers, Bev. "Are you Sumitra Gosh's sister?" Triumphant beam.

She shook her head. Nice one, Clouseau. "We're cousins. I'm Fareeda. Fareeda Saleem. It is OK if I wait here?" The girl cast a wary glance round the car park.

"Course it is." Must be cop shop syndrome. Like white-coat syndrome. Only without the white coat. "She knows you're here?" Bev asked.

"Oh, yes. I called first." A gust of wind caught her hair: it was like a curtain opening. For the first time, Bev had full view of the girl's face. And the damage. She opened her mouth to say something, thought better of it, stuck out her hand. "Bev Morriss. I work with Sumi."

Thin bangles jangled as she reached to return the gesture. "Are you a police officer?"

"Detective Sergeant." Matey smile. It was pretty clear why the girl needed to chill. And have a cousinly chat. "Want to wait in the canteen? I'll take you up if you like. Lot warmer there." If nothing else, Bev fancied grabbing coffee en route to the news conference.

"No, it's OK. Sumi'll be here…"

"Talk of the devil." Bev used her baccy as a pointer. DC Sumi Gosh was unfolding impossibly long legs from a squad car. Enviable effortless grace. Well impressive. When Bev extricated herself from the Midget it came close to indecent exposure.

Sumi locked the driver's door, headed over, couple of files under an arm. "How's it going, sarge?" Her smile faded when she clocked Fareeda. "Why are you here?" Anger? Concern? Impatience? Nope. Bev could read neither expression nor intonation. Sumi was giving nothing away. Except the lie to her cousin. *Oh, yes. I called first.* Like hell. No way was Sumi expecting to see her. "What do you want?

The glance Fareeda cut Bev didn't need an interpreter. Butt out just about covered it. Desperate plea rather than rude dismissal. She took a final drag, shoved the glowing end in the sand-bin. Fareeda wanted a private chat, no skin off Bev's nose. Though she wouldn't mind betting the fist-sized bruise on the girl's face would be up for discussion.

Bill Byford was also in line for a battering. The hostility emanating from the gathered media was almost palpable. The superintendent's taut knuckles and tight lips spoke volumes, though Bev reckoned the tone of the news conference had been set before he even opened his mouth. Since news broke that a serial burglar was at large, early editions of the regional papers and hourly bulletins on local radio and telly had been of one voice: cops' latest cock-up. The decision to withhold information had been described as a cop-out. Abdicating responsibility was one interpretation; Bev's doodle of Byford's neck on a block was another.

For ten, fifteen minutes he'd done little more than issue bare bones and was now wrapping up with a bland appeal for witnesses. The journos' body language screamed: enough already. What they wanted was names of the other victims. More human-interest sticks to beat the cops with. Bev added a pool of blood to her graphic execution, peeked through her fringe at the pack, tried to spot who was wielding the sharpest axe.

Jack Pope was sprawled in a seat on the back row. A former cop, Pope now ran the *Sunday Chronicle's* crime desk, a distant deadline could explain the laidback stance. Tall, dark, and a serious looker, he was an old mate of Bev's – in every sense of the word. In pole position, centre front was Toby Priest, aka the Bishop. Priest, Bishop, Pope? What was it with these news guys? God's sake. They'd be taking confessions soon. Or giving last rites.

Priest was straining at the leash. He'd stepped into Matt Snow's scuffed Hush Puppies as *Evening News* crime correspondent. Snow had a place in the sun nowadays. Well, on *The Sun*. He'd been poached by the red top's news desk three, four months earlier. The hack had hit the headlines himself back then when he was targeted by a killer with exclusives to die for. Several unfortunate sods had, and being on the inside track opened national doors for Snow. He'd penned a book off the back of his lead role, been hawking it round ever since. Far as Bev knew there'd been no takers.

The vertically-challenged Mr Priest clearly felt the guv's offerings weren't up to much either. When Byford threw the conference open, the reporter tossed in spin of his own. "So, bottom line's a psycho's out there and women in the city aren't safe in their own beds." Priest lifted a languid glance from admiring his nails. The pretty-boy features did nothing for Bev, with the ponytail loose he'd look well girlie. "That cuts to the chase, wouldn't you say? Inspector." Surely he was taking the piss? Priest was new-ish as crime correspondent, but he'd been round the block a few times. His demotion of the guv had to be deliberate. The big man didn't take the bait.

"If that's the best you can come up with, son." He gathered his papers to reinforce the point.

"How's this?" Priest shot back. "I understand the guy's out of control, the attacks are getting worse and..." Bev stiffened. Had the Bishop already tracked down other victims? Or had the squad developed a leak? "...that it's only a question of time before he kills." She glanced at the guv, whose lips had virtually vanished. Priest hadn't finished the sermon. "Where's the police warning in all this?" He sniffed. "However late in the day."

Byford rested his elbows on the table's shiny black surface, laced his fingers, and weighed up the loaded question. "Personal safety is an issue." Cynical hacks accustomed to cop-speak straightened backs and sharpened nibs. The guv waited for the buzz to die down. "For all of us. At all times."

Not the admission of failure they'd anticipated. Geed on, Priest played to the gallery, upped the game. "So you're calling Faith Winters a liar?" Bev stifled a snort. That was a leap and a half. Priest stood, waved his rag around, open at an inside page. "You're saying there is no serial burglar, no clown mask, no sand, no rape threat?"

Byford lowered his voice, another sign he was riled. "When exactly did I say that, Mr Priest?"

"You didn't." The reporter had a glint in his eye. "That's the point. If this woman hadn't come forward we'd all still be in the dark." Probably aiming for the guv, Priest slung the newspaper on the table then slumped back in his seat. The paper glided straight past Byford, ended up in front of Bev who now stared down at Faith Winters's picture. The photographer had taken a moody shot through a window, the woman stared out dolefully, hand pressed against her cheek.

"In the interests of the inquiry, I took the decision to

withhold…"

Cheek. Bev frowned. Unbidden, Fareeda's image had sprung to mind. Nasty bruise that. The damson shade meant the damage was no more than a few hours' old. And that chipped tooth? She toyed with the idea of having a word with Sumi, or keeping her nose out? Pensive, she started adding a noose to her drawing.

"Interests of the inquiry?" Priest sneered. "What about the public's interests?"

Byford's voice couldn't get much lower. "I don't need a lecture from you, Mr Priest. Operation Magpie's had top priority since day one. It has major incident status, I've assigned…"

Yada, yada. Bev stifled a yawn. Not just down to the late night. The guv was now lobbing stats in the hope it would throw the hounds off the scent. Mind, the good guys were seriously outnumbered: three rows of journos to just three cops, if you counted Bernie, the police news bureau chief. Ex-Fleet Street, ex-alcoholic, three ex-wives, Bernie Flowers cultivated the John Major look; even his specs were grey. An optical delusion given the guy's past had more colour than a paint factory. Bev's doodle was almost complete, just needed a…

"Sergeant?" Her pen stilled. The guv's raised eyebrow was expectant.

"Guv?" What had she missed?

He tapped the table. "I said is there anything you want to add?"

To what? Better safe than sorry. "Not a word, guv."

"That has to be a first," he muttered.

"If she hasn't – I have." Priest was on his feet again. Regular hack-in-the-box. "When the Sandman kills, will you be resigning? Inspector."

37

The hard-bitten copper with a bottle of Bells in a drawer of his desk was a cliché. That's why Byford kept his Laphroaig in the filing cabinet. It was getting an airing now. A crystal tumbler held a generous measure, Byford's grasp so crushing the glass was in danger of cracking. He only wished his fingers were round Priest's scraggy neck. He took a calming breath, downed the whisky in one, felt the burn.

Unlike all those cops he watched on the box, Byford wasn't an emotional cripple; he didn't do depression, like he didn't eat junk food, chain smoke or drink too much. He couldn't remember the last time he'd taken a drop in the office. Given the late brief, he certainly wasn't celebrating. Not with leads going nowhere, zero from the house-to-house, ditto on the hotlines, apart from the odd offensive remark. The big man refilled the glass, walked to the window. He sipped the liquor this time, savoured it, let it linger in his mouth.

Will you be resigning, Inspector? Five hours since the news conference and Priest's words still rankled. Of course Byford would go if he felt responsible for someone's death. But that wasn't the case here, nor would be, he assured himself. He wasn't the joker dressed as a clown terrorising women. His job was to track down the sick bastard.

Grim-faced, Byford gazed out at the car park below. A prison van was pulling in; security lights flooded the area giving it the look of a film set, special effects provided by raindrops glittering in the beams. Or maybe it was sleet, hard to tell from up here. A couple of uniforms got out of the vehicle, walked across the yard, chatting. Byford took another sip. Shame it wasn't a shoot for *The Prisoner* with the Sandman in the eponymous role. A muscle tightened in the big man's jaw. What he wouldn't give to see the guy

38

in custody.

Was Bev right? Was the perp getting off on it? She had a knack of hitting the nail – among other targets – head-on. The big man turned and perched on the sill. She'd seemed mellower at the late brief, but she'd really gone for Darren New at lunchtime. Problem was the more she opened her mouth, the likelier Darren and some of the others would clam up. A good squad was all about communication and connection. Everyone had to feel they could contribute without a verbal clobbering from Bev or anyone else.

How many times could he let it go? How much slack could he cut? No way could he risk her harming the inquiry. Shame the days were gone when he could just pick up the receiver, have a friendly word. He couldn't seem to get through to her – with or without the aid of a phone. That was another thing... had she really lost her mobile?

He lifted the glass, surprised to see it empty. Another? No. His sleep was shot to bits as it was, and the headaches – a legacy of a near fatal attack two years back – still plagued him. One of his bosses had touched on the subject this morning. A regular update session with Phil Masters, the operations assistant chief constable had turned – however civil the tone – into a snipe-fest. *How are we coping, Bill? Don't be afraid to ask for support, old man.* Even tighter-lipped now, Byford placed the glass out of arm's way, loosened his tie. He wouldn't put it past Masters to engineer a permanent post for Kenny Flint. DCS Flint had only just returned to Wolverhampton after covering Byford's sick leave. Flint was a cop who played by the book. After the last disciplinary, if he'd had his way, Bev would've been demoted – and shown the door. Byford sighed, couldn't stand the thought of losing her completely.

Sod it. He'd get a cab home, pick up a curry. He poured

a single measure, sat at the desk, caught his reflection in the monitor. Wished he hadn't. The bags under his eyes were pack-able. Like the emotional baggage he refused to acknowledge: professional and personal. In denial – isn't that what they call it? The glass went flying when he raised it in ironic toast. Shit. Was he squiffy? Drunk, morose, and an Indian takeaway. He gave a lopsided smile, could see the cop show now: Byford's Beat. It'd make Rebus look like a wimp.

Fish and chips or a big Mac? No contest. Bev had already turned down a big Mac. Tyler had invited her for a quick half down The Prince after work but she couldn't be arsed. Told him she needed an early night. True enough. She'd set up a meet first thing with Donna Kennedy.

The silver Beamer alongside the Midget at the lights had a budding Hamilton at the wheel; prat was revving the engine, giving Bev the glad lamp. She couldn't resist it. Soon as the green showed, she hit the gas, left the Lewis wannabe standing. The MG was like a starting pistol to boy racers. Bev stroked the dusty dash. "That's my girl."

Shame the case didn't have as much oomph.

The squad had been phone-bashing brick walls all day. As for the guv's idea of getting the victims together, it wouldn't happen any time soon. Beth Fowler was staying at her son's place in Brighton. Sheila Isaac refused point-blank to come to the station.

Bev flicked on the wipers though it was more drizzle than downpour. She peered through the smear. Highgate's main drag was lit like a poor man's Blackpool, all ethnic grocers and greasy caffs, private hire cab firms and second hand clothes shops. And just ahead was the best chippie this side of Neptune. And a space right outside.

She was back within a couple of minutes, goodies on the passenger seat. Two portions plus mushy peas was maybe going it, but she was a growing girl. Her smile froze, her hand stilled at the ignition. No. She wasn't. Not any more. Head bowed, she hunched over the wheel, the emotional pain as sharp as the Black Widow's blade in her belly. She gripped the wheel, took steadying breaths, willing the hurt to subside. Her best mate Frankie had witnessed a few flashback episodes, told Bev she needed counselling. Frankie had been told to fuck off. She'd packed her bags, left Bev to it. Baldwin Street now had a spare room. Bothered? She'd get a lodger, a stranger, someone who'd not give her a hard time.

The scream came from down the street. Bev's head shot up, vision blurred; she dashed away a tear with the heel of her hand. Scumbags. She was out of the motor in the blink of an eye. Five hoodies were circling a little old lady outside Threshers off licence, prodding, jostling, name-calling. Sods could easily have snatched her bag and buggered off. Seemed to Bev loads of kids involved in low level street crime only did it for the buzz, the kicks. Generally speaking, they got away with it. Police dished out cautions to save on paperwork. Punters looked the other way. Not this frigging time.

"Leave her alone, you little shits." She'd be on Strepsils in the morning. "Back off. Now." A handful of passers-by did exactly that, the five thugs turned as one, contemptuous leers on every spotty face. They couldn't have been more than fifteen, sixteen, stuffed full of swagger and strut. Seeing Bev hurtle towards them halted the granny baiting for all of two seconds. Clearly they didn't consider a lone woman a threat, all but one returned to hassling the old dear. The probable ringleader, dork with a death wish,

41

bared his lips, barred Bev's path. "What you gonna do about it?"

Everything but Dorkboy was a blur: her focus was absolute, momentum unstoppable – even if she'd wanted to. The defiant wide-legged stance meant his groin was an open goal. She scored – he took the penalty. Bent double, he clutched his crotch, gasped for breath. She was an inch from kneeing him in the face, controlled it just in time. Eyes blazing, she spun round, fists balled. The others had legged it. Shame.

"You're nicked, sunshine." Hissed in his ear. "Don't move a muscle." Not that he could.

The old woman was leaning against the offie wall for support. Bev placed a gentle hand on her shoulder. "You OK, love?"

"Will be when I've got me breath back. Thanks for stepping in like that. I only nipped out for a bag of chips." Sparse white hair framed a face that still showed traces of prettiness, the hand clutching her chest was scrawny and liver-spotted.

"Any time, love," Bev smiled. "Hang on here a sec."

Dorkboy was snivelling in the gutter. She nudged his arse with the toe of her boot, flashed a warrant card. He wiped his nose with the back of his hand. "Police brutality. I'll have you."

"Tell someone who gives a shit. On your feet." She counted five, grabbed his hood, hauled him up. "Pockets. Empty. Now." Another count of five. "Please yourself." She rubbed her hands, reached for the front of his jeans.

"'Kay, OK." Ineffectual fumble.

"Turn them out, dumbo." She tapped her foot. "What's your name?"

"Craig."

"Craig what?"

"Foster." He spread the contents on the damp pavement. The fags were probably nicked. Ditto the iPod. Gum, keys, comb, bus pass were fair enough; God knows why he was carrying condoms. Face like an arse was contraceptive enough. None of it was book-able. She took a note of his address, phone number then poked a finger in his chest. "Listen up, moron. One toe over the line and I nail you. Clear?"

"'Kay." More nose wiping. Not so full of it without his mates.

"Say you're sorry." She nodded at the old woman.

"Wot!"

"Now."

"Sod off."

"Suit yourself. Let's go."

"Where?"

"Disneyland." She reached for her phone. "Where'd you think?"

"OK, OK."

After a grudging apology, he strode off into the night muttering under his breath. Bev turned to the old woman. "Still hungry, love? Hang on there a sec."

Bev had lost her appetite. As she returned from the motor toting her fish supper, something in the gutter caught her eye. A car headlight picked it out again as she approached. Even before she knelt, she knew it was a knife. Was it Dorkboy's? Mostly youths only tooled up for protection. He'd probably dumped it when he realised she was a cop. Not as moronic as he looked then. Cos carrying was the only offence she could've have had him on. If it had prints, she still might. No gloves, nothing to wrap it. Unless…The old woman had wandered across. Smiling, Bev stood and handed her the chips. "Mind if I borrow your scarf, love?"

Fair exchange. No robbery.

Bev in Madame Pompadour gear – all red lace and low cleavage – held a dagger at the Sandman's throat. "Come on, joker. Show us the colour of your money." With the other hand she yanked off the clown mask. "Guv?" While she struggled to get her head round that, Byford's features morphed into the Black Widow's. Bev blinked, rubbed her eyes. When she opened them again, a machete-swinging Toby Priest advanced towards her sprinkling holy water. And she was wearing the mask. Screaming she teetered back and fell into a sand pit full of tiny bodies.

Gasping for breath, Bev bolted upright, flung off the duvet, sweat trickling down her spine. Byford, Black Widow, the Bishop. No prizes for guessing where that lot came from. Freud'd have a freaking field day. Make that month. Of Sundays.

She reached for the glass on her bedside table, took a few sips of water, glanced at the time. Great. Quarter past two. It'd taken ages to drop off anyway. She'd been wrestling with thoughts of Dorkboy. The youth had been lucky in one way. It was only his age that had held her back from inflicting serious damage. What really bothered her was that for a while she hadn't given a toss either way.

An hour later she was still propped up reading the latest Janet Evanovich, wishing her own love life featured a testosterone-fuelled lead called Ranger. Bev gave a wry smile. On her track record that'd be the Lone Ranger. The phone didn't wake her. She answered before it rang twice. "Bev Morriss." And waited. "Hello?"

It wasn't a breather, but she was pretty sure someone was on the line. "Is there anybody there?" Ouija board silly voice. Suit yourself, mate. Maybe a dodgy connection? Mind, there'd been a couple of hang-ups on the answer phone when she got back. She shrugged, gave a wide-mouthed yawn, stretched her legs and laid Ranger on top of the duvet.

The next call did wake her. It was just after four a.m. It was Highgate. And Operation Magpie had now become a murder inquiry.

"Victim's an Alex Masters, fifty-five years old." The cop on the door – PC Steve Hawkins – consulted his notes, his partner Sergeant Ken Gibson was on a mobile. They'd been the first uniformed officers to respond to the triple-nine. A DI and DC who'd arrived just after were now inside the property. Bev tightened her belt: it was brass monkeys out here with frost white-tipping the lawn and diamond-studding the drive. Could be why the MG failed to start; she'd had to grab a lift from Mac.

"How'd she die?" Mac rubbed a flaky patch of skin on his neck.

"She's a he," Hawkins enlightened them, "as in Alexander. Control got it arse about face." Call had been garbled apparently and whoever took it assumed a female victim because the Sandman targeted lone women. "Anyway, the guy died from stab wounds." Hawkins's mouth turned down at the corners. "Blood everywhere."

Bev glanced round. The crime scene was close to the Blenheim Avenue burglary, and not far from Baldwin Street – in distance. Not that she could see herself stretching to a plush mansion-ette in Park View. The cost-a-packet properties backed on to a fair-size private park and lido. Come first light, a search team would be finger-tipping the area. FSI were already hands-on upstairs, the body was in situ in the master bedroom.

"Who called it in, Hawkeye?" Bev asked.

"The wife. Diana. She was screaming, hysterical. No

surprise given what's gone on." Also helped explain the initial confusion. He jabbed a thumb over his shoulder. "She's in there now with a neighbour. She took a couple of flesh wounds. Lucky really. The bastard probably panicked, legged it…"

Bev flapped a hand. "Ta, Steve." Tad early for a speculative heads-up when she hadn't even seen the body.

Hawkeye gave a please-yourself shrug. "GP's on the way, sarge." Bev nodded. Ditto the pathologist presumably. Gillian Overdale always took her time. Then she'd bang on about the weather, the welfare state, women newsreaders. You name it… Bev turned a scowl into a cheery wave as Overdale cruised past in an aging Land Rover. She'd be whingeing about having nowhere to park in a minute. The road was chocker with police motors and a meat wagon waiting to transport the body to the mortuary. Despite the circus, Bev clocked only a couple of twitching curtains. This was posh-ville, residents didn't stand in the street and gawp.

"DI Talbot'd like you to have a word with the widow," Hawkins told Bev. She nodded, that figured. Pete Talbot, who'd taken on much of Mike Powell's duties, was a good cop, but at six-six and near on fifteen stone, his sheer bulk could intimidate some witnesses. A short fuse didn't help either. Course that was a plus when dealing with hard men.

"Pete still upstairs?" she asked. He was, and according to Hawkeye happy to hang around and liaise with Overdale. Top man: saved Bev a brush with Doctor Death. Through the door she caught a glimpse of polished panels, stained glass, stately home staircase. She nodded at Mac. "See what we've got, eh?"

47

The wife was in what Hawkeye had been told to call the drawing room. It had the feel of a genteel though slightly seedy drinking club with William Morris walls and heavy dark furniture, brass lamps cast dingy glows, stags and foxes gazed soulfully from gilt-framed misty landscapes. Dimpled copper scuttles gleamed either side of a huge fireplace, embers glowed in the grate. All it needed was a brace of flatulent black Labs and the tableau was complete.

It took Bev a second or two to locate the source of the noise – and what the sound was. Against the wall to the right of the double doors, Diana Masters was curled in the foetal position on a gold velvet chaise longue. The back of her neck was exposed: slender, white, vulnerable. Her narrow shoulders shook, heartbreaking sobs muffled by an oyster satin nightdress stained with blood. Bev halted momentarily. It was evidence; she should've been told to change. She bit back commenting. The husband wasn't the only victim here. Bev had witnessed this sort of pain too many times, countless lives ruined in the fall-out from violent death.

As she and Mac drew near, an elderly matron type homed in from the left. The neighbour presumably. Her bulky tweed-skirted hips straddled the approach path, and Bev caught a whiff of wet dog and dry sherry.

"I really don't think she should be disturbed right now." Her bulbous pale blue eyes shot glares between Bev and Mac. No one reacted to the sound of ash falling in the grate.

"You a doctor?" Bev asked.

"No." Wattled neck flesh quivered. "Dr Gannon should be here any minute."

"Best get a move on, then." Bev strode forward.

"I don't think so, young lady." Lady? Bev caught Mac

scratching his nose.

"What is it, Joy?" Diana Masters lifted her head, looked as if she was trying to focus – not just bleary eyes. There were a couple of defence wounds near the knuckles on both hands, another thin red weal on a well-toned arm.

"Don't worry, Diana dear, they're police officers and they're just leav…"

Bev barged in, hand outstretched. "Detective Sergeant Bev Morriss, Mrs Masters. This is my colleague, DC Mac Tyler. If you feel up to it, we need to ask a few questions."

Fleeting touch of fingers as the woman straightened. "Of course. I understand. Joy…?" Looked less than ecstatic. "I'm sure the officers would appreciate a hot drink." It was polite but it was a dismissal.

"White coffee, two sugars. Thanks." Bev gave the order. There was a Norwegian wood moment while they glanced round for a chair. Mac spotted a couple of uprights against a wall, carried them across the faded sage Wilton. Doing the interview standing was out of the question, but the seating arrangements felt a bit like an audience with a minor royal. Bev instantly dismissed the notion. Diana Masters had done nothing to warrant it.

"This is Alex's favourite room." She gave a deep shuddering sigh. "I feel close to him here. I hope you don't mind?"

"No worries. It's fine, Mrs Masters." Looking at her now, Bev reckoned pop princess was nearer the mark. The glossy hair with caramel highlights curved razor sharp under a firm jaw-line. Even without make up, the amber eyes were slanted, feline. Put Bev in mind of that singer: Sophie something? It'd come to her. Like a shed-load of other info, some of it useful.

At this stage, she knew squat about the Masters. Initial interviews were about feeling the way, laying down broad brushstrokes, fine detail being filled in by subsequent sessions. By the end, the cops would probably know more about Diana and Alex than their own mothers.

She led Diana gently through the easy ones, full name, age, occupation, family members, anyone who had access to the house. Mac's note-taking meant Bev was freer to register the non-verbal signals; in Diana Masters's case, licking the lips a lot, fiddling with earlobes. Bev was surprised to hear the woman was forty-one, she'd have guessed thirty, thirty-one. There was a daughter, Charlotte, twenty-three, who had her own place in Selly Oak and was on the way over. It was no shock to learn that apart from a few hours' voluntary work, Mrs Masters didn't have a job. Didn't even do her own cleaning, the hired help came in four times a week, young woman called Marie Walinski. Judging by the set-up, it was pretty clear Diana didn't need to earn a crust; the Masters family didn't look short of a bob or three. Then Bev clocked a photograph on top of a baby grand that confirmed her impression. Alex Masters on the steps of the Old Bailey, black gown billowing. No wonder the name had rung a bell. Masters was barrister to the rich and famous. Made Mr Loophole look like Judge Jeffries.

"And of course, Alex is very traditional. He's the bread-winner, I'm…" Early days, easily done. Diana Masters had lapsed again into the present tense. She'd do it for a while yet, certainly until after the funeral. It wasn't denial – sudden death took time to sink in. Soon as it hit home this time she dropped her head in her hands, rocked gently backwards and forwards.

Bev counted to twenty before clearing her throat ready. The widow took the cue. She dashed away tears with the heel of her hand then stared ahead, eyes narrowed as if trying to see sense in events that held none. "I still can't believe it. I was asleep, you see. I'd taken a pill. The noise woke me. I was groggy. Not really with it."

"Any idea what the time was, Mrs Masters?" Essential to establish a timeline or Bev wouldn't have halted the flow.

"I rang the police around a quarter past two, so a little before then, I guess. I thought I was dreaming. A nightmare. A clown! Wrestling with Alex at the foot of the bed. Ludicrous." Her glance sought Bev's agreement, approval. "Then the knife. Jab. Jab. Jab. And the blood." She squeezed her eyes tight. "I screamed and screamed and…"

Sound of clinking crockery. Gentle prompt from Bev. "What happened next, Mrs Masters?"

"Alex saved my life." Head high, she laced her fingers in her lap, spoke with absolute conviction. "The intruder would have killed me too but even badly injured Alex clung to his arm, wouldn't let him go, gave me vital seconds." A lifetime. "I hit the panic button. I couldn't see his face of course but I could tell the alarm had startled him. He stabbed Alex again. I could see that my husband was…"

Dead. Dying. "And then?" Bev said.

"He came towards me. I saw dark glittering eyes through slits in the mask. I knew he wanted to kill me but presumably was desperate to get away too. He came for me with the knife. I held my hands over my face. I thought, this is it – it's all over. I heard a police siren. He called me a… fucking bitch… then I fainted."

Prime witness passes out. Brilliant. "And when you came to?"

"Alex was on the floor. I went to him…cradled him in my arms." She was shaking, sobbing, barely able to get the words out. "But it was… too late. I'm so sorry…"

Bev glanced at Mac, tapped her watch. "You've been a

51

great help, Mrs Masters." Tactful as she could, she told the woman the nightdress would have to go to forensics, said a colleague would sort it. "Try and get some rest now. We'll talk later."

The neighbour came in with the coffee as they took their leave. That didn't halt their progress. It was the widow's remark as they reached the door.

"The irony is, Alex stays in London three evenings a week. He wasn't due home last night. Until the fight broke out, I didn't even know he was here."

8

"What d'you make of it, then?" Mac's focus was on his plate but the question didn't relate to the state of his breakfast. He and Bev were in the canteen, grabbing a bite before the brief. She'd opted for the full Monty, too. Giving away last night's fish and chips might've been good for the soul, but her body had paid for it. Since the early shout she'd been running on empty, felt dizzy and nauseous at one stage. Though that could've been the sight of Masters's body when she'd nipped upstairs to have a word with Pete Talbot.

Not normally given to spouting Shakespeare, soon as she'd entered the bedroom a quote had sprung to mind. Now it just slipped out. "Who'd have thought the old man had so much blood in him?" Well it was close enough.

Mac jabbed an admonitory sausage. "Masters was fifty-five. That's not old." Mac was fifty-two.

Bev rolled her eyes. "Ignorant pillock."

He shrugged. "I see where you're coming from, though. What was it Overdale said? Fourteen, fifteen wounds?"

"She reckons the post mortem might reveal more." Bev spread Daddies' sauce on a fried slice, added bacon, egg and tomato. "Frenzied attack is what the papers'll call it."

"They'd be right, wouldn't they?" Mac hadn't seen the body. There'd been no point both of them entering the crime scene.

"First time for everything." Satisfied with the filling, she topped it with another piece of bread. They ate in silence for a while. The place was filling up: uniforms, support staff, plastic plods – dick-lites as Bev called them. She

53

spotted Sumitra Gosh at the counter, lifted a fork in greeting. Maybe Sumi hadn't noticed. Maybe Sumi had other things on her mind. Mac clearly had. "The press'll crucify Byford."

That they would. She'd spoken briefly with the guv earlier. The big man looked as if he was weight-lifting as in world on shoulders. "He'll cope."

"Reckon the wife's away with the Mogadon fairies every night?" Mac asked.

"Uh?" Byford's missus had been dead ten years. Then the penny dropped. Diana Masters. Maybe she only needed help sleeping when she was alone in the house; maybe she was a chronic insomniac. Bev shrugged; who knows? It was on a growing list of things to find out. She gulped a mouthful of tea, scraped back the chair.

"Where you off to, boss?" Mac glanced up. There was still half a pig on his plate.

"Catch you at the brief."

"Hold on. 'fore you go." He offered her a napkin.

She scowled. "And that's for…?"

He pointed at her chin. "Out, out damn spot."

Mac quoting Lady M. There's a thing. Bev was still smiling when she sat at her desk, tapped a few keys and waited for the screen to come up with the goodies. Stone me. They say you shouldn't speak ill of the dead but by God Alex Masters was no oil painting. And she was studying a pic on the barrister's own website. Even in the rudest of health he was an ugly squat little bloke. Savile Row's classiest pin-stripe three-piece wasn't gonna disguise the pot belly. The head looked too big for the body, the hair was like wire wool, the squashed nose needed re-setting and the face could do with ironing. OK, beauty was skin deep but Bev bet the bloke had a hell of a big... bank balance.

She hit a few keys, waited for a page to download, mused a bit more. Was it money that made guys like Masters attractive? Or was it Henry Kissinger's theory about power being the ultimate aphrodisiac? The widow's grief had seemed genuine enough, maybe she saw beyond the surface. Not Bev, though. Give her a looker any time. Like the guy in the Fighting Cocks. If he didn't do drugs and it didn't go against her recently adopted rules of engagement she'd see Jagger lips again, no sweat.

Bingo. Here it was. She remembered seeing the article before. According to *The Times* on-line, Alex Masters had power, presence, charisma, call it what you will, in spades. Skimming the article, she reckoned you could make that pick-up trucks. Before marriage to Diana Scott, he'd sown more oats than the Archers. Professional strike rate was on a par. In legal circles he was known as The Raptor: razor tongued, cutting wit, sharp suits. Nowadays he was mostly associated with high profile court cases where A-list celebs were fined peanuts for offences ordinary mortals mostly got sent down for. In the past though he'd been a top criminal prosecution lawyer. Big bank balance? Masters was minted.

Footsteps in the corridor, banging doors, busy buzz building up. The brief. Shit. She grabbed her bag, put on a topcoat of lippie, gathered the stuff she'd printed out. "Sorry, mate – gonna be late." Masters's coarse features vanished from the screen as she closed the page.

Lucky to get a seat, or what? Bev glanced round a packed incident room, spotted a spare next to Carol Pemberton by the window. Bag dumped at her feet, she had a closer butcher's. It wasn't quite standing room only – two-thirds of the available officers were out in the field. Or the park.

One theory had the burglar gaining access by scaling the railings at the back of the Masters property. No CCTV coverage there. Luck or judgement? Bev knew where she'd put her money. The perp had certainly entered the house through a kitchen window. A pane had been removed with cutters, glass covered in perfect dabs and DNA. Yeah right.

The squad would hear the minute anything broke. FSIs were still on site, area search was underway, uniforms were knocking doors. Information was being called in, filed back. The clack from printers was pretty constant, ditto ringing phones. Jack Hainsworth was co-ordinating it, making sure it was disseminated. The Inspector collated and cursed in roughly equal measures. Bull-necked and big-mouthed, he hailed from Leeds but was no archetypal Yorkshireman. Hainsworth was less bluff more bolshie-bugger. And he didn't issue threats, he meant every word. Highgate's Mr Nice Guy. Not. But he was a sharp operator. And every member of the team knew he or she had to raise their game. Cos the guv had just finished telling them. Alex Masters's murder had upped Operation Magpie's ante. And then some.

As usual Byford was perched on the edge of a desk. The swinging leg indicated how keen he was to get on with the job. "Do we know if anything was stolen, Bev?"

Hadn't had time to ask. "Don't think so."

"Think isn't good enough," he snapped. "You spoke to the widow, didn't you?" Below the belt, the big man must be feeling the pressure.

Bev tensed. "She was wearing her old man's blood. We didn't talk about baubles. Sir."

Byford clenched his jaw, let the dig go, gave a terse nod when he noticed Mac had his hand in the air. "From what

Mrs Masters said, guv, it seems unlikely the perp had time to nick anything. She woke around two a m to find him attacking her husband. Way it looks, Alex Masters caught him in the act. The alarm going off would've panicked the guy and he fled empty-handed." Not quite. Bev pursed her lips. The burglar had taken his own belongings. Not so much as a grain of sand had been left.

"Why wasn't the main alarm on?" Question from a new-ish DC. Bev was about to answer when DI Pete Talbot piped up. Despite his bulk, she'd not noticed him hiding away at the back. He'd still been at the scene when Bev left, now looked as knackered as she felt.

"My guess is because Alex Masters was in the house. He was in his dressing gown, which makes me think he may not have been in bed when the perp entered. We know he arrived home after midnight." Next door's security camera had footage. "Maybe he felt like unwinding after the drive, fancied a nightcap, a bit of music. He wasn't expected back at all that night according to what the wife told Bev."

"That's right." She nodded. "According to Diana, he split his working week between London and Birmingham. Apparently followed the same pattern for a couple of years. A neighbour said the same. Obviously we need to run checks, but it looks as if anyone who knew the family…"

"Or made it their business to find out." Byford glanced round then tasked two DCs with tracing Masters's movements on the day he died. The Sandman would almost certainly have known them. Serious players didn't just show up in a striped jumper carrying a swag bag. They recced a location for days, weeks sometimes, recorded comings and goings, established habits. Everyone has a routine – not just comedians. And the Sandman was no joker. Seemed to Bev the burglaries had been planned to the last detail, carried out to the nth degree. Unless... She straightened, eyes narrowed, finger against lip.

"What is it, sergeant?" Byford recognised the pose.

Sergeant? Still pissed with her, then. "He cocked it big time last night, didn't he? Instead of finding Diana Masters on her own, the perp comes face-to-face with her old man. He was lucky not to get collared. Now he's looking at a life sentence."

"And?" Byford's leg swing had gone up a gear.

"What if it's not the same guy? What if some wannabe picked up the MO in the papers? Within hours of details about the mask etcetera being in the public domain – our man goes from hot-shot to toss-pot. Strikes me as weird, that." Encouraging copycats had been a factor in the guv's original decision not to release the information.

"Could be," he said. "Might just be coincidence. Either way, the killer's still out there."

"Not for much longer, mebbe." The Yorkshire accent carried across the room. Every head turned. Jack Hainsworth had a smug look on his face and a sheet of paper in his hand. "CCTV opposite the house? Guess who's been framed?"

9

Twenty minutes later as many bodies as would fit in the viewing room were squashed round one of the monitors. A despatch rider had biked the tape from Moseley to Highgate. Darren New cracked a stale line about popcorn. Then the guv pressed play. The relevant sequence hadn't been cued so they stood through a minute or two of suburban street life: scintillating shots of empty milk bottles, overflowing wheelie bins, lamp posts, lots of privet. An emaciated fox provided the only action when it limped across the road. Bev crossed her legs, dying for a pee, debating whether to nip out.

"Needs fast-forwarding," Daz pointed out. "Look." A piece of paper with a note of the relevant time frame had been stuck to the box. Thank God for that. Bev wasn't sure how much more excitement she could take. Great detection rate though – given CID's finest was gathered. Reminded her of an old gag: how many cops does it take to screw in a light bulb? None, it turned itself in. Punch-line was different in West Midlands Serious Crime Squad days: depends how many cops planted it. She considered sharing, trying to lighten the tension. Looking round she doubted Peter Kay could raise a smile. Anyway, it was show time…

Byford hit Play again, few seconds of build up and then… the big entrance. The perp came tearing through the Masters's front door, halted briefly at the gates to the drive. Sharp focus, perfect shot. Of a man in black, average height, average build. All very Mr Norm – except for the clown mask. "Take it off for God's sake," Byford muttered.

The guy glanced from side to side before dashing to the

left and out of frame. For several seconds no one spoke or moved, every gaze fixed on the screen as if expecting the perp to make an encore, take a bow.

Daz started a slow handclap but the guv cut him a glance that would've silenced the crowd at a police concert.

"Right." Byford balled his fists. "I want every frame of footage from every camera in the vicinity viewed. I want everyone on it traced. And I want every vehicle on it checked. The perp didn't disappear into thin air."

"Never know, guv." Pollyanna Morriss speaking. "The geek squad might work a bit of magic." Amazing what the guys in technical operations could do.

"The pictures need a miracle, sergeant. So unless Christ's on the payroll…"

"That who I think it is, boss?" Mac cocked his head at a print-out pic on Bev's desk – his crossed ankles were up there, too.

"Doing in my chair, Tyler?" She slammed the door, stomped across the floor of her office. "Feet. Now." Finger click.

Sheepish, he swung down desert boots, vacated the hot seat. Bev snatched the print-out, gave it a good shake. It was dotted with pastry flakes and grease spots. Alex Masters looked as if he had the lurgy. Mind, that was an improvement on his current condition. "What you been eating?"

"Cheese and onion pasty." Mac mimed empty pocket linings. "I'd've saved you a bite if I'd known."

"There's a gob full on this." She grimaced, checked her watch, raised an eyebrow. Don't have to be having fun for time to fly. Half past lunch o'clock already.

"I take it pretty boy's the vic?" Mac hadn't actually seen Alex Masters – dead or alive; not even spotted the photo at the house. She filled in the guy's back story: ex-criminal prosecution lawyer, barrister to the rich and famous. Byford was already up to speed: Bev had just come from his office. She'd intended sharing the information on Masters during the brief, but Jack Hainsworth's dramatic denouement had brought the curtain down early. Not that it was the main reason for her visit to the big man. She'd dropped by to pass on news from technical operations – if not good then slightly less bleak. The images of the perp weren't as black as Byford feared. She'd spent an hour or so with techie manager Brian Whelan. Though there was still a bunch of buttons to twiddle before getting final results, it was looking a tad brighter.

"Brian reckons there might be more than meets the eye to the Park View footage." Bev stood at the side of her desk, leafing through paperwork.

Mac turned his mouth down. "Like what?"

She was binning the boring stuff: crime stats, performance reviews, today's initiative. "Logo on the jacket. " She tapped her upper arm. "Another on the rucksack." Both needed enhancing.

"Rucksack?" Mac queried.

"Yeah, I didn't spot it first time round either." No one had. The communal focus had been on the face, well, the mask. "Nor the socks," she added.

"Socks?"

Distracted nod. "Two pairs, Brian reckons."

"Two pairs?"

"You got parrot genes, mate?" She dithered about ditching the print-out of Masters's *Times* profile, decided to leave it be. "Yeah. Thick wool socks over his shoes." Or trainers, boots, ballet pumps. Guessing game, wasn't it? The perp was au fait with enough forensics to know to mask his footwear as well as his face. FSIs covered up to protect crime scenes; crims did it to protect themselves. Proof – as if the cops needed more – to know they weren't dealing with a goofball. Also the best indication yet that the Sandman had wheels. And that the motor couldn't have been parked a million miles away. Byford's instruction to check every camera in the immediate area now had added imperative.

Mac had been gazing at the *Times* article. "Masters was an ugly bugger." He pulled a face. "Would you give him one, boss?"

"Not now, I wouldn't." She sniffed. "Got the time, Mac?" Her watch was in full view and there was a clock ticking on the wall.

"Uh?" Puzzled frown.

"I need a lift." She was already shucking into her coat.

"Knew you were on the cadge," he said. "The Mac's a giveaway."

Hitch-hike thumb in the air. "Yeah, well, I can see you're rushed off your feet."

He was now. "Where you want dropping?"

"Baldwin Street. Motor's gotta be sorted and I need to catch a few zeds." Donna Kennedy had called first thing. The Sandman's third victim wanted the interview rescheduled for this evening. Probably double-booked or something; she'd struck Bev as a bit of an air-head. Blonde, late-forties Donna had a touch of the Stepford wife, except Simon Kennedy had been dead more than a year. Though Bev hadn't much time for the woman, calling round this evening was no sweat. It was this morning's four a m shout that was a problem.

"Sleeping on the job, boss?" Mac winked as held the door for her. "Part-timer." Like he'd not already slipped home for a kip and a shower.

She caught a mixed citrus whiff. "Changed the after-shave?"

"No!"

Olfactory hallucinations: she was smelling things. Definitely needed a break. Counter-productive to keep going when you could barely keep your eyes open. Anyway unlike the paperwork, the overtime budget wasn't a bottomless pit.

"This lift, boss?" They were strolling down the corridor.

"Yeah?"

"Cost you."

Eye-roll. "How much?"

"Pieces of eight." Strangled squawk. "Pieces of…"

She laughed. He gave good parrot. "In your dreams, Percy."

10

"Little sods. They give animals a bad name. Need caging, the lot of 'em. And I'd chuck away the keys." The belligerent rant came from an old bloke whose head only just came up to Bev's shoulder. They were standing on the pavement outside her Baldwin Street pad, both staring glum-faced at the vandalised MG. Alfie Yates was a neighbour, born and bred in the house opposite, they'd lived a stone's throw apart for three years. Neighbourhood Watch? Bev hadn't even noticed the little man until he introduced himself a minute or two ago. Alfie was making up for lost time. Rabbit-rabbit.

Half-listening, she vaguely wondered why he'd never hit her radar before. The job probably. One of the drawbacks. The culture and anti-social hours meant personal hinterland – never mind community involvement – was mostly bare. Bev could count on the fingers of one digit the number of people she felt vaguely close to. Right now she wished she was next to the git who'd given the Midget a crap make-over.

Hands jammed in the pockets of her leather coat, she circled the car, totting up the damage. Two arms and a leg, she reckoned. Jagged lines had been gouged down both sides, glass shards from the wing mirror winked from the gutter, the soft top had shit air con. Stanley knife? Screwdriver? Metal comb? Bloody sharp whatever it was.

Alfie was waiting for a response, but she wasn't sure her voice wouldn't crack. She loved the motor more than some old boyfriends – including their bodywork. As for the MG's? Lips tight, she traced a finger along one of the raggedy tracks, emitted a fringe-lifting sigh. She peered inside. What was with the scarf on the passenger seat? Shit. What with everything else kicking off, the old lady and the lost supper had slipped her mind. Mental note: surrender knife.

"Police've been round," Alfie told her. "Called them myself first thing. Though what good the Old Bill'll do. I say old..." Derisive sniff. "Spotty-faced kid, all of twelve." His volley of tuts set loose dentures clacking like castanets. "What's your line of work, Bev?"

"Air hostess." Didn't miss a beat. Might've had something to do with the Boeing flying over. "I'm away a lot."

He gave her an old-fashioned look, but didn't comment. She felt a bit mean lying, but telling people what you did for a living wasn't worth the hassle. Alfie was a retired postman apparently. He had a round face, and his bald crown looked as if it had a white fur trim. Several chins concertinaed into an un-demarcated neckline. He put Bev in mind of a monk. There was no sackcloth, but plenty of ash. Alfie's angry words were punctuated with sign language from a wildly gesticulated Sherlock pipe.

As to the cops not nailing the bastards, Bev tended to agree. Even in the best of times, criminal damage didn't get much of a look in on the police priority list, right now most cops' eyes were peeled for the Sandman. She'd pull the attending officer's report when she got back to the nick, but since first sight of the ruined paintwork, her gut had told her this was personal. Maybe she'd kicked one butt too many. She wasn't on MySpace or Facebook, they were too in-your-face from a cop's point of view. But Bev didn't need a social networking site to know where the bad guys lived. And vice versa. Should they feel moved to find her.

"Mindless yobs," Alfie sneered. "No discipline, no respect. Streets aren't safe anywhere these days."

Bev narrowed her eyes. Dorkboy? Could this be down to

the yob and his gang? She tapped fingers on thigh. Nah. Probably not. There were likelier lads in the frame. She ran a few names through her head, all but missed Alfie's next diatribe.

"... the whole bloody road." He took it in with a sweep of the pipe.

She stepped back from the fall-out. "Say again, Alfie?"

"One end o' street to t'other. Five cars and a van they done over last night. Well, I say last..."

She frowned. "Sorry, Alfie, you saying it wasn't just my motor?"

"No, lass. What makes you think that?"

Wry smile. "Must be getting paranoid."

He tapped the side of his nose, gave a broad wink. "And y'know what they say about that?" He was still chortling as he crossed the road, waving the pipe. At the door he turned, shouted back. "Don't worry, lass. I'll keep an eye on the place. When you're on your travels."

Travels? She'd be lucky to take a flight of stairs.

Bev's pessimism was well-grounded. It was mid-afternoon before the motor was sorted, or at least on the road to being sorted. Carl, a mechanic at the Easy Rider garage she used in Stirchley had driven over with a swapsie, a VW Polo to tide her over. She'd not long waved them off, leaving neither time nor inclination for a kip. Sleep was the last thing on her mind anyway, too many notions buzzing round in there already.

One of which she wanted to moot to Diana Masters.

It was getting on for half-four when Bev parked the Polo outside the house in Park View. PC Danny Rees had drawn the short straw again. He was on the door, meticulously recording comings and goings, logging it was called. Well exciting. Just thinking about it made Bev yawn. Thinking one step further, it meant the forensic boys hadn't pulled out yet. Big job on their hands though. She peered through the windscreen. Sky was blue ink with a smattering of star glitter. Not surprisingly, the search team was calling it a day. Some of the guys stood chatting round the back of a white van, metal shelving and steel cases visible through the open doors, a couple of searchers still trying to find the way out of their paper suits.

Bev gave a wolf-whistle as she locked the motor. "Wotcha." There were a few waves and Hi, sarges. Rubbing her hands, she strolled to join them, wishing to hell she'd brought gloves. "Any joy, lads?" Nothing earth-shattering or surely she'd have heard?

"Big fat screwdriver do you?" Tall, stick-thin guy with a pencil moustache. Robin? Robert? "It was used to force the frame in the kitchen window."

Was he winding her up? "You joking?"

"Not me, but the perp's got a sense of humour." He told her it had been found in one of the Masters's flower beds, only a cursory attempt made to hide it. Lab work would confirm the forensic match, but to a trained eye the screw-driver had definitely caused the marks in the wood.

There had to be a punch-line but she couldn't read it in his face. "'Kay, so why aren't I laughing?"

"He'd only nicked it from next door's garage." The neighbour had been looking for it, actually in the garage at the time, happened to glance into the Masters's garden and saw the action. "Knew it was theirs straight away, sarge."

"How come?"

"Her husband carves his initials in all his tools apparently." He wiped the back of his neck with a crumpled hankie.

"Her?"

"A Mrs Cummings. Joy, I think she said."

Bev arched an eyebrow. They had come across a bit of joy then. "Prints?"

He snorted. "Now that is funny."

The screwdriver was so clean it squeaked. Not a solitary whorl. It had been carefully wiped before being left almost in full view. Bev stamped her feet, more to keep the blood flowing than signal frustration, though there was a smidgen of that, too. The Sandman obviously wanted the cops to find it. Why? Because nicking neighbours' tools to gain access was the sign of a pro. In this case – a two-fingered wave to show the cops how clever he was. Like they needed further proof. The guy was savvier than a smart arse convention.

"We can't go on meeting like this, Danny." Bev winked.

"Sarge." Still on door duty, PC Rees blushed as he stood to one side to let her in. Wiping her boots on the mat, Bev was still smiling when a waif carrying a tray of crockery stepped gingerly down the Masters's wide staircase. The tray looked too heavy for the girl's slender frame. Her dull blonde ponytail was scraped back so tight it brought tears to the eyes and accentuated what were already sharp features. The shapeless cheap-looking gear had charity shop written all over it. The girl had to be the hired help. Marie, was it?

"Hiya." Bev raised a hand. "I'm Detective Sergeant Morriss. Bev. Can you tell Mrs Masters I'm here, love?" She'd told the widow four-thirty on the phone, it was only a few minutes after.

"Sure. Would you like to come through to the kitchen?" Bev did the honours with the doors. Cups and saucers rattled as the girl laid the tray on a heavily scarred butcher's table. "She was having a nap. I'll just see if she's awake."

Lucky for some. Bev stifled a yawn. Mind, if the widow wasn't ready... "Cup of tea'd be nice while I wait."

Slight hesitation then: "No prob." She pulled one of the Bentwood chairs out from the table, Bev ignored it, took a nose round. The racing green and buttermilk colour scheme wasn't to her taste. Kitchen itself was a weird blend of retro and high tech gleam machines. Probably need an engineering degree to work the Gaggia; mind, it could double as a mirror. She peered at her reflection. Save a bit of time in the mornings – you could apply the slap waiting for your espresso to perk or whatever it is espresso does.

Perp's point of entry was easy to spot: lower right casement window was boarded up. Bev homed in for a closer look, clocked traces of dab dust on the sill. Not that there'd been any prints. A guy canny enough to wear socks over his footwear was hardly going to oblige by leaving greasy finger-marks all over the shop.

Mother's little helper was fixing a pot of Earl Grey. Bev pulled a face. No problem with the Jaffa cakes though. The girl looked as if she could do with scarfing a few packets herself, not so much slender as painfully thin. She was keeping her back to Bev. Chatty little thing.

Bev ran an exploratory finger along the granite worktop, played with one of the brass weights that went with a set of scales. It slipped through her fingers and landed in the sugar bowl. Without a word, the girl fished it out, ran it under the tap, put it back in its proper place.

Suitably chastened, Bev shoved her hands in her pockets, carried on with the tour. She twitched a lip at the celebrity cook books. The blessed Delia was bang next to the hairy bikers; the naked chef rubbed shoulders – make that spines – with the domestic goddess. Maybe the Masters had done a lot of entertaining? Mr and Mrs Dinner Party. Bev pursed her lips, somehow didn't see Diana getting steamed up over a hot Aga.

She perched on a corner of the table, swinging a foot. "How long you worked here, love?" The girl turned, leaned against the sink, her gaze seeming to weigh up the question. Her eyes were the palest blue Bev had ever seen. Before she spoke, she tightened her already taut pony tail. "Not long."

Shame that. She might've had a clue where the bodies were buried. Mental grimace. Not the brightest expression. Given Alex Masters's corpse was in the morgue. She winked. "What d'you think of it so far?" Then reached for a biscuit.

"Help yourself." Bev's hand froze halfway to her mouth. The girl grinned, raised a palm. "Only joking." An apologetic smile softened her face, the teeth were perfect, tongue pierced. Bev might have pigeonholed her too soon: Little Miss Chatterbox appeared to have hidden depths. Drown if she wasn't careful.

"This job then?" Another prompt. " D'you like it?"

"Yeah. It's cool." She pushed herself up, started pouring the tea. "Not like being a cop though. That's dead cool. Do you get to do all the murders?"

"Not personally."

Cartoon frown then she cottoned on, giggled like a schoolgirl. "D'you need a degree and stuff?"

Stuff mostly. "Why? Thinking of joining?"

"No way. Just wondered." Laughing, she pushed a mug in Bev's direction. "You know where the sugar is."

Bev couldn't read the girl at all. Either her humour was an acquired taste or she was taking the piss. She stifled another yawn. Blood sugar must be down; she bit into a second biscuit. "When you're ready, love. Sooner I've had a word, sooner I can get off." Bev narrowed her eyes, used the Jaffa cake as a pointer. "Is that Mrs Masters?" She strolled over to the Smeg where she'd spotted a photograph partially obscured by four or five fridge magnets. Diana Masters was barely recognisable from the grieving widow she'd met first thing. Stunningly attractive woman, dolled up for a night out. Charity do? Dinner? Something of the sort.

"What's she like, then? Your boss?"

"Ask her yourself. Dickhead."

"Sergeant." Bev's head whipped round. Diana Masters was standing in the doorway. "I see you've met my daughter."

11

Why hadn't the girl put her right? Bev was seething.

"Don't mind Charlotte, Sergeant. She's upset." Diana Masters was still framed in the doorway. Her placatory words broke a prickly silence. Bev noted the woman's immaculate make-up, the classic black dress. Widow's weeds. Before she could fashion a reply, the girl kicked off.

"Too right I'm upset." The girl jabbed a finger at Bev. "And *she* doesn't mind. She doesn't give a shit. She's an arrogant, slack, insensitive, condescending... pig." Sharp words, hard face, shining eyes.

Bev felt a blush rise, her heart rate was up, palms tingling. "Finished?"

"I've barely started, 'love'. You walk in here like you own the place, snoop round, talk to me as if I'm a simple-minded pleb. How dare you?"

Lecture from a lippy git she could do without. Bev opened her mouth to bite back. Then stopped. Did the girl have a point? She'd just lost her old man. Was Bev guilty as charged? Had she crossed the line? Again. Either way, the situation needed cooling. She had to have Charlotte Masters on board; the girl might hold vital information. Pissing off a potential witness wasn't the best way to elicit it. Damned if she was apologising though. She raised both palms. "What can I say?"

"Sorry wouldn't be a bad start."

"Sorry."

The pale eyes held a contemptuous glare. "God help us if the police are all like you." She was probably older than her slight frame and heavy irony habit suggested. Bev revised her original estimate upwards to early-to mid-twenties. The girl curled a thin lip. "Talk about scraping the barrel."

That was a barb too far. "You could've said something. Instead of…"

"… making you look a fool? Didn't need my help, love." Fighting talk but she was shaking like a leaf. And she still hadn't answered the question.

Bev tapped a foot. "Why didn't you let on?"

She folded her arms. "If you must know, I was curious. I wondered just how far you'd go. You and your ignorant arrogant attitude. No wonder the police are always getting it in the neck."

A strange sound staunched the flow of vitriol, and halted Bev who was mid-stride towards the girl. They glanced round in synch. Diana Masters, head in hand, was slumped against the door, tears dripping from her wrist.

Bev moved first. "I'm so sorry Mrs Masters." Genuinely gutted. It was only a few hours since the woman had witnessed her husband's murder. Last thing she needed was a dogfight in the kitchen. Bev placed a gentle arm round the woman's shoulder. "Can I get you anything?"

"Why don't you just get out?" the girl answered.

"Please, Charlotte. She's only doing her job." Mrs Masters's beautiful face was masked in pain. Mask. The main reason for Bev's visit; she'd wanted to question Diana about the clown mask. She led the widow across the kitchen, settled her in a chair. Shallow breathing, shaking, the woman was showing classic signs of a panic attack. Was there any mileage pushing it now? Bev stifled a sigh. "Take it easy, Mrs Masters. I'll drop by tomorrow."

"Don't bank on it. Love."

Bev turned back at the door. If looks could kill, Charlotte Masters would swing for her.

The bedroom lights were low, boosted a little by the glow from scented candles: cranberry and cinnamon, Christmas leftovers. The smells reminded him of Christmas Eve, the first burglary. Under the mask the man was smirking. He studied his reflection, loved the effect the flickering shadows had. No wonder it scared the rich bitches. If he was the nervy sort it'd put the wind up him. He snorted. Like that'd happen any time soon.

He turned his head this way and that in the triple mirrors, angled the glass so it reflected the clown face over and over again, each image a little smaller, a little more distant. Diminishing returns? The man sniggered. No way. Easy gains. Offing Masters had been a breeze.

Hands palm down on the dressing table, he zoomed in for a close-up. Through the slits, pinpricks of light danced in his pupils. Dark glittering eyes. That's what the old woman said when she'd mouthed off to reporters. He'd read it in the papers. So it must be true. Read a few other things as well. One of the rags wanted the lead detective to resign. He'd seen the cop on the news trotting out the usual platitudinous crap. By God, he'd like to bring the smug bugger down. None of the feds had a clue.

The media had started calling him the Sandman. How cool was that? Sighing, he shifted back on the stool, observed from a different angle. Just as he was having the most fun it would soon be over, time to hang up the mask. Not to worry. There were compensations. He reached for the phone.

Mac hadn't even placed the glasses on the table before Bev blew. "See, here's the thing… if your dad's on a slab down the morgue surely you don't go round dicking off a cop?"

He sat opposite, shoved her Pinot across, raised his glass. "Cheers, boss."

They were in the Prince, just down the road from the nick. Apart from cops, the place was full of old codgers, all very dominoes and Double Diamond. He couldn't remember when she'd last agreed to go for a jar. Though not her shout, this quick post-brief half had been Bev's call. It soon emerged she was after a sounding board, not a drinking partner. Mac was on bitter and sank a few mouthfuls.

"Well, do you?" Tight-lipped, she tapped a beer mat. He pointed at her glass, waited until she at least tasted the wine. He'd heard about the verbal dust-up with Charlotte Masters. She'd talked him through it on the way here, the unexpurgated version. She'd treated the brief to the barest of bones. Most of the squad's focus had been on follow-ups from the CCTV cull, possibility of a couple of leads there.

"Like her ma said, maybe she was upset." He hauled two packs of roasted peanuts from his pocket.

"Doh." She caught one single-handed. "Course the girl's upset. Her dad's dead. You'd think she'd have better things to do than play silly buggers with me."

Mac kept his eyes down. Pissing people off was becoming Bev's default mode. Sometimes not even deliberately. "OK... if it wasn't something you said..."

"If?" She glanced round, dropped the volume. One old geezer was adjusting his hearing aid.

Mac bit his lip, counted ten. "If it wasn't something you said... what are you driving at?"

She leaned across the table. "I know it sounds off the wall, but... what if she's hiding something?"

He raised a sceptical eyebrow. "About the murder?"

"Drugs maybe?" She shrugged. "Something a bit dodge."

He shovelled in a handful of nuts, chewed it over. Bev leaned in closer. "Maybe by alienating me she thinks she can distance herself from the police." The statement had a question in it – as did her eyes. She was seeking reassurances Mac couldn't give. Surely the notion sounded lame even to Bev?

"That's bull, boss. She's Masters's daughter. Important witness. She knows she'll have to talk to the cops, just not..." Talk to you. He didn't say it. Didn't need to.

"Cheers, mate." Face flushed, she banged the glass on the table. Like half a dozen old boys, he watched her stalk out the bar, coat flapping like the wings of a fallen angel.

Greensleeves. Why do people spend good money on door-bells with naff tunes? Bev scowled, pressed the buzzer again, stamped her feet. Despite the cold she was well steamed up. Mac tower-of-bleeding-strength Tyler. It was like the *Greensleeves* lyrics, all those doing-me-wrongs and discourteous-castings-off. She'd wanted Mac's reassurance, not his if-it-wasn't-something-you-saids. Raw nerves and struck chords. She pursed her lips. Deep down, Bev feared Charlotte Masters had every right to feel aggrieved. And that dropping hints about the girl being up to no good was classic defence strategy: attack being the best back-coverer. On the comfort front, Mac hadn't exactly overdone the routine. She sniffed. His stand-up was probably crap too.

It wasn't just the Masters spat that was needling her. She was ravenous, dog tired and it was arctic monkeys out here. She gave a deep sigh, glanced up. Not a cloud in sight, ice chip stars winked against a black velvet canvas. Very Lucy in the sky with diamonds... But where on God's earth was Donna with the wisdom pearls?

She checked her watch: just after seven-thirty. The

arrangement wasn't even down to her; Kennedy had rescheduled it from this morning. Mind, ever since the first meeting, she'd had Donna filed under D for ditzy. Had the visit slipped Mrs Butterfly Brain?

For a third time she rang the bell, let her finger linger for at least half a verse. Delighting in your company? *I should be so bloody lucky.*

Was there a light on upstairs? Bev stepped back. Not a pinprick anywhere. Lots of rosy glows elsewhere in Marlborough Close. It was like a mini Dallas: white houses, balconies, lots of wings. Very urban ranch, darling. The close was one of Harborne's upmarket enclaves. She snorted. Not like her own dear Baldwin Street where motors weren't safe from marauding lowlifes. She'd walked the road earlier while waiting for the mechanic to show, hadn't spotted any other broken glass in the gutter. Still not sure what to make of it. Maybe other car owners had already cleared the damage. She wasn't paranoid. Couldn't be a cop if you were. But as Alfie had implied, it doesn't mean they're not out to get you.

She felt for the Maglite in her bag. Right now, it was Donna Kennedy she wanted in her sights. She sauntered back to the door, bent to peer through the letterbox. This had so better not be a waste of…

Shit a brick. An icy chill shot down her spine. Shivering with shock now as well as cold, Bev's heart pounded. It was all she could do to keep the torch steady, but the flickering beam cast more than enough light. Donna Kennedy lay curled on her side on a Persian rug, sightless green glass eyes seemed to stare straight through Bev. Reproach? Remorse? Revulsion? Bev's next thought unleashed a shock wave that made her scalp tingle. Had the Sandman returned? Had Donna been a threat? Would key information be buried alongside her body? Had the cops unwittingly left it too late? Bev fumbled in her bag for the phone, took a final glance before setting the circus in motion. The woman's waxy white face wasn't set in fear. The death mask said something, but it was an expression Bev couldn't read.

12

The suicide note was more legible. Five minutes later and Bev stood in the hall wrestling with frustration and fury, a single sheet of ivory paper fluttered in her hand, the writing firm, the message clear. Donna Kennedy had killed herself because the Sandman had taken everything that made her life worth living. She described the humiliation of the attack and its terrible aftermath. How what had happened made her feel ashamed, vulnerable, violated. Bev bit her lip as she reread the final desperate words.

Night and day his eyes menace me, follow my every move from behind that grotesque clown face. Everything scares me now. I trust no one. I'm weak and lost and life is worthless...

The Sandman had imposed a death sentence – and as good as executed it. Bev squeezed the bridge of her nose. The poor woman hadn't been ditzy. Donna Kennedy had been driven to despair, clinically depressed and dying inside. So she'd swallowed enough happy pills to externalise the process. And made sure she'd never feel anything again. Bev placed the note on the hall table, raised an ironic eyebrow at a charity shop pen near the phone. Charity sure hadn't begun at home here. She knelt at the dead woman's side and gently stroked Donna's fine fair hair from her once-pretty face. She hoped to God the woman had finally found some peace.

Bev's was shattered by more bars of *Greensleeves*. Bloody racket. She rose and walked to the door half expecting to see the police doctor she'd called. You didn't have to be Quincy to know Donna Kennedy wasn't going anywhere under her own steam. The death still had to be certified by a medico.

"You looked as if you could do with a drink." The neighbour who'd let Bev in hovered on the doorstep offering hot chocolate. Small, round, twinkly-eyed, grey-permed, a Mrs Tiggy-Winkle made flesh.

Touched by the kindness of strangers, Bev managed a weary smile. "You're a star, Mrs Wills." Latex gloves peeled off and pocketed, she wrapped chilled fingers round the warm mug. "Thanks a mill."

"Reckon you can polish this off?" Bev's eyes lit up; a Penguin nestled in her palm. Talk about bird in the hand…

"Do bears sh…sing in the woods?" Whoops.

"If you need me – you know where I am. And I think you'll find what bears do is shit." Cheeky wink.

Bev watched open-mouthed from the door as the little woman scurried through a gap in the hedge, herbaceous short cut. Maybe she was missing Strictly Come Something Inane on the box. Bev narrowed her eyes. Missing something. A notion niggled that she was failing to spot something as well. When she bit into the Penguin, her mouth watered. Maybe the sugar hit would kick-start the mental juices too. As for Mrs Wills – the telly addict aspersion was unfair. The woman had just done her a good turn. And Donna Kennedy. The mutual key holding arrangement had emerged during Bev's initial interview with Donna. Thankfully it had sprung to mind before she forced the door.

Closing it now, Bev leaned against the wood, took a few sips of chocolate, studied the layout, the body. Why was Donna's final resting place the hall? Surely it made more sense to pop your pills – and clogs – in bed? Had she been heading for the stairs when she collapsed? Bev had found empty blister packs scattered across a kitchen surface, half-full tumbler of water on the draining board. Christ. The poor woman hadn't even used booze to blur the edges. Had she miscalculated the dose and the dying time? Sense? Calculations? Logic? Hello! The woman was topping herself, not auditioning for *Countdown*.

But why call to rearrange the interview? Was it a cry for help? Chewing it over with the last bite of Penguin, she wondered if the final act had been spur of the moment madness. Or if Donna had hoped to be found before the pills took effect. Bev swallowed hard: frigging screwed that up then. What a futile waste of a life. She closed her eyes, clenched her jaw. The sympathy was fused with anger now. Why couldn't Donna have clung on just a gnat's longer? Could she see no light at the end of the tunnel? In the darkest of Bev's dark days, ending it all had never crossed her mind. Homicide, sure. Suicide, never. She still dreamt occasionally of blowing away the mad bitch who'd killed her babies. Snuffed them out before they'd drawn breath. She took a calming one of her own.

Maybe if Donna Kennedy'd had kids she'd not have cut the mortal coil. Far as Bev knew there were no close relatives. Not that finding out was down to her. The death wasn't suspicious. No one had forced Donna's hand, doors or windows. Apart from uniform, Bev had called off the troops. Soon as officers arrived she'd shove off. They'd tidy up here then dig into the family tree, see if anyone needed the news breaking. Shit job that was.

Thinking of which… She stifled a yawn, pulled her mobile out of her bag. This wouldn't be a bundle of laughs either.

Byford was eating at the kitchen table, red wine at one elbow, latest Henning Mankell at the other, Bob Dylan blowing in the wind for company. One of the detective's new-year-new-man resolutions was to avoid the microwave and rubbish ready meals. Tonight he'd pushed out the culinary canoe. The fresh pasta was cooked to perfection, and the Matriciana was to die for. The Chianti was going down a treat too. Displacement activity? Probably. He sure needed something to take his mind off work. He knew it wouldn't last soon as the phone rang. Scowling he snatched the handset, glanced at caller ID. "Make it snappy, Bev. Dinner's on the table."

"Donna Kennedy's in the chiller. That snappy enough?"

Tight-lipped, he traced a finger along his eyebrow. Another death down to the Sandman? His heart sank as he considered the ramifications, professional and personal. The media had already written Byford off. The final edition of the *Evening News* had run a readers' poll: Cop out – or in? Isn't it time this man goes? Flattering picture they used: looked as if he had special needs. The paper had gone in the bin. Outside. Byford reached for his glass. "Go on."

"Topped herself. Overdose. Antidepressants." He heard her tapping foot add punctuation. "No suss circs. Uniform are here. Ditto the doc. I'm off home. Bon bleeding appetit."

Deep sigh. "Sergeant. Please." No point slapping her down. She'd clocked up sixteen hours flat, the exhaustion was audible. Bet she hadn't eaten either. He wandered to the stove. "What were you doing over there anyway?" Plenty of sauce left? Easily rustle up another portion of penne? *No. Don't even think about it.*

"I told you." Tut. "She switched the time of the interview." He grabbed his wine, leaned against the sink, listened as she filled in the details, how she found the pills, position of the body, letter left on the hall table. She threw in her take on the woman's mental state, her notion that it may have been a cry for help.

"Or plea for attention."

"Maybe…" She paused. He pictured her at the other end: blue eyes narrowed, lips turned down. "Think she was scared of not being found, guv? There's no kids in the picture, no close family. Maybe she couldn't handle the thought of lying dead for days?"

"So she called you? Thinking you'd get there, take care of the fall-out?"

"Cheers, guv. Feel better already."

He sipped the wine. "Suicide's genuine? No doubt on that score?"

"You'd have none either if you'd read the note. Bastard killed her though."

Didn't need spelling out. He heard a door slam, the rasp of a match, deep intake of breath. She'd kicked the habit when they lived together. Raised eyebrow. Well, said she had. He glanced round; Bev touches still graced the place: blueberry candles on the windowsill, a Playgirl apron hanging on the back of the door. A present. Not that he'd worn it. Nor the Santa hat on top of the fridge. She'd left before Christmas.

"Is it possible she knew him without even realising it, Bev?" The Sandman.

"Anything's possible…" A 'guv' was swallowed by a yawn. "Guess we'll never find out."

Forensics might though. He'd get a guy round there. Couldn't dump the sorting on Bev, she needed her bed. "Has the press got wind of it yet?"

"Not that I know."

It wouldn't be long though. He rubbed a hand over his face. Maybe the media was right. Maybe he should go. Maybe he was getting too old for this lark. Or maybe he was sick and tired of spending every long empty evening alone in a house that had only recently seemed too big.

"As I say, guv, I'm off. Catch you lat…"

"There's enough here for two." Smoke exhalation this time: breathing space? His own was bated. He'd regretted the offer soon as it slipped out. Hadn't he?

"Best freeze it then. Oh and guv? I'd like the Dylan back."

She must've heard it playing in the background. The greatest hits CD was another Bev relic. He frowned. Actually, no. She'd bought it as a gift. To tune his musical palate, she'd said. The line was dead or he'd have pointed out her mistake. Bob was still banging on though.

It's all over now, baby blue.

What you're doing, young lady, is cutting off your nose to spite your face. That's what her mum always trotted out when Bev was being a bloody-minded kid. Her dad called it wearing the stubborn-blinkers. She sighed, flicked on the Polo's radio to drown out the silence. Either way she'd sold herself short tonight. Lost out on a plate of decent grub and missed spending a bit of quality time with a decent bloke. Make that the most decent bloke she'd ever come across. Metaphorically speaking. Smart move or what? She whacked the wheel with her palm. Ouch. Why beat herself up? It was Byford's bloody fault. Make it snappy, Bev! Who'd he think…?

Christ on a bike. She hit the horn, swerving to avoid some binge-head who'd stepped off the kerb. It wasn't even chucking out time. Like that counted. Moseley village had its share of alco-fools any hour. Still loved the place though. It was so popular sometimes you couldn't get into the hippest pubs. Bouncers controlled drinker numbers by counting 'em all out, counting 'em all in. Mind, some nights the main drag resembled a war zone.

Make it snappy, Bev. Cheeky sod. While he'd been stuffing his face, chucking booze down his neck and listening to *her* Bob Dylan, she'd been holding the police fort freezing her arse off with a stiff for company. And her stomach still thought she'd had a gastric bypass. The lights were on red at Saint Mary's Row, she hit the handbrake, toyed with picking up a take-out from the Taj Mahal, or dropping by the Sicilian pizza place? Nah. CBA. Can't be arsed. It'd be BOT again. Beans on toast.

Make it sodding snappy!

By the time she pulled up outside the house, her mood had dropped down a few gears. From seething through pissed off to the current how-dumb-can-you-get? She'd as good as told the big man to go fornicate while taking a running jump in the fast lane of the M6. Like she could so afford to alienate him professionally. And personally? There were times every nerve in her body ached to be in his arms, but that would mean letting him get close. How could she when she had reverse-Midas? As in everything she touched turned to shit. She dropped her head to her chest and hugged the steering wheel.

It was why she failed at first to spot the two figures huddled in her doorway.

13

Fareeda Saleem was only on her feet because Sumi Gosh was clinging on to her cousin's shoulders for dear life. Even then Fareeda was bent double, arms clutching her stomach, and issuing soft low moans with every breath. Bev's doorstep was stained with what appeared to be drops of blood.

"I couldn't think where else to go." Sumi's words didn't say a lot, it was an understated plea writ large across stricken features. The young DC was normally never less than cool, calm and professional. Sumi was rattled now, rapidly losing it, equally patently this was no place to be.

"How 'bout a hospital?" Bev could barely hide her incredulity – and censure – that Sumi had seen fit to show up here with someone clearly so sick.

"No… please!" Fareeda lifted her head briefly, long hair swishing like black satin curtains. Pain deepened the shade of her already dark eyes, and Bev caught a flash of blind terror.

"I can't get her to go." Sumi stroked the younger woman's back, made soothing sounds. "She's afraid."

You don't say. "Look, Sumi…"

"If you'd rather we…" She cast a sideward glance: pride, propriety, decorum.

Bev had the key in the lock. "First on the left. Sling us your coats." The sitting room would do. Until she'd talked sense into them. Fareeda needed medical attention. Was she pregnant? Miscarrying even? When they'd met in the car park at Highgate, Bev hadn't spotted a bump – only a big fat ugly bruise. Maybe there was a baby – and the two were linked. "Hang fire, I'll get the door for you." She stood back while Sumi, still supporting her cousin, steered a course to the nearest sofa, started settling her, reassuring her with soft words.

Bev had a zillion questions on hold. "Back in a min," she called. There was a first aid kit in the kitchen, and they might need hot water. She yanked out drawers, searched cupboards, scanned shelves. Where was the bloody thing? Under the sink. Where else? Quick check of the contents revealed antiseptic, witch hazel, pain killers, enough bandages to wrap an Egyptian mummy. Should do the trick. Shame there was no medicinal brandy: Sister Bev needed a drink or three.

"May I get some water for her, please?" Sumi stood in the doorway, her elegant taupe linen suit spattered with blood. Gracious as always, she seemed to be finding eye contact difficult. And however proper her manners, bringing an injured woman here was out of order.

"Sumi. She needs a doctor."

The floor tiles were clearly fascinating. "She'll be OK."

"Is she pregnant?"

That caught her attention. "Are you mad?" Her guffaw verged not on humour but hysteria. Straight-faced, Bev crossed her arms, waiting. "That was rude. I'm sorry. But Bev, I doubt Fareeda's been alone with a man who wasn't family in her life."

She didn't labour the point but Sumi's answer hadn't exactly addressed the issue. Bev turned her back, took a Coke glass from a shelf, headed for the tap. Like a lot of apprehensive people, Sumi felt the pressure to talk, blurting out: "She's only just eighteen, Bev." Like that figured?

"And?" Again she wasn't going to spell it out. Sumi was being disingenuous. Or in denial.

She spread her hands. "Trust me. Fareeda's not expecting.

If you knew her, you'd realise the idea's preposterous."

"Then why's she…?" A wail cut the supplementary. Fareeda might not be pregnant, but she was scared and in pain. As to the answer, Bev was pretty sure she could take a crack at it. In the overhead lighting in the sitting room, it was obvious someone had taken a crack at Fareeda.

Her beautiful face was beaten black and blue, the damson shade matched her kameez, the silk ripped at the neck. Her nose was probably broken; the bleeding had just about stopped. Her top lip was split, the lower swollen to cartoon proportions. No one was falling about laughing. This was the discernible damage; Bev knew damn well it wouldn't be the full extent.

Hands on hips, she stood over the teenager so fired up she could barely spit out the words. "Who did this?" Her teeth hurt they were clenched so hard.

Fareeda mumbled something but Bev couldn't decipher it through sobs and the lisp; two teeth were missing at least. She cut a glance to the older woman. "Sumi." It wasn't a question. It was an order. Non-negotiable.

Sitting next to Fareeda, stroking her hand, Sumi shook her head. "I don't know. She won't tell me."

"She'll tell me." Bev knelt on the carpet, coaxing, cajoling. Fareeda barely responded let alone revealed detail: what happened and, more to the point, who'd made it happen. In effect the girl was protecting her attacker, a man who'd used her as a human punch bag. Bev felt desperately sorry for her.

"OK, have it your way." She rose, turned at the door. "Get your coats."

"Please, please don't make me go." Tears ran twin channels down the teenager's bruised and bloody face. Bev reckoned you'd need a heart of brick not to be moved.

"I'll drive."

"No!" Fareeda screamed.

"The hospital. You need checking over, then I'll take you down the station for a statement."

She gave a defiant stare, the first indication she still had some spirit left. "I'll kill myself before letting you do that."

"The fuck you will!" Shaking with fury Bev stormed across the room. "Never pull that line on me again. Got that?" Maybe she should tell Fareeda she'd spent the night with a corpse, a woman who'd swallowed her bodyweight in happy pills. Another victim of sick violence.

Fareeda dropped her head, fiddled with the bunch of bangles round her wrist. "You don't understand."

"Got that right, kid." Bev frowned, couldn't catch Fareeda's mutterings. Patience wearing thin, she snapped: "Say again."

Eyes brimming, she tossed her head back, raised her voice to a loud shout. "Get this right too. If I speak out they'll kill my mother. Maybe my sister, my niece. They don't care." Tears dripped from her chin, splashed into her lap.

Bev knelt again, took the girl's hands in hers. "Who will, Fareeda? Why will they? Tell me, love. We can stop them."

Head high, the teenager held Bev's gaze. "And if you can't?"

She glanced at Sumi who was biting her lip looking shattered. Bev lifted a finger, too whacked to think properly. "One night. Then we'll see." She shook her head, gave a deep sigh. "I need to sleep on it."

It was three a m when the phone rang. Fareeda was in Frankie's old room, asleep, presumably. A shocked and sober Sumi had taken off home shortly after seeing her cousin to bed. Bev had grabbed a slice of toast, knocked back a half-bottle of Pinot and hit the sack. She'd zonked soon as her head touched the pillow. Now she wanted to stuff the bloody thing over her head. Groaning, she fumbled for the receiver, snapped out her name.

Nothing. No one. Nada.

"I don't frigging believe it." She punched in 1471. Caller withheld. There's a surprise. Half an hour later, still tossing and turning she swung her legs out of bed, grabbed a dressing gown from the back of the door, headed for the loo. The gown was an unwitting legacy from Oz Khan, her erstwhile lover and former DC, now a sergeant in the Met. Its brushed cotton used to smell of Oz. After he'd gone she'd bury her nose in the fabric, breathe in his scent wallowing in what-ifs and maybes. Then she'd lost his babies and turned down his offer of a life in London. A boil wash had done the trick on the cotton. Shame it didn't work on lingering emotion as well.

She sighed ran both hands through her hair, picturing Oz's face: sculpted cheekbones, full luscious lips, dark chocolate eyes like deep limpid pools. Chick-lit? Dick-lit more like. Mills and Bev. She gave a lopsided smile then flushed the loo, washed her hands. Quick glance in the mirror confirmed she looked like shite. Tough. Given what she'd witnessed tonight, it wasn't the worst look in the world.

Back on the landing she heard a noise from the spare room. She pressed an ear against the door heard Fareeda's stifled sobs. She reached for the handle, pulled back at the last second, knew further probing tonight would be futile. Fareeda was on a psychological knife edge. Bev was pretty mixed up as well: compassion, concern, but also still a touch of anger. Fareeda had said one thing that made sense.

"You don't understand."

She was bang on. And until Bev did, she'd leave the girl in peace. Tomorrow she'd make it her business to try and get her head round the issue. Drifting back to bed she swallowed a yawn. Nothing else on the books, was there? Apart from nailing the Sandman. Easy sodding peasy.

From behind a horse chestnut tree on the opposite pavement, a dark figure watched the house. The trunk wasn't wide enough to conceal the observer completely. Had Bev glanced out, she might have spotted the outline of a body, the glow of a cigarette. The watcher thought the risk worth taking. When the bedroom light was turned off, the observer emerged from behind the tree, padded over the road. Gloved hands carried a package which they carefully placed on the step. Late Christmas? Early birthday? Either way the cop was in for a surprise.

WEDNESDAY

14

Bev's nose twitched, a lazy smile spread across her sleepy face. Proper coffee. Was there a better smell in the universe first thing? Arms above her head, she stretched full length in bed cogitating. Cut grass? Sweet peas? The sea? Suntan skin? Chips and vinegar? Bacon sarnie? Strawberries? Bread baking? Candy floss? Dark chocolate? Rive Gauche? Yeah yeah yeah: point taken. But dark roast Kenyan came pretty damn close. Eyes wide, she bolted upright. However pukka it was, coffee didn't brew itself.

Almost tripping over the duvet, she was halfway downstairs before last night's events fell into place: the caffeine fairy had to be her house guest Fareeda Saleem. As Bev entered the kitchen, the teenager peeked through long glossy black hair, then pushed a mug across a work surface. Service with a shy smile.

Bev winked. "Could get used to this." Her Snoopy jim-jam bottoms were at half mast; she hauled them up with one hand, concerned gaze covertly raking the teenager's damaged face. "How you doing, kid?"

"Fine." Knee-jerk response. Touchy subject. Far as Bev could see the swelling on her bottom lip had gone down a fraction overnight, bruised eyes still resembled over-ripe damsons. Emotionally she seemed to be holding it together, and was evidently keen to change tack; two slices of bread were on standby for the toaster. "Ready for breakfast?" Given the crumbs and buttery knife on the table she'd already had a bite. Kids!

"Definitely get used to this." Bev flashed a smile, grabbed the coffee. "Give me five mins, yeah?"

It was nearer ten when she came down suited, booted and abluted. On the basis she still looked like an extra from *Shaun of the Dead*, she'd opted for a sharp blue skirt suit. Hopefully some sartorial edginess would rub off on its wearer, unlike the hastily applied slap that just about concealed two broken nights' sleep.

Bev paused at the door, loath to disturb Fareeda who stood at the sink gazing through the window, miles away. The girl wouldn't be admiring the garden; nothing there to write home about, even when it wasn't ink-black outside. It didn't seem as if Fareeda was studying her haunted reflection either. Bev reckoned her mind's eye was watching an action replay, a mismatched big fight. Dwarfed by one of Bev's white cotton nighties, the girl looked featherweight.

Bev checked her watch, gave a rueful sigh. At 7.22 there was no time for small talk let alone big issues. The guv's eight o'clock brief wasn't optional, she had to get a move on. Fareeda must've caught movement in the glass, she turned to face Bev. "Thank you so much for letting me stay."

"No sweat." Her hungry glance fell on breakfast. "Ta for this, kid." She snatched a few sheets of kitchen towel off the roll, wrapped it round the toast. "Have to eat on the hoof. If I don't hit the road…"

"You said one night." Unwittingly perhaps, Fareeda's fingers stroked a swollen discoloured cheek. "Do you want me to leave?"

Despite what was probably emotional blackmail, Bev had already made up her mind. She wanted Fareeda to be safe, untouched by inhuman hand. That meant knowing where she was. "Make yourself at home, eh? We'll take it a day at a time." She cocked her head at the table. "And get rid of those crumbs. This ain't a flaming hotel, you know." A warm smile and wink took the heat out of her words.

The girl nodded, eyes brimming, fingers kneading a slender forearm. "Thank you so much, I…"

"Later." She raised a palm. "We'll talk then."

Later. Like she'd deal with the sodding parcel on the doorstep. After nearly tripping over the damn thing, she scooped it up, glanced at the tag and tucked it under her arm. It'd be the desk clock she'd spotted on eBay: the flashing blue light would give her Highgate mates a laugh. Mind, she'd have another word with Postman Pat, he was lucky the bloody thing hadn't been nicked.

"Hey, Morriss! This is your lucky day." The familiar voice shouting across the car park was almost drowned out by contractors digging up the road at the back of the nick. They were replacing water mains or something, drilling seemed to have gone on for weeks.

Bev reached into the Polo's passenger door, a smile curving her lips. She knew who was predicting her fortune without looking round. It wasn't so much the quasi Delboy delivery, more the sarky, "Morriss". The only guy she knew who didn't call her Bev or sarge was Mike Powell. The DI wasn't a sexist git just because of that. There were loads of reasons. Was it good to have him around? Betcha.

"Mystic Mike." She yelled back, not even trying to hide the smile in her voice. Still without a backward glance she locked the motor, then juggling shoulder bag, files and parcel headed for the rear of the building. This time of morning the air was chocker with exhaust fumes, aftershave trails and wafts of perfume. She always reckoned her nose could detect Highgate's early birds. Quick sniff, quirky frown. Not that one though. Powell was just behind her now. Had he finished at Hendon? Or had the guv requested his early release? Given Operation Magpie's increasing complexity, the squad's workload was growing fast – same as the pressures. If she was the guv she'd split the inquiry, have one team concentrate on the burglaries, the other focus on the murder, pool everything at joint briefs. "You back with us then, sir?"

"Can't keep a good man down, Morriss." He upped the pace; fell into step beside her.

"Yeah, but what about you?" The cheeky wink finally established eye contact. And boy was he looking good. She might have told him if her teeth weren't clenched against the cold. Sod it, if the temperature didn't buck up she'd soon be investing in thermals. Heated bra would be good.

"God. You look rough." Mike Powell: Mr Charmer. Or was that snake? She opened her mouth to bite back then stopped. There'd been no edge to the remark, his concern was probably genuine. Even more reason to ignore it.

"Equality awareness course, was it, at cop school?" She was wide-eyed innocence, knowing full well Powell had been tutor not trainee. Lecturing in Intelligent Management, Mac had heard. Sounded like an oxymoron to her.

Powell could've got the door but held back deliberately. She gave an exaggerated sigh as she struggled to open it. "Glad you passed. A* was it?"

"Patronising, isn't it? Blokes holding doors for wimmin." He'd purposely crossed his what-women-want wires to wind her up.

"Patronise ahead." She nodded at the first fire door, arms still laden. This time Powell did the honours, even stooped to pick up the parcel and a file she'd dropped. She had to admit he looked almost tasty. His skin glowed, the blond hair a tad longer now, curled at the neck. The dove grey suit swelled in all the right places. "Joined a gym, have we?" She sensed his appraising gaze as they walked; he'd be limping if he didn't watch what he said.

"*I* have." He left it at that: subtle for Powell. Perhaps he'd learned something in class after all. Their catch-up chat was intermittently put on hold as colleagues passing in the corridors welcomed the DI back with Hi Mikes and the odd high-five. Hendon had been badly hit by a flu out-break, he told her. So many people were down with it loads of sessions had been cancelled, including his. Either way he'd have been back next week, his three-month stint was up this Friday.

"And you just couldn't wait to get back in the saddle, eh?" They'd arrived at Bev's office.

"I know you can't live without me, Morriss. Heard you were pining away."

"Get the hearing aid checked if I were you." Her fingers closed on the door handle.

"Pardon?"

She rolled her eyes. "That is so old. Try a refresher course next time."

"Touché, mon babe." He tapped his forehead, walked away, whistling what sounded like *I heard it through the grapevine.*

Still smiling she bummed the door, off-loaded files and bag, shucked out of her coat. What was Bob Dylan doing on her keyboard? Of course, last night's phone call. She'd told the guv she wanted her CD back. She sniffed. He could at least have given it to her in person. She lifted the case, turned it over. Big of him, he hadn't even left a note to say thanks. Actually. Eyes creased, she tapped the desktop. Felt the hint of a blush. Her greatest hits were at home. This had been a present for the big man. *A present.* Like the package on the doorstep this morning. Powell had waltzed off...

He walked in without knocking, dumped parcel and file on her desk, loosened his tie. "Must be getting as ditzy as you, Morriss."

"Time of the month, sir?" Deadpan, she grabbed bag, file, notepad, water bottle. "Brief's in five. Don't be late. First day back and all that."

Byford had clearly been busy. Still was. The big man was up at the front, back to the squad, standing towards the end of a row of five incident charts. His sleeves were rolled back and a charcoal grey jacket was slung over the nearest swivel chair. Bev headed for a seat by the window, glanced at the guv's handiwork in passing. The first four charts covered sequentially the Sandman burglaries, the fifth was devoted to the murder. In the centre of each board was a close up of the victim: Beth Fowler first, Sheila Isaac, Donna Kennedy, Faith Winters, finally, Alex Masters. Each pic was circled in thick black marker, lines led off to smaller circles. In his distinctive italic script, Byford had added names, locations, main players, key points. And a crop of question marks. He was still working on the murder chart.

Byford's headmaster stance might have subdued the atmosphere, or maybe Donna Kennedy's suicide had dampened the team spirit. Whatever was to blame for the downbeat vibes, it was so quiet you could hear the guv's felt tip squeak.

Bev slouched back, hands on head, legs crossed, and sussed out the action. Mac was texting, Pembers was biting a nail, Powell leaned against a wall leafing through one of the zillion files he needed to catch up on, Peter Talbot and

Jack Hainsworth were shuffling printouts, the two new-ish DCs were reading through their notes probably in the hope they'd be word perfect when it came to delivering input, Daz was doing *The Sun* crossword. Bev sighed, circled an ankle. Byford still had his back to the gathering, pen still squeaking. She spotted Sumi Gosh behind a desk a few rows back, gaze fixed on a computer screen. They needed to get their heads together, sooner rather than later. After signally failing to attract Sumi's attention, she tried air mail. Missive scribbled on a sheet of A4, she folded it into a paper plane, sent it flying into Sumi's air space. It crash landed into Darren New's who re-modelled a wing tip before re-launch.

"What are you playing at?" If the guv had yelled, it would've been less ominous. Everyone in the nick knew the softer his voice the harsher the sentence. A pointer tucked under his arm, Byford was replacing the top on the marker pen, steely glare on Darren.

"Sorry, guv, I was…" The words petered out, but the bobbing Adam's apple said a lot.

"Being puerile," Byford sneered. Bev's ankle was like a windmill in a force ten. What was bugging the big man? He'd be handing out detentions in a minute. "If I could afford to lose an officer you'd be off the squad."

That was well over the top. Bev straightened, bristling. "Daz didn't start it. If you *need* to take it out on someone – have a go at me." Her eyes blazed, heart raced. It was as good as calling him a bully who needed a whipping boy to cover his own failings. As if that wasn't enough, she'd issued a public challenge for him to take her on. In the diss-the-boss stakes, it was a double whammy: insubordinate – and insolent.

Byford clenched his jaw two, three times. She stared,

arms folded, aware the squad was holding its collective breath. Talk about sailing close to the wind; this was more like the eye of the storm. When he spoke, the words were little more than a whisper. "When we've finished here, you report to my office."

"Sir." Loud and clear.

"Donna Kennedy committed suicide last night." Business mode, normal delivery. Byford's roving gaze took in every officer present. "Her death – far as I'm concerned – is as much down to the Sandman as Alex Masters's murder." No one argued. "We stop him before there's another." Earnest. Unequivocal. And total bollocks. They were no nearer an arrest than they were on the first day of the inquiry. Byford walked the line of charts, used the pointer as he named each victim, paused a few seconds to let the incident's import sink in.

Facing the squad he said: "The targets weren't selected at random. He didn't just flick through yellow pages. There have to be links between the women. We've looked before. Clearly we've not looked hard enough. We dig deeper. I want ideas."

The sound of a pneumatic drill shattered the silence, broke the still uneasy tension. There was the odd laugh, a weak one-liner. Byford nodded at the open window, the nearest DC took the hint and closed it.

"How about a property angle?" Mac scratched his cheek. Bev frowned. Burglars often had a favoured point of entry: louvred windows, french doors, whatever, they rarely deviated from an MO. The Sandman wasn't fussy how he got in; they'd already dismissed this line of inquiry. "Maybe the victims have had dealings with the same estate agent?" Mac had a different line in mind. It was a reasonable next move. Up to now they'd concentrated on establishing personal connections: family, friends, neighbours, colleagues. Same with any case: start small, work out. If the women had thought of selling their houses, it meant keys could be floating around. Not the likeliest scenario but at least the ball was rolling. The team ran with it.

"What about banks? Building societies? Do they use the same branch?"

"Motors? They all drive. Maybe they visit the same garage?"

"Go to the same gym?"

"Hairdresser? Library?"

"Callers to the house? Gardener maybe?

"Window cleaner?"

"Milkman?"

Potential leads or clutched straws – they'd all have to be checked if only for elimination purposes.

"Volunteers?" Byford lifted an eyebrow. A couple of DCs raised their hands.

"Don't bother calling Diane Masters." Head down, Bev jotted notes on a pad. "I'm seeing her this morning."

"You're not," Byford said.

She looked up smartish. "It's arranged."

"I'm not getting into it here. See me later." Open-mouthed she watched as he perched on the edge of a desk, rolled down the sleeves. "Chris? Forensics, please."

She glowered through her fringe as the FSI manager Chris Baxter took a sip of tea, coffee, whatever, from his Buffy mug. A slight flush highlighted his freckles as he swallowed, then dabbed thin lips. "As you know, we lifted fibres from the railings at the back of the Masters property." Black cotton. Didn't amount to much until they nailed the Sandman and got a match. If they nailed… "We're still waiting on a few test results but apart from that it's more of the same." Which meant SFA. Sweet forensic all.

Byford's lips tightened. Frustration wasn't in it. Each crime scene had yielded an embarrassment of potential goodies, they could run donkey rides on the sand alone but not a grain had been traceable. Or rather it was – to any builder's yard in the UK. Ditto the tethers. The three-ply nylon cord was manufactured by the mile and available in almost every hardware store across the country.

"Any joy with the knot man?" Daz asked. Bev stifled a snort. She doubted Prof Ed Mclean would appreciate being referred to as the knot man. It made him sound like a bondage act on *Britain's Got Talent* instead of Europe's leading forensic knot analyst. They'd found Mclean via the National Crime Faculty at Bramshill. Cops used the NCF register when they needed input from expert witnesses or behavioural investigative advisors – posh for profilers, or the Freud Squad. Either way, soon as the cords had been through the local forensic mill they'd gone down to Southampton for Ed Mclean's specialist take.

"Talked to him briefly last night." Baxter ran fingers through thinning ginger hair. "Like with the previous cases, the knots used on Faith Winters are simple half-hitches, and were tied right-handed. Though that could be to disguise the fact he's left-handed." Chris's blush had deepened a shade. No wonder. The local forensic ace had come up with identical info days ago. She'd like to know how much the pro was being paid. Talk about old rope and easy money.

"And that's it?" Byford asked.

"He's cross-checking burglaries with similar MOs, but…"

"Best not hold our breath?" The guv sighed. It wasn't the inquiry's only instance of hopes being raised then dashed by forensic let down. Way back at the first crime scene, traces of sweat and skin had been extracted from one of the cords, knots were usually a good place to lift DNA. Only snag? Lab tests showed it was Beth Fowler's. Bev wouldn't be surprised if the Sandman had planted the bloody stuff. He could be a cop, he knew so much. She frowned. No way. Yes way? Either way – given her current standing, it wasn't an idea she'd be sharing any time soon. She plumped for safer ground. "Anything back on the knife you bagged at Blenheim Road, Chris?" Knife. Shoot. She'd not handed in Dorkboy's blade from the other night. Must still be in the Midget. Mental note: get on to it, Beverley.

"It's in the initial report. There's a copy on your desk." Must've missed it under all the other stuff. She spread empty palms. "Tests aren't complete," Chris said. "But the blood's not human." Coincidence more than convenient discovery, then? Couldn't really say the news was a shock; Bev had never shared Danny Rees's rose-tinted theory. "Shouldn't take long to determine what animal it's from," Chris added. "Not sure where it'll get us though."

Movement on the CCTV front was equally disappointing. A couple of DCs had interviewed owners of vehicles parked overnight in the vicinity of the Masters place; every one checked out. Of the five people who appeared on the tapes four had come forward after media appeals. All four had been eliminated. Which left one mystery man.

"Get on to the news bureau," Byford told one of the detectives. "Tell Bernie I want the CCTV frames issued to the press by midday at the latest."

Bev made mental notes as she listened to more negative feedback: no headway with mask suppliers from Mac, ditto stolen jewellery from Carol Pemberton and Sumi. One of Bev's notes made it on to paper: exhibits, check.

"Stick with it, everyone." Byford rose, retrieved his jacket. It was almost a wrap. "If there's no early break, I might take the *Crimewatch* option. I had a producer on the phone last week wanting to send up a researcher." There's a surprise. Bev could see the reconstruction now. Man in clown mask, terrified woman tethered to a bed, low light, menacing shadows, sprinkling sand, spooky soundtrack. Good telly, wasn't it? Long as you don't have nightmares.

"Want me to look after that, guv?" Powell casually stroked his neck.

"Mike. Sorry. I got sidetracked." The guv cracked his first smile of the day. "Should have welcomed you at the start. Good to have you back on board." Bev raised an eyebrow. A sidetrack now, was she? "Just so everyone knows," Byford continued, "soon as DI Powell's up to speed, he'll take senior investigating officer role on the murder inquiry. Pete Talbot'll remain SIO on the burglaries. I'll stay in overall charge, and I'll be looking to split the squad into two teams." There'd be joint briefs, he said, and smaller strategy meetings with the SIOs and other key players as and when.

The reasoning was sound. The inquiry was already becoming unwieldy. With more and more information being gathered it was increasingly vital to prioritise and disseminate it properly. As Tony Blair didn't say: communication, communication, communication.

Byford slipped into the jacket. "Anyone want to add any-thing?"

Not a word apparently.

15

It didn't happen often. Bev was speechless. As in goldfish.

"Don't be under any illusion," Byford said, "she's this close to slapping in an official complaint." Bev glanced at the guv's finger and thumb – they were butt-joined. Post-brief, she'd tailed the big man to his office expecting a dressing down. Now they faced each across his executive desk, he'd not even asked her to sit. Charlotte Masters had phoned Highgate first thing apparently. She'd seen Byford's name in the press, knew he was the officer in charge. Currently he was only just keeping a lid on his anger. "Objectionable, amateur and incompetent were among the adjectives she used." He glanced at a Post-it note on the desk. "Not forgetting a disgrace to the force."

Four or five screaming gulls patrolled a roof opposite. Sodding racket. Shame she hadn't got a gun. She waited until Byford closed the window. "Charlotte Masters wants me off the case, that's all."

"Don't be ridiculous." Thanks for listening, guv. "She found you obnoxious."

"Obnox…" The voice couldn't get any higher. She cleared her throat. "Obnoxious?"

"She said it – not me." He jammed a hand in his trouser pocket. "The girl's upset, for God's sake, her father's been murdered."

"Turn on the waterworks did she?" Bev studied her nails.

"If that's your attitude, no wonder the girl's got a grievance." And thanks for the vote of confidence, guv. Byford took a deep breath before ploughing on. "I assured her you were one of my best officers, experienced, sensitive, dedicated, professional."

"'preciate it." Sheepish mutter.

"I've not finished. Ms Masters doesn't share my view. If she goes ahead, sergeant, it won't just be the interview you'll lose." She followed his glance to a fat personnel file on top of the out-tray. Her name wasn't visible but she'd seen the file often enough. She'd faced so many disciplinaries, she should have a seat on the board. Meant Byford had already been on to Human Resources for her paperwork though.

She toed the carpet. "I did apologise to her."

"Not always enough, is it?" He walked to the water cooler, poured himself a cup, drained it. "What did you say to upset her?"

Guilty as not even tried. She objected loudly. "Make out like I deliberately pissed her off, why don't you, oh you did."

"I won't tell you again, sergeant." The voice was danger-ously low. "Don't answer back."

She licked dry lips before giving him a précis of the exchange with Charlotte Masters, then: "It was six of one and half a dozen of the other. I was out of line maybe but she could've put me straight."

"It's not down to a witness to 'put you straight'. Sort your-self out, sergeant." He reached for the phone. "I'm asking Mike Powell to go out there this morning." She shrugged. Being Powell's second fiddle was better than sitting on the subs' bench. "Carol Pemberton can go with him."

She stopped just short of stamping a foot. "Putting someone else on it's playing into the girl's hands. Sir."

"D'you really think I'm so easily manipulated?" He shook his head. "And it's not a game."

Course not. But Diana Masters was a key witness. Pleading her case didn't come easily to Bev, but she rated

Powell's interview skills as patchy to middling. "Me and the widow are like this, guv." It was pushing it a tad to show crossed fingers. Not that showing closeness was why Bev usually employed the gesture. "Look, if I run into Charlotte, I'll give her the full-on Morriss grovel." Her eyes shone. "One more chance? Please?"

"I gave you one." He stared at her for five, six, seconds. He'd missed a bit shaving, but now wasn't the time to mention it, she reckoned she knew what was coming. "You threw it back in my face." At the brief.

Yep. She raised both palms, felt a blush rise. "I was totally out of order there. I apologise. It won't happen again."

"Damn right it won't. Consider this a verbal warning. Next time it'll be in writing." He nodded at the door.

His eyes were harsh as the words. There was no leeway however hard she searched. "Sir." She turned, walked away, head high. Pleading was one thing, but she'd not get on her knees. Halfway out of the office, she heard the receiver hit the cradle.

"Bev." Eyes brimming, she glanced back. "One last chance. That's it."

He held up a single finger to drive home the point; her vision was blurred, she was seeing double.

PC Danny Rees was on one knee in the middle of the pavement head-height with a little girl who looked like Alice in Wonderland's kid sister. Bev raised a curious eyebrow as she drove past. Following the action in the wing mirror, she parked the Polo a few doors down from the Masters place. Flushed and frowning, young Danny looked a little out of his depth. The kid was in floods of tears, clinging to the hand of a whippet-thin, thirty-something blonde, presumably the mother. They were all rabbiting on, but from where Bev sat it was a silent movie. A grey winter blanket sky added to the monochrome impression, Park View seemed leeched of colour bar the little girl's scarlet coat, and a couple of magpies arguing the toss over a dead rat in the gutter. Two for joy? Yeah right.

For all of a second or three, she considered giving Danny a hand. Nah. She lit a Silk Cut instead. This was the rookie's deal and he needed the practice. More to the point she was itching to interview Diana Masters. Soon as Mac rolled up, they'd get the show on the road. Fanning smoke through the window, she glanced at the clock on the dash, tutted. The rush hour was over: trust Tyler to get caught in traffic. Normally they'd have travelled together, but after the blistering encounter with the big man she'd ached for her own space. Last thing she needed was Mac coming over all paternal, trying to get her to open up.

Frowning, she glanced in the rear view mirror. The silent movie now had sound effects. What was that kid's problem? Talk about throwing a wobbly. Mind, Bev knew the feeling. Since the guv's bollocking, her mood swings made an emotional rollercoaster look flat. The hurt and gratitude had morphed into self-righteous pique. She took a deep drag. Frig's sake – she was hunting a murderer not looking for a best mate. Course she'd be civil to Charlotte Masters, but she'd not be cowed by anyone. If she had to watch every word she said, the suits might as well gag her. It'd go with the straitjacket. Fighting crime was crazy enough without both arms tied behind the back. Anyway bottom line was this: if push came to shove they could stuff the job.

"All in a day's work, eh, sarge?" Danny was squatting at her window, nodded at the kid and woman as they strolled past the motor.

"What's up? Someone nick her jelly babies?" Bev cracked

a half-smile. Danny was easy on the eye, and had a decent line in banter – a rare breed at Highgate.

"Nah. She wants me to look for Crumpet."

"Thought you had a girl?"

The blush was endearing. "Missing cat. Me being a policeman she wants me to get a search party out. I told her I was a bit busy, like." Bev nodded, knew Danny was now on the team mopping up house-to-house inquiries, not everyone had been at home during the first wave. "Said they should get posters up, see if…"

"When'd it go AWOL?" She took another drag, eyes creased against the smoke, toying with a notion.

"Couple of days, why?"

"Where'd they live?"

He nodded up the road. "Big place round the corner, with the hedge?" Close to where uniform had found a knife stained with animal blood. A discovery Bev had always seen as dead convenient. "What's up, sarge?"

"Dunno yet." It was a hell of a leap from missing moggie to master criminal. She frowned, trying to think it through.

Danny removed the helmet, smoothed shiny dark hair. "Her mum was giving her a hard time as well, reckoned she was telling porkies."

"Lost me there, Danny. This cat missing or what?"

"Yeah, it's missing, but the little girl says someone ran off with it. Wants me to put the bad man in prison." Indulgent smile, shake of the head.

Bev stiffened. "Did the kid actually see a bloke take the cat?" Curt.

The smile faltered slightly. "The mother says she makes things up all the time."

"Did she see a bloke take the frigging cat? Christ, Danny, you were here when we found the knife."

"You think…?" She'd never seen blood drain from a face so quickly.

"I don't know what I think, 'cept there's an outside chance the kid might have clocked the perp. You'd best…"

"On it, sarge." Like a bat on speed. He was halfway down the road before she'd hit fast dial for forensics. The tests needed narrowing down. If it was cat blood on the knife, they needed to know pronto. Busy line. "Damn."

"Where's the boy wonder off to?"

Jeez-us. Mac was at the window now. Not such a pretty sight. "Tell you later." She'd get on to the lab after the Masters interview. The cat thing was probably a wild goose chasing red herrings down a dead end. No sense wasting even more time now Tyler was here. She stubbed the baccy, grabbed her bag. "What kept you, mate?"

He pointed at the ashtray. "Could have you for that. The Smoke Free Exemptions and Vehicles Regulations 2007 states quite…"

"Nothing in the known universe could you have me for, mate." She locked the motor, headed towards the house. "So? What kept you?"

He hitched his denims. "D'you never listen to the radio?"

It'd been on; she'd not been tuned in. "Just give, eh?"

"Some nutter's on top of Selfridges."

"Pissed off at the prices probably." Cynical snort.

"Police cordons, traffic diversions. It was like a circus down there."

He'd come from Highgate to Moseley via town? "Took the scenic route did you?"

"I fancied a quick nose. Powell's there calling the shots."

"Why Powell?"

"The guy on the roof's dressed as a clown."

The Selfridges building is a Doctor Who spaceship fashioned by Steven Spielberg out of Salvador Dali. A massive blue whale covered with silver discs, it's beached in the Bullring and dwarfs neighbours including the faux-gothic Victorian church of Saint Martin's. Powell reckoned it was surreal enough without a clown mincing along the top. Gazing upwards, he also reckoned Dali would've appreciated the spectacle. The crowd certainly was: scores of shoppers, office workers and the odd wino were enjoying a free show. Uniform was doing its best to keep everyone back, but the thin blue and white line was severely stretched. Powell slipped through the police cordon and headed for the action.

"Eh, you!" A burly uniform grabbed the DI's shoulder. "Where'd you think you're going?" The loud Birmingham accent set Powell's teeth on edge. Eyes blazing, he shook off a ham-sized fist, flashed his warrant card. The lack of recognition was mutual.

The older man eventually gave a token salute. "Sorry, sir. PC Knowles. Andy." They were getting heavy with the crowd, he explained, because there'd already been a couple of public disorder arrests, two youths hacked off with the disruption chucking their weight around – and their fists. A few sickos had even been yelling at the guy to get a fucking move on.

"Tossers." Powell clenched his jaw, recalled an incident in a neighbouring force when a baying crowd acting like animals, goaded a teenager to jump to his death from a multi-storey car park. It was the last thing they needed. "Negotiator here yet?"

"On the way, sir." Knowles added that more troops and a uniformed inspector were inside liaising with maintenance people, having a look at the building's layout. Knowles ran a fat finger round his collar. "God knows how he got up there."

Powell shuddered. He was acrophobic. Just looking at the bloke gave him palpitations.

"Has he said anything?"

"Barely a word. Being honest, I reckon he's pissed." The PC sneezed into his hankie, sounded like a horny elephant. Someone in the crowd yelled, Bless you. Knowles scowled. "Some of this lot seem to think it's a joke."

Laughter and cheers broke out as if on cue. Powell's gaze followed craned necks and pointing fingers. And froze. The guy had a gun. "Shit. Get everyone…"

"It's a water pistol," Knowles snarled. "He was blowing bubbles a while back. Playing up to the cameras, isn't he?" There was a nearby line of snappers and wannabe auto-cuties with clipboards – as well as the world and its aunt taking mobile phone footage.

Powell finger-combed his hair then took a closer look where the lenses were trained. The figure on the roof was in full clown costume: loud yellow-checked jacket, red baggy half-mast strides, striped black and white socks. The fun guy even sported a spotted bow tie. And Powell would be surprised if the bloody thing didn't have flashing lights and whiz round. He was beginning to think the only thing linking this nutter to the Sandman was spin.

Control had taken half a dozen triple-nines from anonymous callers. Punters who'd have read the papers, seen the telly, spotted the clown mask and maybe triple-jumped to conclusions: two plus two equals a pile of garbled Chinese-whispers. Powell sighed. It happened a lot. Mixed messages, mischief makers, genuine mistakes. Either way, he reckoned this was a waste of CID's time. He'd have a word with his uniform opposite number then pull out. Turning to leave, he caught a yellow flash in the corner of his eye. Just for an instant, he fancied the spread arms of the jacket resembled a canary's wings. And though Powell would always recall the incident in slow motion, the clown then took a running jump.

16

Diana Masters opened the door herself. Her chic black suit was probably Chanel; the row of shimmering pearls accentuated the classy image. She looked pretty good for a recent widow, or maybe she knew how to mask the grief. Close up it didn't work. Bev noted mauve shadows under the artfully applied concealer, puffiness around the kohl-lined feline eyes. "Sergeant Morrison, isn't it?" She stroked the necklace, her Sloane Ranger voice slightly hoarse.

"Morriss, Mrs Masters. This is my partner, DC Tyler." Bev's was a tad hesitant, unsure what the reception would be.

"Morriss, of course, forgive me." Ghost of a smile, fleeting handshake. "Charlotte's had to go out, so if you want to talk to her as well, I'm afraid…"

"We'll catch her later, no worries." Phew. Bev wiped her feet – and her mental sweaty brow – then told herself not to be a wuss. It only put off the inevitable. The hall smelt of beeswax, the banister gleamed. A crystal vase with stunning red roses had appeared on the dark wood console table since the last visit. Someone had been busy.

A few steps in and Mrs Masters halted, raised her voice. "Marie? Can you rustle up coffee for three, please?" She tilted her head until the order received muffled confirmation from Marie who was likely in the kitchen. Nothing seemed to have changed in the room where they'd first met, though this time the widow eschewed the chaise longue, drifted towards the fireplace, gestured wordlessly at a pair of green leather wing chairs. She slipped off kitten heels, and with shapely black-stockinged legs tucked neatly beneath her, nestled into the arm of a matching chesterfield. "I seem to spend most of my time in here." A sad-eyed glance took in the surroundings as she circled her wedding ring. "Alex loved this room. It's where I most feel his presence." She gave a self-deprecating smile. "If that doesn't sound too cheesy."

She'd made the same point last time. Bev still couldn't see it. The space was dark and depressing, the deer-laden landscapes dire; she'd junk the lot in the nearest ditch. As to proximity to the dearly departed, the aesthetically-challenged Alex Masters was right beside his widow – in photo form. A leather-bound picture album lay open on the settee, four or five more lay scattered on the faded carpet. The current spread showed the couple's wedding, traditional post-ceremony poses, wall-to-wall smiles, lots of tender touches, loving looks. Diana Masters had clearly been leafing through the past. They needed to edge her into the present.

"I know this is a painful time, Mrs Masters, but there are questions we have to ask."

She folded lightly bandaged hands in her lap, neat nails were Barbie pink. "Of course."

They'd decided to press ahead with the interview despite the circus kicking off in town. Not that Bev thought the rooftop stunt amounted to a row of beans. Soon as Mac told her the guy was prancing about in full clown costume she'd more or less dismissed him as a serious contender for the Sandman. The perp they were hunting was sadistic, calculating, professional. No way would a cold-blooded killer pull a crazy trick that guaranteed prison and a porridge diet. Even if she was wrong, however events in the Bullring panned out, the woman opposite had vital information. All Bev and Mac had to do was draw it out.

"If you could talk us through again what happened the

night your husband died, Mrs Masters?" Bev slipped a copy of Mac's notes from her pocket, needed to compare what the woman said now with the original version: omission, deviation, addition could all be telling. When a witness was word perfect it could mean they'd memorised the lines thinking they'd be less likely to divulge incriminating material. Course, they could just be telling the truth.

Diana Masters took a deep breath and swallowed hard. She repeated how the sounds of a scuffle woke her from a deep drug-induced sleep. For a few seconds, she'd thought it was a dream, a nightmare, her husband wrestling with a man in a clown mask. The intruder rained blows time and time again. She didn't even realise there was a knife. Until the smell of blood brought home the terror. She repeated her belief that her husband sacrificed his own life to save hers. By grabbing the killer, Alex gave her precious seconds to reach the panic button. His reward was another vicious onslaught. She bit her lip. "How can people like that live with themselves, sergeant?"

What could she say? She shook her head. "Did your husband speak at any stage, Mrs Masters?"

"Speak?" She looked confused, not rabbit-in-headlight variety, more slightly thrown. "No. No, I don't think so. He was struggling to breathe, fighting for his life." She barely reacted when a phone rang somewhere in the house.

"You said the intruder approached you?" Bev asked gently. It was always going to be the hardest line of questioning. The widow closed her eyes, massaged her temples. Bev exchanged glances with Mac. "Take your time, Mrs Masters." Uncle Mac mode.

She was clearly psyching herself up. When she spoke, the words spilled out fast and furious. "He came within three feet. All I could see were his eyes. Black. Shiny. Aroused.

He wanted to kill me. I'm convinced of that. It was only the alarm that stopped him. He had to take a split second decision to finish the job or escape. He panicked, called me a…"

A tap on the door halted the flow. Bev cursed mentally. Interruptions they could do without. Marie, presumably, came in with a silver tray, set it on a low table. She looked like Kate Moss a decade ago on a bad day: lanky hair, pouty mouth, pasty complexion. "Someone called Tate on the phone, Mrs Masters, shall I…"

"I'm busy. I'll call back." She swung her legs down, sat forward, started pouring coffee into white porcelain cups. The girl hovered with a gormless expression on her face. "That's all, Marie. Thank you."

There was milk, sugar, biscotti on the tray. Mrs Masters told them to help themselves. Mac took advantage of the enforced break; he needed a leak, though that wasn't the term he used. While they waited, small talk was strained: the weather, the widow's charity work, the William Morris wallpaper. Jeez. They'd be on the price of onions soon. Bev hid growing impatience; the interview was at a critical stage. Before Mac even sat down, Bev took up the questioning. "You were about to tell us what the intruder said, Mrs Masters?"

"He called me a fucking bitch." Her bottom lip trembled. "No one's ever spoken to me like that in my life." Lucky you. It was almost a daily occurrence for Bev.

"Was there anything in the voice you recognised, anything that reminded you of anyone?" Long shot given it was just two words.

She shook her head. "I only wish there were, sergeant."

"Difficult one this, Mrs Masters." It was the same question she'd intended putting to Donna Kennedy before her untimely death. "Is there any chance at all you know the man?" Not easy implying someone has a psycho in their social circle.

Predictably, she bristled. "Of course not." Her hand shook and the cup rattled as she placed it in the saucer.

"Please, Mrs Masters, just think about it. Was there anything about him that was even vaguely familiar? Smell, stance, way he walked?" The squad had assumed from the start the perp wore the mask to prevent the women providing a description, but what if they knew what he looked like. And if they'd seen his face could provide an identity? As the guv said, the Sandman didn't flick through yellow pages, looking up V for victim. He appeared to know a fair bit about the chosen individuals. Maybe the likes of Donna, Faith Winters and Beth Fowler couldn't handle the possibility that someone they associated with at whatever level could wish them harm, let alone carry out an attack. At least Mrs Masters was giving it some thought now, clearly replaying the scene in her head.

"I think he was quite a young man, twenties perhaps? Powerful, strutting, arrogant, what's the word…?"

"Macho?" Bev suggested.

She nodded, concentrated again. Bev counted fifteen seconds before the widow shook her head. "It's no one I know, sergeant." It didn't have to be an intimate acquaintance, Bev persisted. She talked her through possibilities: garage mechanic, travel agent, wine waiter. Again Mrs Masters considered the suggestions before dismissing them. It was the same take on links between her and the other victims. Mac had brought photographs of the women. Diana Masters studied each image carefully. She frowned, hesitating over Faith Winters's picture. Breath held, fingers crossed, Bev asked if she'd come across the woman before.

"Only on the news, I'm afraid." The widow dropped her head. "I don't actually know her."

Bev's heart hit her boots. Gently she pushed again and again, old ground, new ground. The only certainty established was that nothing had been stolen during the incident. Eventually they reached the point where it was counter-productive. "God knows I want to help, sergeant." Mrs Masters ran both hands through her hair. "I'm so tired I can't think straight." Each strand seemed to fall back into perfect place.

Resigned, Bev said they'd leave it for now, took a card from her pocket. "If anything comes to mind, Mrs Masters, even if you're not sure it's important, ring me any time."

"Thank you." She gave the card a quick glance, placed it on the album. Grilling over, she sank back, visibly relaxed. But something was bugging Bev, seeing the pictures reminded her. They'd now traced Alex Masters's movements on the day he died. He'd returned to his London chambers late afternoon after the unexpected collapse of a big case. He'd told a partner he intended clearing a backlog of paperwork, gave no indication he was thinking of heading back to Birmingham. Clearly, he'd changed his mind. Security cameras clocked him leaving the building just after eight p m. He'd eaten at a bistro round the corner before collecting his Audi from an underground garage. More cameras and a paper trail showed he'd stopped for gas and coffee at Cherwell Services on the M40. Next door's CCTV had footage of him arriving home at midnight, parking the car and letting himself into the house.

"One more question, Mrs Masters. Any idea why your husband didn't call? Let you know he'd be back?"

"He did call."

"But you…"

"Around eight. To say goodnight. He sounded tired. He said he was going to eat then go back to the apartment." A bachelor pad in Docklands, according to the DC who'd run the checks.

"And he didn't call again?"

She sighed. "I guess he may have tried…But when he's away, I generally go to bed early, take a pill. And you know, sergeant." The widow glanced at her husband's photograph, a sad smile tugging her lips. "Despite appearances, Alex was an incurable romantic, quite impulsive from time to time. It could be he wanted to surprise me."

He'd sure done that.

PC Danny Rees, mobile glued to his ear, was perched on the bonnet of Bev's motor. The Polo was a rental: Rees was on borrowed time. "Shift your arse, Rees." If his bony bum had dented the bodywork, there'd be hell to pay. Not to mention the Easy Rider garage. Smartish he jumped up, backed away, palm raised in apology, still gabbing on the phone. Park View was pretty quiet this time of day, posh, affluent, definitely not ASBO territory. People in these parts had letters *after* their name. Bev lit a Silk Cut, picked a fleck of baccy from her tongue. "What you reckon, mate?"

Mac unwrapped a Mars bar, jabbed it in her air space. "You should stop smoking."

"Yeah right. Diana Masters. Top line." Travelling back to the nick in separate cars meant it'd be a while until they could pick over detail.

"I think she was doing her best." He took a bite, then: "Seems genuinely cut up to me. What'd she say about the will? 'I'd give away every penny if it brought Alex back.'"

Pass the sick bag. Mental slapped wrist. As to the attack,

the widow had related – though not verbatim – the same sequence of events. That augured well for authenticity if not totality. What Diana Masters had seen was so traumatic the brain was probably suppressing the full picture: subconscious censorship, cerebral defence mechanism. Witnessing murder was bad enough, how much worse when the victim was someone you love? Diana had adored Alex Masters; Bev didn't doubt that for a minute. Neither did Mac.

"Worshipped him, didn't she?" He winked, shoved in the last bite of chocolate. "What's he got I haven't?"

Apart from eight million quid? Smoke curled from Bev's flared nostrils. "How long you got, mate?"

Danny joined the confab, pointing the phone at the Polo. "Sorry about that, sarge." Gleam in the eye, he tucked the mobile in a tunic pocket. "Heard the latest?" Clearly, he was gagging to share.

"Shipping forecast?" Bev drawled. "FTSE? Give before I keel over in a frenzy."

He glanced round like it was classified information. "There was this nutter on top of Selfridges…" Past tense.

She flapped a get on with it hand. "And?"

Pursed lips. It was his story and he was telling it. "Dressed as a clown. Police were there, fire, ambulance, the works…"

"Danny?" She flicked ash on the ground. "What's happened to him?"

"Him?"

17

Jessica Kathryn Harvey. Twenty-two. The picture on the dog-eared student card didn't do her justice. Pensive, DI Powell fingered the plastic wallet, recalled again the flawless skin and perfect features of the young woman who'd died in front of his eyes. She reminded him of someone, or maybe it was just the titian hair. Maybe it was a painting he had in mind.

He sighed. Back at his desk now, he couldn't shake off the incident: the sickening thud of the impact, shocked gasps from the crowd, then a stunned silence that seemed to last for ever. Unbidden, the phrase dead weight repeated again and again in Powell's spinning thoughts – like a stylus stuck in a groove. He'd reached her first, longed to brush away the rough grit from her ivory cheek. Desperately she'd opened her mouth to speak but words were beyond her. The mask lay a few feet away, red shining lips parted in wide garish grin. It must've flown off in the fall. Powell balled his fist. Why? For frig's sake, why?

He slumped in the chair, loosened his tie. God, he could do with a drink. Times like this he almost wished he smoked. Had Jessica Harvey been on the wacky baccy? Or the booze? Some mind-altering substance? Had she been so wasted…? He closed his eyes. Saw again the lovely undamaged face. It was her body that had been smashed. Surely her mind had already been broken?

Maybe the mother could shed some light. Poor cow was driving down from Whitehaven to identify her only child. He had to put it behind him. Jessica Harvey's suicide was uniform's baby. Why was that a relief? Why couldn't he stop thinking about her? The introspection was uncharacteristic and useless. Focus and move on, man. They had a killer to nail, he sure couldn't see the Sandman handing himself in any time soon.

"You're trying to tell me that's the Sandman?" Byford slung the paper across his desk, leaned back in the chair, legs spread. Bev averted her gaze, looked instead at "that"; a child's drawing, crude primary colours. Five-year-old Daisy Towbridge had come up with the artwork in exchange for a bag of Gummi Bears from PC Danny Rees. Under her mother's watchful eye in the kitchen of their Moseley home, Daisy had crayoned a likeness of the man she claimed took her cat. Unorthodox, sure. Inadmissible, deff. Potential? Maybe. Unconvinced, Byford picked up a pen: class dismissed.

Bev stood her ground. "Think of it as first draft, guv." She'd been equally sceptical until she'd heard the full story. Danny had spent time chatting to the girl and – showing a bit of initiative – organised the impromptu sketch show off his own bat. He'd asked Bev to be there when he ran it past the big man.

She tilted forward slightly, read upside down. It looked as if Byford was immersed in some poor sod's Performance Development Review. More sodding paperwork, more sodding accountability. Like there weren't enough hoops to jump. Every officer was monitored every bloody month nowadays. Why not go the whole pig roast? Make the snoop-test weekly, dish out gold stars or detentions on a Friday afternoon. Sod the rain forest. Danny looked gutted, too. She'd give it another shot. "Come on, guv, at least think it over."

Byford sighed, lay down the Waterman. "She's five years

old, sergeant."

"So?" Blank look, empty palms. "Obviously we'd need to bring her in, organise a child witness officer, police artist. Working on it together, they might come up with something worth feeding the press." She'd already checked Al Copley's availability. He was Highgate's top imager, known inevitably as Picasso.

"Again sergeant." He tapped a finger on the desk. "She's five years..."

"Age isn't IQ, guv." Come on, Danny, help me out here.

"She's bright as a button, sir," Rees enthused. "Well advanced for her years." Bev masked a smile. Not quite Danny's earlier, pithier, precocious brat.

Byford raised a sceptical eyebrow. "Reads a lot of fairy tales, does she?" Bev exchanged glances with Danny. Ground was less certain here. Daisy had a lively imagination according to her mother. Even so, it was a weird tale to make up and stick to. She'd told Danny that when she couldn't sleep, she sometimes looked at the stars through her bedroom window; even had a kid's telescope. On the night Faith Winters was attacked, Daisy had spotted a man in the street trying to coax her cat. She'd banged the window; he'd glanced up, grabbed the animal and done a runner. Mrs Towbridge confirmed she'd found Daisy sobbing and had put it down to a nightmare.

"Even the mother thinks it could be the truth now, sir." That was no lie. Julie Towbridge had conceded her judgement might have been hasty.

Byford narrowed his eyes; Bev read the sign, pushed on. "If the e-fit, sketch, whatever's no good – we don't release it. No harm done."

He picked up the Waterman, tapped it against his teeth. "We don't even know it's cat blood on the knife."

123

No. But she'd now asked the lab to fast track the tests. "Should hear later today."

"The guy could be anyone, Bev. Who's to say it's the...?"

"Thing is, guv, we're not exactly drowning in leads. I know it's long odds, but if the kid did clock the Sandman..." She left it hanging; he'd be aware of the consequences of failing to follow it through.

Byford raised an eyebrow, reached for Daisy's daub. "Think Al Copley's around this afternoon?"

Oh, yes. "Want me to check?"

"Keep me posted." He flapped a hand towards the door. They were almost out of the office when Byford called, "Nice work, Rees. Oh and Bev?" She glanced back. He had a knowing look on his face and a PDR aloft in his hand. "Guess whose?"

"Cheers." Bev toasted Danny's brownie points from the guv with a steaming mug of canteen tea. The young cop had offered to buy her a drink as thanks for holding his hand at the audience with the big man. They'd grabbed a table near the radiator. Not hard in the post-lunch lull, tougher finding anything half-decent to eat. The ratatouille looked like puke and she'd turned her nose up at the liver and onions. Mind, Fareeda's toast was still festering at the bottom of her bag. She'd ferret it out when she got back to her desk, assuming she still had a desk, she'd not seen it since the early brief, it could have been swept away in a sea of paper by now. And why did Danny look so ecstatic not. "What's up, mate? You should be well chuffed."

Gazing at the Formica, he circled his finger in a pool of spilt milk. "Why didn't I see it, sarge?" Missing cat: blood-stained knife. "If you'd not been there..."

"Bollocks." True actually. But she'd been in the game a

124

damn sight longer, and her middle name was suspicious. The rookie needed positive rope not a kicking. "Who was it got the kid drawing?" She blew on the tea. Al Copley was primed and set to go soon as the girl and her mum showed. "Masterstroke that was, Danny."

He gave a lip service smile, still beating himself up. She'd been there, done that, knew it was a waste of time. Glancing round, she spotted Sumi at the counter and raised a hand. Sumi mouthed a See you later. Bev glanced at her watch: four hours to be precise.

"And the way you played it with the boss?" Danny interrupted her not particularly welcome train of thought. "I thought Byford would never go for it. He was eating out of your hand by the end. I wouldn't have known where to start."

She shrugged. "The guv and me go back a long way, Danny." Shame there didn't seem to be so much ahead. And that the time had gone when it wasn't her hand he wanted to eat from.

"Yeah, but…"

"No, but." And quit the whinge-fest. "Get over it, Danny. You've got the makings of a decent cop. Just remember – look, listen, and learn. Don't be afraid to ask questions and never believe a word anyone says. Keep your eyes open, your mind focused and your mouth…"

"This the lesson according to Saint Bev? Mind if I take a pew." Smirking, DI Powell placed a tray on the table, parked his bum on the next seat. Powell didn't suffer her offal aversion; the plate was swimming in liver. She nearly gagged on the stink. "Don't mind me," he said, waving a magnanimous fork. "You were banging on about your mouth." He nudged the new boy. "This I must hear."

"…and your mouth zipped." She gave a disingenuous

grin. "'less you've got something worth saying." Powell opened his for a comeback but Bev got in first. "'specially when you're eating. Sir." She winked at Danny, drained the mug, scraped back the chair.

Powell muttered, "Lippy tart," as she walked away. God, it was good to have the DI back. He was PC as a Playboy mag. She smiled then remembered the Bullring fiasco, turned back. "You got the short straw this morning, sir. Sorry to hear that." Couldn't have been a barrel of laughs. You'd not wish it on your worst enemy. Tight-lipped, he waved the fork in what she interpreted this time as dismissal. She stepped back smartish but not before noticing his eyes. It looked very much to her as if the DI was tearing up. She walked away without another word. On rare occasions, even Bev knew when to button it.

Soon as she dropped her bag on the desk, Bev opened the office window, breathed in deeply. She could still smell Powell's liver. Lips puckered, she sniffed her jacket. Picked up traces of almond body lotion but that was about it. Bloody stink was clinging to the back of the throat. Like a bad crime scene.

Powell on the verge of tears, though? She narrowed her eyes. Maybe he was mellowing in his early middle age. She gave a thin smile. Nah. It was probably the onions. Snorting, she sat down, recalled an incident from DI Powell's glory days as a PC, his *Silence of the Lambs* moment. She'd dined out on the story for months; even now there was a smile on her face. Super-cool Powell had seen the movie when it first came out and watched Jodie Foster dab Vick under her nose to mask the reek of corpses. FBI technique, wasn't it? Course the DI slathered it on at the first rank opportunity. A pungent PM if she remembered rightly. He'd come in next morning with a top lip like he'd done ten rounds with Rocky. Station wags called him Vicky for years. She preferred Clarrie.

Enough of this. She sighed, surveyed her desk. The paper mountain looked more like the Urals. Get the old crampons out, girl. She fumbled in her bag, took out breakfast-lunch-high tea and pulled a face. Covered in fluff, hair and bits of tobacco, the toast lost what little attraction it had held. A further scrabble elicited an almost full pack of Polos. Her eyes lit up: beggar's banquet. After half an hour at the admin rock face, the door nudging open was a welcome distraction. She knew who was there without looking up. "Don't you ever…?"

Mac bustled in. "Couldn't, could I?" Closing the door with his bum he ambled over, bags in hand. Top man.

Arching her back in a lazy stretch, she gave an unwitting flash of lacy black bra. "God, you know how to treat a woman, Tyler."

Hastily redirecting a lecherous ogle, Mac slipped the goodies in front of her. "Choc chip muffin and a caramel macchiato? Must be where I've been going wrong." Perched on a desk corner, he told her he'd been chasing mask suppliers, nipped in to Starbucks on the way back.

"Catch anything?" Mouth watering, she peeled the paper from the cake, licked the crumbs.

"Nah." He'd shown an image of the mask lifted from CCTV footage, but none of the outlets stocked it. "Gave me a few places to try though." She muttered something through a mouthful of muffin. "Say again, boss."

Wiping her face with the back of her hand, she told Mac they had a date for later. "Charlotte Masters. Fixed it on the phone." Surprisingly easily as it happened. Maybe the girl had seen sense or Bev's grovel master-class had paid off.

"Back at Park View?" Distracted, Mac cast uneasy glances round the office.

Bev breezed on regardless. "You'd-a thought. Dutiful daughter caring for grieving momma and all that. But she wants the meet at Selly Oak…" Bemused, Bev paused as Mac hopped off the desk, made for the bin, gave it a good shaking, studying the contents. "… she's got her own pad there." She finished the sentence though she might as well have been talking to herself. "Lost something, mate?"

"No offence, boss, but there's a funny smell in here." Mac spotted the brownish stain first, pointed a stubby finger at the package on her desk. "Hell's that?"

She frowned. It wasn't that she'd forgotten the parcel; she'd been keen to break the back of the paperwork first. Looked on it as a carrot after the stick. Mouth down, she pulled the box nearer, tore open the paper. Whether it was the sight or the smell that greeted her, she slapped a hand to her mouth. "What the fuck?"

It was animal rather than vegetable. And it certainly wasn't a novelty clock.

18

The heart wasn't going anywhere. Bev had her back to it gulping fresh air through the now wide open window. "Where is she, mate?" Querulous. "Thought you said she was in the building?"

"She is," Mac said. As luck would have it he'd clocked the police pathologist chatting to Vince Hanlon at the front desk no more than ten minutes back. Gillian Overdale popped in on path business from time to time, but it was pure happenstance she was around when they needed expert opinion. Paging her had seemed the best and quickest way of finding out exactly what they had on their metaphorical hands. "She's on her way." He peered into the box again: fat, muscle, valves, ventricles. Mac was no medico but it looked human. "Chill."

"Chill? Chill?" She lowered the volume. "How chilled you be, matey, if someone left a bleeding heart on your doorstep?"

She'd never know. There was a rap on the door then the pathologist poked her head round. "What have you got for me then?"

Thank God for that. Arms folded, foot tapping, Bev nodded at the opened box on the desk. "You tell us, doc."

Overdale barged in looking as if she was on the way to a Cotswold shoot. The tweeds, brogues, distressed Barbour were typical of her habitual county look. The pudding basin steel grey bob did nothing for her shiny moon face. Through gold-framed bifocals, Overdale took a good look at the heart. "You don't need me, sergeant." Was that thin lip twitching? "You'd be better off with a butcher."

Bev didn't see the funny side, her fists were balled. "Perhaps you'd like to be more specific." Ultra polite.

She sniffed. "It's a cow's. They look human but they're bigger."

"A cow's? You sure, doc?" Mental cringe. Dumb question, or what?

"I can't tell you her name and address, sergeant, but yes, pretty sure."

"Anything useful you can say?" Thin smile.

"It's past its sell-by but not by much or the smell would be worse. So it's fresh-ish or it's been frozen." Was she taking the piss? "Seriously, sergeant. It was probably kept in a fridge until whoever it was did whatever they did." She retrieved her steel case from the floor. "But as I told you – it's not my territory. Try Waitrose." She was still sniggering when she reached the door. "The meat counter."

"Boss." Mac's low warning and extended arm halted Bev in her tracks. Gritting her teeth, she slammed a fist into her palm. "Cool it, sarge." Mac in placatory mode. "Here y'go." He proffered a bottle of Highland Spring. Body temperature. Where'd he keep these things? Pulled a second from a different pocket. She drank greedily, wiped her mouth with the back of a hand. Chances of tracking down where the organ came from, or more to the point who left it, were on a par with discovering weapons of mass destruction in the Vatican.

Mac perched on the desk, arms resting on beer belly, genuine concern in his warm brown eyes. "So who'd pull a trick like that, boss?"

She'd given it serious thought since first setting sight on the bloody thing. Someone obviously wanted to freak her out. Was it a warning, a message, a sick joke? But who? And why? Pound to a penny it was someone she'd pissed off big time. She affected a who cares shrug. "Where shall I start?"

The dark-haired man sat on a velvet kidney-shaped stool studying his gym-toned physique in the dressing table mirror. Light bulbs round the glass were switched on Hollywood style; heavy gold velvet drapes were drawn against both casement windows though it was only mid-afternoon. An older woman, her back to the man, lay on the king-sized bed behind, an ivory negligee revealed lightly tanned and slightly parted thighs.

The man was naked – apart from the clown mask. Preening this way and that, he admired his taut lean body, repeatedly flexed well-defined muscles. He shuffled forward, adjusted the mask, called the woman's name to make sure she was watching, then ran a moist pink tongue along the red rubbery lips. Their glances met in the mirror. An observer might have found the man's lascivious gesture faintly ridiculous. For Diana Masters it was almost the ultimate turn on.

"Do stop that, Sam." The lazy smile was indulgent, her normally sleek hair damp and mussed, perfect make-up smudged. "I have to get ready." She pointed a mock schoolma'am finger. "And you, Mr Tate, should not be here." Plus, if he felt anything like her, he'd be shagged out.

"Always time for a quickie, Dee." Confident bordering on arrogant, the young man rose, padded slowly towards her, flicked a long black fringe from eyes that were nearly as dark. "You know you want it." She couldn't take her eyes off him, everything about him was beautiful. And growing more so. Teasing and playful, he flaunted the fastest growth area inches from her open mouth.

Slowly she turned on to her back, deliberately flashing her inner thighs. "No more than you do, darling." Diana meant the refusal though. It was a risk Sam even being here. They'd kept the affair secret for six, seven months. They'd met during one of her stints at Oxfam; he worked in the hair salon opposite. The attraction had been instant, unstoppable. They'd come so far – a cock-up now wasn't an option. Though deadly serious, she smirked at the unintended mental pun. Obviously the house wasn't crawling with cops any more, but there could be a knock on the door any time, that dreadful Morrison woman back again with the fat man, or any of the interchangeable woodentops. There'd been so many. Imagine! They'd wanted her to have a family liaison officer around the place. Ludicrous. Risible. On the other hand, wasn't the risk part of the thrill?

She knew the answer when he tried to enter her. Her laughing protest was merely token; both knew she could never say no. His dark sensual eyes glinting through the slits turned her on even more. But now she wanted the complete picture. Careful not to cause damage, she gently removed the mask, laid it on the bed; both aware it would be needed again – business and pleasure. Parting her lips and legs, she drew his beautiful face towards her. There was nothing in the world that Diana Masters wouldn't do for the Sandman.

Byford squinted as he held the image at arm's length. "I don't know, Bev. Releasing it could be more hindrance than help." Thank God he'd dropped calling her sergeant, but more than that she hoped the guv's verdict on the e-fit was down to dodgy eyesight rather than Daisy Towbridge's vision. For the better part of two hours, the little girl and her mother had been ensconced with Al Copley and a child witness officer working on a composite of the cat thief's features. Byford now held the image – and its future – in his hands.

Over his shoulder, Bev studied the face again. "It's not bad, guv." Unlike a lot of visuals produced by over-anxious or over-avid witnesses, Daisy's effort didn't resemble half the population, and if Bev's instinct was smack on it could depict the Sandman. The likeness was the end result of patiently-posed, carefully-constructed open-ended questions aimed at not making the kid feel prompted or pressurised into coming up with something just to please the grown-ups. Bev had popped her head round the imaging suite door and reckoned the chances of Daisy doing or saying anything she didn't want were slimmer than Bev's of landing Johnny Depp. What the little girl had delivered was this: a guy in his twenties, not bad-looking, long black hair, dark, deep-set eyes, wide mouth, prominent cheek bones.

Byford sniffed. "Looks like that chap who used to knock about with Kate Moss." Bev pulled a face. That narrows it down. "Pete something or other…?" he expanded.

She mirrored the guv's squint. Couldn't see it herself. She leaned against the filing cabinet, ankles crossed. "So what you going to do?"

He slipped the image on to his desk and wandered to the window. "Hang fire, I think."

"But guv…"

A screech of tyres from the car park below as much as Byford's raised palm halted her protest. "She only caught a glimpse, Bev."

"Under a streetlight. With a good pair of young eyes." Twenty: twenty, she'd checked.

Perched on the sill, he looked at her without speaking. The big man wasn't convinced. Was it worth pushing the forensic tack again? The stain on the knife was definitely cat blood, she'd found Chris Baxter's updated report on her desk. Along with… she blinked, censored a flashback of the cow heart. She'd mentioned the gross gift to the guv. With nothing to go on, he agreed there wasn't much they could do, apart from Bev keeping an even closer eye on her back than normal. Cops don't win the popularity vote. What she wanted was the superintendent's authorisation.

"How 'bout the tests on the knife? Don't they swing it, guv?"

He shook his head. "It's still a load of ifs and maybes, Bev."

She held his gaze. "All we've got, guv."

"Doesn't mean it's worth having."

She sighed, knew the score. She was probably clutching short straws in a basket with too many eggs. And if the guv was right and they released a misleading image, it would likely provoke a load of duff intelligence from the punter. The cops would then end up being pointed in the wrong direction – which had to be even worse than their current position of not having a clue where to go.

"Third left after the Queen's Head, boss." Mac cut a sideways glance through the passenger window then bit off a chunk of Granny Smith. Dodging the juice, Bev raised an incredulous eyebrow. Wonders would never cease: Mac scoffing fruit. "That one of your five-a-year, mate?"

"Sarge made a funny," he drawled. "Ho ho." Progress was slow. The Bristol Road was rush hour chocker, traffic stop-start, headlights picking out greasy puddles from an earlier shower. Patchy fog was hovering now, clouds of the stuff swirled round the tops of streetlamps, diffusing the orange glows.

Sneaky smile still playing on her lips, Bev checked the

mirror, flicked the indicator. "What's with the apple then? You on a health kick?"

Fidgeting slightly, he subtly loosened the seatbelt. "If you must know, I want to shift a bit of weight."

"Hire a crane." The snort was unstoppable. She caught a glimpse of stony profile. "Sorry." Whoops. "Hey, mate, there's nothing wrong with being... cuddly." Her search for a mollifying alternative took a smidgen too long. Mac gave it a short shrift sniff. She wondered idly if he had a new woman in tow. His divorce must be going through any time. Had to be rough living miles from your kids, must get lonesome now and then.

"Hey, Twiggy." He tilted his head to the right. "Over there. House with the baskets."

"Touché, Tyler." There was a tight space up ahead. She reversed the Polo, applied the handbrake. "Finish your apple, mate. I'll take a breath of air." Leaning against the motor, she scoped out the street. Bank Avenue, Selly Oak, was Edwardian villa territory: bow windows, low redbrick walls, stained glass fanlights over solid front doors. Good nick mostly, except the odd multi-occupancy: Birmingham uni was in walking distance. She turned her mouth down, reckoned Charlotte Masters must be doing all right. The only pad Bev could afford at the same tender age was a one-bedroom maisonette over a Balsall Heath laundrette.

She glanced at her watch: half five. Coming here meant they'd miss the late brief. The guv was cool about it, even cracked a wan smile when she described it as time off for bad behaviour. Best not put a foot wrong in this encounter with Ms Masters. And she hoped it wouldn't take too long. She needed to pop back to Highgate before calling it a day. A spot of unfinished business on the Fareeda agenda. Still, two birds with one stone: she could pick up breaking developments on the Sandman front at the same time. Assuming there'd be any. The car gave a sudden lurch as Mac shifted his weight getting out. Still feeling a tad mean over the crane crack, she hoisted her bag and bestowed a full wattage beam. "OK, mate?"

"Yeah. Let's get it over." He sounded as thrilled as her. Mind, she'd given him the back story, Charlotte's complaint and the subsequent bollocking. As Mac opened the gate, he nodded at a brace of baskets hanging either side of the door. "Is that what I think it is?"

Bev peered closer. "Not weed is it?"

"Doh." He rolled his eyes. "Looks like leylandii to me." Her blank look made it clear: gardening was a foreign country. "Think beanstalk," Mac enlightened. "As in Jack — only it grows quicker."

She raised the brass knocker, left it pending. "Didn't he nick a golden goose?"

"Hen. And it laid gold eggs. Didn't you learn anything at school?"

Their eyes met, lips twitched in sync. Both knew the trivial pursuit was only putting off the serious tack. "Go on, boss, get on with it."

She rapped the door a couple of times, tightened her belt along with a mental girding of the loins. Despite the earlier bravado she felt an unaccustomed edginess. Bev didn't do timid, but Charlotte Masters had marked her card. And not with a dance request. The door opened in a heartbeat.

"Bollocks." The girl slapped a hand to her mouth. She wore a scruffy Afghan coat and was now knotting a leopard print scarf round her neck. "I thought you said tomorrow. My head's all over the place. Sorry."

Bev had her doubts: the girl's father had been murdered.

136

Was it likely she'd forget details of a police visit? Maybe the grief was getting to her? Maybe she was losing her grip? Or maybe she was just being arsey? "As we're here...?" Bev forced a smile; she'd give a month's salary to read the girl's thoughts.

Eventually voicing assent, Charlotte stepped back. "Yeah, sure."

The living room was off a pale terracotta hallway. It was Habitat meets Pier with lots of taupe and light wood, vibrant splashes of teal and scarlet courtesy of a shed-load of scatter cushions and tasselled throwbacks. Bev caught a smell of joss sticks: jasmine? vanilla? And a more pungent undertone. If her suspicion was correct it could explain a lot.

"Take a seat." Charlotte slung the coat over a chair. "Get you a drink?"

"Thanks, no." Bev answered for both of them. "We'll ask a few questions then shove off." They'd share the interview load this time, good cop, good cop.

"Fire away." The laidback stance on the opposite sofa seemed deliberately exaggerated. The faded blue denims and cheesecloth shirt were casual to the point of slack. Bev hadn't noticed before how plain she was: if ever a girl needed a touch of slap... The hair was again scraped back in a ponytail, and still looked as if it could do with a wash. The contrast with her mother was acute. Unlike Diana Masters, Charlotte clearly thought grooming was something to do with horses.

Bev had intended opening with a bridge builder but given the girl's more amiable attitude plunged straight in. "Tell me... have you noticed anything odd near your parents' house in... say, the last two or three weeks?" Charlotte pouted, apparently casting her mind back.

A clock ticked, water pipes gurgled; Bev nudged. "A stranger hanging round? Cars you've not seen before?"

More pondering then she shook her head. "I'd like to help. Thing is I'm rarely there these days. I moved out four, five years back."

"College?" Mac cocked a casual eyebrow.

"University of life." With a smile the girl looked almost pretty. It wasn't just her softer features. Charlotte seemed a different woman: chilled, no hard edges. Home territory, perhaps? Or spaced-out? The dope smell was stronger in here. Bev reckoned a spliff or two could explain Charlotte's mellower mood and earlier confusion. Not so much losing grip as deliberately letting go. Emotional pain relief? Cannabis as coping mechanism? Each to their own. Bev sniffed, filed the discovery under F for future use and L for leverage. She pressed on: "I guess you visit from time to time?"

"Hardly ever." Not unfriendly, though the smile was thin. She spread her arms wide. "I love this place. And value my independence."

"What do you do for a living, Miss Masters?" Sounded like polite interest rather than pointed question. Bev was glad Mac had broached it.

The girl hesitated slightly before giving a careless shrug. "Bar work. The Hamptons? Brindley Place?" Cool, upmarket bistro down by the canal. Either Charlotte earned a fortune in tips, or she'd won the lottery. This house certainly didn't come cheap. Head down, the young woman picked a loose thread on her jeans. "My parents help with the mortgage."

Ah. Say no more. Bev's lip curved. That'd be the bank of dad: Diana didn't earn pin money at Oxfam. Would mummy be as generous now she held the purse strings?

"Can you think of anyone who might want to harm your parents?" Mac still had the baton.

Her head shot up. "You said the burglary had nothing to do with my father." Smarting eyes sought assurances from them both.

Mac gave what he could. "We always look at every possibility."

Charlotte's hand shook as she reached for a scuffed patch-work bag, pulled out a crumpled pack of Marlboro. Empty. Scowling, she chucked it on the table, tapped twitchy fingers on thigh. "I don't understand," she murmured. "Who'd want to hurt Daddy?" She must know how ridiculous that sounded; someone had killed him. Charlotte's father may have been in the wrong place at the wrong time – he was no less dead. The young woman scrabbled in the bag again, found a crumpled tissue, dabbed her eyes. "She says he wasn't even due home."

Who's she? The cat's mother? The old saying sprang unbidden to Bev's mind. She'd mull over the implications later maybe: right now there were more obvious points to pursue. "What about your mother, Miss Masters? Can you think of anyone who'd want to harm her?"

"How would I know? I'd be the last person she'd confide in." Bev's interested was piqued. She watched, waiting out the silence, as Charlotte tapped a finger against her lips. "Look, I may as well tell you… we're not exactly… close." Bev's jaw gaped involuntarily. "I'm sorry if that shocks you." Charlotte sounded anything but. "Diana doesn't really approve of me, you see." The smile was bitter and didn't reach her bloodshot eyes. "I don't fit her image of beautiful dutiful daughter. I'd rather you know so she can't play the emotional blackmail card again."

"Emotional blackmail?" Bev prompted.

"Happy Families." She sighed. "What a joke. I only went to see her because she said it'd look bad if I wasn't there. Diana and I don't get on, we have zilch in common and now daddy's dead… I don't have to pretend any more." Tears glistened on her cheeks and though she was shaking her voice was steady. "I'm OK. Carry on."

"Were your parents happy, Miss Masters?" Mac voiced the question that was on the tip of Bev's tongue.

"From what I could see – they adored each other." Did the couple only have eyes for each other? Was that why Charlotte flew the nest when she was so young? Was she jealous of her mother? Bev filed more thoughts as Mac showed the girl photographs of the other burglary victims. Even from the extensive media coverage, Charlotte didn't recognise the women. "I'm sorry. I'd help if I could." Releasing the ponytail, she ran both hands through lank tresses then re-tied it even tighter. Subliminal message? Get out of my hair.

Bev settled back in the chair, crossed her legs. The interview lasted a further twenty minutes – went nowhere. Frustration wasn't in it. She'd known cases where one inspired line of questioning had led to the breakthrough; this had been a series of dead ends. Signalling a wrap to Mac, she rose, reached for a card in her bag. "If anything comes to mind – call me. Any time."

At the door, she glanced back, gave an ostentatious sniff. "Good turns and all that…"

19

Google honour killings UK, and you get over four hundred thousand hits in 0.29 seconds. Slice of quattro formaggio pizza in one hand, can of Red Bull pending, Bev was tapping into some of the more credible posts. After the Charlotte Masters interview, she'd dropped Mac at the Prince, managed a pit stop for food and air freshener at Sainsbury, and was now taking a crash course in a subject she knew too little about. To have any chance of connecting with Fareeda she needed at least an idea where the girl was coming from. She sniffed. Probably overdone the air spray; office smelt like a cheesy pine forest. Better than cow heart though. Taking a slug of Red Bull, she glanced at the clock on the monitor. Ten minutes before Sumi was due – best make the most of it.

Elbow on desk, chin in hand she focused on the current screen. The *Independent* article should be pukka given its source. According to ACPO, the association of chief police officers, *seventeen thousand women a year were subjected to honour related violence.* And they were talking iceberg tips. Bev took another slug, tossed the fringe from her eyes, hit another link. *Young women with Pakistani, Indian and Bangladeshi backgrounds were three times more likely to kill themselves than the national average.* Then another link. *Victims of violence are likely to suffer thirty-five attacks before reporting to the authorities.* And yet another. *Police estimate there could be up to twelve honour killings a year in the UK.* And the hits kept coming…

She blew her cheeks out on a sigh, rolled back the chair, drained the can. Stats and facts; people and pain. The figures didn't tell a fraction of the real story, didn't show livid bruises, shattered bones, broken spirits. Or dead bodies. Closing her eyes, she recalled a Met inquiry she'd been on the periphery of a few years back. A young Kurdish-born woman raped and strangled, body crammed in a suitcase, driven to Birmingham for burial. In a Handsworth back garden. Killing ordered by her own father. Why? She'd walked out on an arranged marriage, fallen in love with another man. Bev sniffed. So why'd all the reports carry quote marks round the phrase, honour killing? Like there was any doubt. The cops hadn't exactly covered themselves with glory either. Bev could still see the grainy mobile phone footage of the victim warning police she was in danger. The media had dubbed the video evidence from beyond the grave. Much fucking good it did the victim. Bev's fingers crushed the can. God, she needed a smoke. If Sumi didn't show soon, she might nip...

Or not. There was a tentative tap on the door. It certainly wasn't Mac.

"Sorry I'm late, sarge," Sumi said. "I couldn't get away." The young DC had been fielding calls in the squad room, the lines were going crazy.

"No prob." Bev was the same, couldn't resist a ringing phone. Never knew if it was the big one, the witness with the case-cracker. Daft to think cutting edge detection and forensics skills solved every crime, the majority of success was down to intelligence from the public. Not that it was all quality gen. "Anything earth shattering?" Bev offered a slice of pizza, tried not to notice there were only two left, she'd bought the family size.

"Not for me thanks." Sumi smiled. "As to earth shattering – you know what it's like after a media appeal."

"Sure do." Loony tune central. Byford had apparently

142

done turns that afternoon for local telly and radio, the Park View footage had also received a few airings. Bev frowned. Come to think of it, the local rag's claws had been sheathed lately. She reckoned Toby Priest's cop-out poll must've gone in the guv's favour – or it would've been plastered all over the front page.

"People mean well mostly, but…" Sumi held out empty palms.

Did they? Bev wished she had Sumi's faith. Or maybe not. Given her recent reading matter. She opened her mouth to get down to Fareeda business, but Sumi hadn't finished.

"Have you heard about Byford?" He'd decided to go ahead with *Crimewatch,* announced it at the late brief apparently, and according to Sumi it was about the only positive step that had emerged. Bev turned her mouth down. Not sure she'd describe network exposure as a move forward. "Hey sarge, do you think…?"

She thought Sumi was stalling. "Enough already. What're we going to do?" No need to clarify. Sumi knew the situation as well as if not better than Bev.

The animation dropped from Sumi's features. Bev noticed feathery lines at the edges of her fine eyes. "I wish I knew, sarge."

"It's Bev, OK?" She rose, walked round, perched on a corner of the desk, closing the gap between them. "And course you know, Sumi. It needs reporting."

"What does?" Her voice rose, she straightened, crossed her legs. "She won't even tell me what 'it' is?"

Secrets and lies; fear and despair. Bev held the other woman's gaze. "She didn't walk into a door, Sumi. Whoever did it will likely do it again. Prob'ly worse next time." What was it she'd just read? Victims are likely to suffer thirty-five attacks before… "This isn't the first time, is it?"

Sumi bit her lip. Bev winced at the teeth marks. She clenched a fist. Unfair maybe but she saw these walls of silent protection as complacent complicity. Sumi was a cop, westernised, but under the skin…

"I think it may have happened before." She dropped her head. "She just won't talk about it." Sumi had phoned her cousin four or five times during the day, tried getting Fareeda to open up. The girl wouldn't even say why let alone who. Bev sighed in sorrow and anger. After the net search, she knew vicious beatings could be down to something as innocuous as a girl taking off her scarf in the street, wearing hair gel, having an unknown number on her mobile.

"Tell me about Fareeda. What does she do, what's she like?" Sumi relaxed slightly. Fareeda was shy, quiet, bright, an A-star science student, into music, reading and TV. "You know, sarge, usual teenage things." Sumi gave a tired smile. Bev didn't return it, she'd learned squat. "Beatings aren't the norm, Sumi." And she'd uttered not one word about Fareeda's family set-up. The girl was Muslim: it struck Bev this was all about family. She pushed herself off the desk, paced the office. "You had a word with the parents yet?" Fareeda was old enough to leave home, but somehow Bev didn't think that would cut much ice with mum and dad. And the age of consent wasn't why she'd asked. She suspected the father was implicated in the attack. Why not come out and say so – instead of pussy-footing round what Bev saw as the women's misplaced sensibilities?

Sumi shook her head. "I phoned to tell them she's OK, safe, but she's begged me not to make contact again." She looked down at her hands. "She doesn't want to go back." Inadvertently she'd said it all.

"Where'd they live?"

Eyes wide, Sumi hesitated. Made no diff. Bev had already done a bit of homework, knew Fareeda had four brothers and the family lived in Small Heath. Sumi knew how easy it was to get hold of information. She gave Bev the address. "Don't go round, sarge. It'll make it worse if you get involved."

If? "Fareeda's holed up in my spare room, Sumi." And how much worse could it get?

"She needs a bit of space so she can get her head together." Sumi held out her palms. "Just a few more days where she feels safe. Please, sarge?"

Maybe it was the stink of air freshener that brought it back: the unwanted gift on her doorstep. Shit. "Sumi." She aimed for casual. "Last night? When you and Fareeda came over to my place? Is it possible you were followed?"

Sumi hadn't been aware of a tail, but neither had she been checking assiduously. Fareeda had texted the previous evening begging for help. Sumi had driven to Small Heath and collected her cousin from a bus shelter several streets from the family home. They'd motored round aimlessly for twenty minutes or so before heading for Bev's. This was some of what Sumi shared with Bev before they left Highgate at a rate of knots in separate cars.

God knew what went through Sumi's mind, but Bev's unease increased en route. Before hitting the road, they'd called her landline and Fareeda's mobile several times, no one had picked up.

"Come on, come on." Bev tapped the wheel. Seemed every sodding light was against them, and dense fog was no help. She flicked on the wipers again, rubbed the windscreen with a sleeve. The smear reduced visibility even further. Nice one, Bev.

She'd not seen the possible Saleem connection either. Outside chance maybe, but it was there: the dumped heart could be down to one of Fareeda's relatives. A warning to Bev to back off. That could mean a clear and present danger. She'd not given the thought house room when she'd compiled her list of likely suspects. Quite a few of the crims she'd nicked had featured Neanderthals who grunted predictable watch-your-back warnings from the dock. Even Dorkboy had made the cut on the basis their run-in was recent, more than that, he'd lost face with his crew. Briefly she'd considered the Sandman, but only because he already occupied so much of her headspace. If any cop was in the Sandman's sights, Byford had the big media profile.

A guy ran across the road just as the lights changed. Cutting it fine or what? She muttered *wanker* under her breath. Actually going on the gait and natty gear, he looked vaguely familiar. Driving away, she clocked him in the mirror. Yep. Jagger lips. Mick, was it? Rick? She knew he lived off Moseley's main drag; it's where they'd ended up that night. She'd had no duvet action since. Cop's life was a great contraceptive.

Baldwin Street was just up ahead. Sumi was right behind. Bev indicated left, scanned both sides of the road. She was locking the Polo when Sumi pulled up in an unmarked Astra. It was just after eight. The house was in darkness.

20

Sam Tate stared into the small oval mirror and toyed with the idea of giving the Sandman a little fun. Up-lit in the beam of a torch, his benignly smiling alter ego seemed to concur with the notion. Tate wouldn't have believed it possible but, disembodied and cast in monochrome shadows, the clown mask was even scarier. Good. Tate cocked his head, expanded his chest, liked what he saw.

Inexplicably, an old Beatles song leapt to mind – *I am the Walrus*. In his head, he changed the lyric to Sandman. It appealed more to his already inflated ego. The media had bestowed the title, but he liked it, got a thrill seeing it on billboards, hearing it on the radio. The Sandman had something of the dark about it. And not the Michael Howard variety. He sniggered under the mask. Muffled, the malevolent sound spooked the rich bitches even more. That's why he did it. Look at this one: eyes like dinner plates, trembling so much the bed was shaking, wheezing like an old biddy on forty-a-day. Fully aware of the effect his eyes had, he met her terrified gaze in the glass, then drifted towards her, loomed in so close he felt her warm breath through the slits. A pitiful moan escaped as she tried to move her face. "Please... please... don't."

"Shut it," he snapped. "I won't tell you again."

Biting down on her lip, she nodded compulsively. He skimmed the Maglite over her body, made sure it lingered on the pert boobs, the slight swell of her belly and the pubic – now public – arena. Spread-eagled, her thighs were open to the slow stroke of the torch. He broke out in a sweat, felt the stir of a hard-on. Naked and tethered she was at his mercy. He could do whatever he fancied and no doubt about it, Libby Redwood was a looker. Not like the crones Dee usually picked. Face it, he'd be doing the poor cow a favour. Sure looked as if she needed loosening up a bit. He pinched her nipple with gloved fingers. Stupid tart flinched. Next time he used the knife. He narrowed his eyes. Surely, a quickie would do no harm? The rucksack was already packed with rich pickings. He'd be in and out in no time. Another inane snigger. Or maybe not. If Dee found out she'd kill him. On the other hand… if no one was left to spill the beans. He played the beam on the blade of the knife.

"Don't hurt me," she whimpered. "Please don't hurt me…"

Witch must be a mind reader. Carefully, he laid the weapon on the bedside table, the ostensibly merciful gesture apparently underlining the clown's larger-than-life smile. For ten, fifteen seconds he stared down at her then: "Me, me, me." Each mocking word punctuated by a stinging back-handed slap. The woman's face was screwed in fear, tears flowed down blood-drained cheeks. Beneath the mask Tate's fine features were set in ugly contempt. Was it worth the hassle? Nah. He couldn't be arsed. With the endgame in sight he wouldn't want to screw up.

Bev hit the light switch. A quick scan through narrowed eyes revealed nothing out of place, nobody in situ. Quiet though. She cocked her head; the house had an empty feel. She chucked keys and bag on the hall table, shucked out of her coat. "I'll take a look upstairs."

Sumi nodded, didn't need telling to take the ground. Bev entered the bathroom first. Pristine. Not so much as a hair in the sink. Damn sight tidier than normal. Same story in the spare room, hardly a sign Fareeda had slept there. Bev registered a hike in her heartbeat, tingle in the palms. Unwanted images flashed in her head, other searches she'd taken part in leading to skeletal remains, decomposing flesh, bloated bodies. For God's sake. Get a grip.

She checked the wardrobe, bed, drawers, nosing round for any sign of life. It was tucked away at the back of the bottom drawer. "Well, well, well." A pregnancy tester. She recognised the brand immediately, had chosen it herself what seemed a lifetime ago, two lifetimes ago. Briefly she closed her eyes, banished more uneasy thoughts, concentrated on the implications for Fareeda's present and future. The girl certainly wasn't running the kit in for a friend. So much for Sumi's blind faith in her cousin's non-existent sex life.

Sumi's scream put complex thoughts on hold. Bev dropped the pack back in the drawer, took the stairs three at a time. Shaking and terrified Fareeda leant against the hall wall, clinging to Sumi. Stroking the girl's hair, Sumi said she'd found her hiding in the cupboard under the stairs. Crouched in the far corner, she'd been peering out from behind a mountain of empty boxes, DIY gear and discarded furniture. Toss up who got the biggest shock. Sumi was calmer now, her relief almost palpable. Fareeda looked fragile, bowed if not broken.

"Get her settled, Sumi." Bev nodded towards the sitting room. "I'll fix a drink."

A sense of déjà vu accompanied Bev to the kitchen. It didn't seem five minutes since they'd first gone through this routine. Slight deviation now though, after filling the kettle she opened the fridge, poured a generous Pinot Grigio, sank it before the tea was brewed.

Sumi and Fareeda were huddled together on the sofa. Sumi's arm lay protectively round her cousin's shoulder.

Bev bummed the door to. "Here you go." Along with Pinot, the tray held two mugs and a pack of digestives. She slipped it on to the coffee table then sat cross-legged on the floor opposite her houseguests. Waiting for enlightenment she took a sip of wine, then another. Neither woman met her glance. She was half tempted to see how long the silence would stretch, but the genial host was morphing into Basil Fawlty: knackered, rattled and pissed off. It had been a long day and she was running out of sympathy for a girl who it seemed to Bev wouldn't lift a finger to help herself.

"You gonna sit there all night – or maybe tell me what happened?" Something had obviously spooked Fareeda. Unless she'd been playing hide and seek. On her own.

"Sorry. I'm still a bit shaky." Fareeda's bangles slipped and jangled as she blew her nose, wiped her eyes on a tissue. "Someone broke in."

Bev stiffened. "Someone's been in the house?" Was the bastard still here? Fired, she sprang up, fists balled, ready to take off in pursuit.

"He's gone." Fareeda raised a palm. "I heard him leave."

"Why were you still in the cupboard then?" Sumi posed the question a damn sight more gently than Bev had been about to.

Curtains of hair concealed her face as she dropped her head. "I was scared in case he came back."

Adrenalin falling, Bev dropped to the floor again. "From the beginning, Fareeda. Now."

Shredding the tissue in her lap, the girl told them there'd been a knock on the door. She'd looked through the landing window saw a man on the step. She watched him take something from his pocket, then heard what she thought was the sound of a key in the lock. Panic set in at that point. Without thinking, she ran to the cupboard, shut herself in.

"He went straight upstairs, I heard his tread above my head, I was so scared I could hardly breathe. Any minute I thought…" The voice broke, but her gaze was steady, her eyes brimmed with unshed tears and pleaded for Bev's assurance, understanding, whatever.

In Bev's head, fury vied with sympathy. Getting involved in Fareeda's messy life had inadvertently led an intruder into her own. Unwittingly she thought of the Sandman's victims. Beth, Sheila, Donna, Faith, Diana. Imagine the horror they'd gone through. Tonight was a breeze by comparison. But this wasn't down to the Sandman. Both the timing and Fareeda's attitude had convinced Bev that this was the Saleems' baby. She fought to keep her voice level. "Don't piss me about, Fareeda. Who was it?"

Bev sensed Sumi's shocked gaze but kept her own glare on Fareeda. The girl straightened, bristling. "How the hell do I know? I've never seen him before in my life. I told you, I panicked. I ran. I wanted to get away. I wasn't thinking straight."

Bev stared at the girl's beautiful damaged face. Fareeda was more than capable of lying through her missing teeth. The pack upstairs was proof positive of that. A protective wall of silence appeared to be part of the family structure. She toyed briefly with asking how far gone the girl was, decided the question would likely get a more productive response when big cousin Sumi wasn't around. Blurting it out would destroy what – if any – trust Fareeda had in Bev, showing discretion might make it easier to bond when they had a one-to-one chat. Keeping mum? Bev curled her lip. Crap expression.

Bev's face was an open book; Fareeda had clearly read the scepticism. "Honest, Bev, the man was nothing to do with me. I should've realised before but…"

She raised a palm. "Yeah, yeah, you weren't thinking straight. So now you are?"

"The man was white, mid-twenties, thirties? I'm not good with ages." Her rueful smile wasn't returned. "He was dark-haired but definitely not someone in my circle. There's no way…" Eyes wide, she clammed up, aware she was in danger of giving away too much. Bev could easily fill in the blanks: there's no way my family would hire a heavy who wasn't Asian. Assuming Fareeda wasn't lying about the guy's colour. Maybe Sumi was thinking along the same lines. She turned Fareeda to face her.

"If you know the man, Fareeda – now's the time to say so. We can't help if you don't give us the full picture."

"I'm telling the truth." She folded her arms, truculent. "Why would I make it up?"

Bev took a mouthful of wine, rolled it round her tongue. It still seemed a hell of a coincidence: within hours of the girl's arrival, animal matter had been left on the doorstep and an intruder had broken in. Or not? She almost choked on the wine. What was it Fareeda had said about a key in the lock?

Drink spilled as she slammed down the glass, dashed into the hall. Were the scratches round the lock fresh or normal wear and tear? Bev rubbed her chin, heard the sound of more jumping conclusions. Despite what Fareeda said, it didn't necessarily figure the guy had a key; the lock could've been picked. Either way she made a mental note to call her friendly neighbourhood locksmith first thing. Wouldn't be the first time. She ought to ask for a discount. Deep in thought she stepped out, scanned the street in both directions. Nada. Natch. Even the fog had lifted.

She closed the door, leaned against it for a while still thinking things through: the cow heart and tonight's break-in could be connected with Fareeda, but not the damaged MG, the early hours hang-ups. She narrowed her eyes, her gaze fixed on the stairs. The earlier search had been incomplete. Hand on banister she headed for her bedroom.

21

It took fifteen, twenty seconds for Diana Masters to pin-point the sound. Being roused from a deep sleep didn't help her disorientation and the ring tone was unfamiliar, the phone had never been used before. She groaned when she registered the time. The clock's glowing green digits showed 02.17. Jesus this had better be worth it. Her fingers scrabbled on the bedside table, as she homed in on the mobile. It was a recently acquired pay-as-you-go, and the number was known to only one other person.

"Sam?" Sleepy, still confused, she ran a hand through her hair.

"Diana, we have a problem."

She bolted upright, instantly alert, goose bumps not entirely down to the temperature. "What do you mean – a problem?" It was nothing trivial. His tone told her that, and he rarely called her Diana.

"Someone saw me leaving the Redwood place tonight." She heard him swallow, detected incipient panic in his voice.

"Someone *saw* you?" Incredulous. Concealing her censure was a huge effort. She swung her legs out of bed, paced the room, thoughts swirling – none of them good. She waited for Sam to elaborate, not willing to make it easier for him, not keen to learn more, knowing ignorance wasn't an option.

"It's worse. He recognised me."

Her legs almost gave way, she sank on to the edge of the bed. "But the mask?"

"He followed, watched me take it off." His voice cracked.

She sensed he was on the verge of tears. Tough. His stupidity bordered on criminal negligence. Criminal! Christ. That would be funny – if they weren't neck-deep in ordure.

"How the hell did you manage that, Sam?" Cold, clipped, mentally clutching for even the shortest damage-limitation straw.

"I'm sorry, babe. I didn't see anyone around. I thought I was in the clear."

"Thought?" Had she badly misjudged the guy? They were supposed to be equal partners. OK, she was older and had the intellectual edge, but he was sharp, a quick learner and they shared the same dream and drive to realise it. Not drive. Ruthlessness. She caught sight of her reflection in the mirror, surprised how good she looked given how shit she felt. Not that it gave her any pleasure. Not with Sam whingeing on like a wuss. She recalled the last time he'd been here, preening in front of the same mirror, titillating her with the same bloody mask. She tapped a finger against her lips. Please let this flaky state be a temporary aberration. If he went to pieces they'd be well and truly fucked. She took a calming breath, injected warmth she didn't currently feel into her voice. "Come on, Sammy, we can work it out."

"There's more." Another swallow. "He's been on the phone. He wants a cut."

Blackmail. Her scalp pricked. Thank God for that. It meant the greedy oik wouldn't go running to the cops. "A cut?" She stroked her slender neck, gave a lazy smile. "I'm sure we can manage that."

"Diana. He's not talking peanuts." She knew Sam well enough to suspect he was holding something back. And he wouldn't be saving the best till last. "He knows about us." Diana closed her eyes: could it get any worse? "He wants you to make the drop. He knows how much your old man was worth. He wants half a million."

She snorted. Like that was going to happen. Then frowned. They'd been so careful. Who could have found out? And how? And what the hell were they going to do? God, she needed time and space to think this through. Sam wasn't going to come up with an answer. She had to be strong, or Sam would fall apart. They'd come a long way, they were on the home stretch and she'd be damned if some bastard was going to stop them reaching the finishing line. Feline eyes narrowed as she worked on the seed of an idea. It would need a lot of nurturing but there was too much at stake not to give it their best shot.

"Darling." There was a teasing smile in the endearment. "When I say cut… I'm not necessarily talking cash. After all, the Sandman's a dab hand with a knife… is he not, Sammy?"

When she ended the call ten minutes later he sounded calmer, which was lucky. Until the blackmailer made contact again, it was a waiting game and they'd need nerves of steel. Duplicity and cunning they already had in spades. She'd told Sam to drop by tomorrow. She knew a guaranteed way to help him unwind. Diana lay back on the bed, reached out a hand to switch off the light. It would be OK. And she'd missed enough beauty sleep for one night.

It wasn't exactly hidden, but Bev missed it during her increasingly tetchy sweep of the bedroom. Maybe she'd been expecting something bold and in-your-face, given whoever it was had taken a hell of a risk coming here. Who'd the bastard think he was? How dare he invade her space? Hot and dusty after crawling under the bed, her temperature as well as her temper was rising. She was at the bedroom door, unclenching a fist so she could switch

156

off the light when she spotted it: a new item on the summer holidays cheesy tat shelf.

Eyes creased, she walked towards the far wall where she kept her tacky knick knacks. Her mate Frankie had a collection, too. They'd been amassing the gross and garish since they were kids, trawling tourist dives from Blackpool to Benidorm seeing who could bring back the winning gewgaw. Harmless fun, teenage kicks – the egg-timer was an impostor, though. And had a sting in the tail.

Tight-lipped, she took it from the line-up where it was tucked between a lime-green T-rex and a day-glow pink guppy with Barbara Cartland eyelashes. The egg-timer wouldn't qualify for a place; it wasn't kitsch enough for one thing. The hourglass in a wooden frame was a traditional design, not trashy rubbish. Secondly, it wasn't totally useless: an egg-timer had a purpose – presumably this one also had a message.

She perched on the bed, timer nestling in her palm, slowly she inverted it, watched the sand trickle down. She tried to read beyond the obvious, and not to read too much. But if this was from the Sandman, he'd made it personal. The suggestion? That time was running out?

It was past midnight before Bev hit the sack, knackered, drained and still grappling with thorny thoughts. Was it the Sandman who'd been in her home? Was the timer a warning, or a challenge? She'd kept the find to herself during the subsequent two hour session with Sumi and Fareeda. The talk had dragged on and on, going nowhere slow: Fareeda stone-walling at Olympic level, Sumi sincere but ineffectual in getting her cousin to divulge who'd inflicted the injuries. Bev had gone through coax and cajole mode to bribery and coercion. Nothing worked. The girl was adamant, she just wanted a few days to get her head straight. And her nose and teeth, presumably. Bev had it in mind to pay a house call on the Saleems, nothing heavy, just a quiet word. She'd take advice on that from the one person she knew who might be able to give her a decent steer. Assuming Oz was still talking to her. She'd know soon enough, she'd left a message on his answer phone.

Throughout the discussion, the pregnancy kit had burned a hole in Bev's mental pocket. But by the time Sumi called it a day, it was too late to bring up the issue. Too late. And Bev was too distracted and if truth were told not feeling particularly well-disposed towards the girl. Jeez. Bev was only human. Mañana would do. Fareeda wasn't going anywhere, and was under strict instructions to bolt every door and window in future to stop further unauthorised entries.

Bev lay on her back, gave a jaw-breaking yawn. So much for an early night. The egg-timer was on the bedside table; she reached for it now, held it in both hands and watched the slow trickle of sand. Was it a challenge from the killer? *This is your mission should you choose to accept.* The line from the Cruise movie had sprung to mind unbidden. She gave a thin smile. If she was honest, hadn't she instinctively made the decision the instant she picked up the timer knowing she risked destroying prints?

A personal challenge she could take. No doubts on that score. With a black belt she was more than capable of kicking ass, going too far even; inflicting – and taking – serious damage. She'd been there more than once; the danger since last year's attack was willingly going there again. Having been through the worst – she had no fear, little restraint. Personal risk wasn't a factor. But the professional?

She turned the timer again, watched the sand glisten in the lamplight. If she went out on a limb over this, played the Maverick card, she could kiss goodbye to the cops, never mind the stripes. Teflon Girl they'd called her after the last disciplinary. Mind, there were times she still felt like telling the suits to stuff it anyway. On the other hand if she told the guv what was going off, he'd put a 24/7 tail on her. He'd done it once before behind her back; she'd hated it then, wouldn't tolerate it now. Baby-sitting she didn't need. And the last thing she wanted was to scare off the perp.

Anyway, what had she got to lose? Metaphorically or actually everything she valued had already gone. Her babies. Byford. Oz. Bring on the sodding violins, Beverley. She snorted, gave a wry smile. The sand had run out. She placed the timer back on the table, turned off the lamp, snuggled under the duvet. "Bring it on, sunshine. Any time…"

THURSDAY

22

It was pitch black when the phone roused Bev from a deep dreamless sleep. Bleary-eyed, fuzzy-headed, several cylinders short of an engine she made a grab in the dark, heard something tumble and crack. Shit. Great start. Had the timer gone for a Burton? No going to work on an egg today, then. Come to think of it where was Burton? And why'd people go there? And could she care less? Sharpen the act, cobweb-brain. She shook her head. At least she'd located the mobile. If this was another hang up... She snapped out a peremptory, "Bev Morriss."

"Wakey wakey, rise and shine." Mike Powell. The DI wouldn't be asking about the state of her health. "How quick can you get to the General?"

Duvet flung off, she flicked on the lamp, clocked the time: 06.17; registered an intact egg-timer, and the picture frame she'd knocked over: her and the guv on a weekend in Bath. Mouth turned down she calculated rapidly. The hospital was a ten-minute car ride, quick shower, face on, piece of toast. "Half an hour, forty minutes."

"Forget the slap, Bev. Make it twenty."

Her hand stilled on the bathroom door. It was more than the fact he'd used her first name, there was something in the tone she couldn't pin down. "Why the rush?"

He'd not had a shave; she could hear the rasp as he rubbed his chin. "Because the latest victim might not last that long."

Latest? Her scalp tingled. "You talking Sandman?"

160

"Got it in one."

She was rooting through the wardrobe for a suit. "I'll hold the shower."

06.33 and it was sheeting down when Bev hit the slick stone steps at the General's wide front entrance. She'd used half of one of the intervening sixteen minutes to scribble a note to Fareeda: new locks being fitted – bolt them! Then with the DI's words ringing in her ears, she'd shot three reds, slewed a ticket-less Polo across two parking bays and made a dash for it. Race against time? God, she hoped not. After only a short sprint rain streamed off the leather coat and trickled down her spine; she knew her bob would look like a skull cap. Inside, the heat was tropical, her skin felt clammy, and she was out of breath. She fanned her face with a hand. Steam would be rising any minute, some of it from her ears given what she'd learned en route. Powell and Control had fed more detail via police radio. Tight-mouthed, she loosened the coat; bastard Sandman had excelled himself.

The victim was Libby Redwood, thirty-seven, Kings Heath address. She'd been found semiconscious by her sister. The women had been due to catch an early flight to Paris, the sister – Kate Darby – driving them to the airport. Getting no reply at the house, alarm bells had rung. The Sandman – indeed any criminal activity – had been the last thing on Ms Darby's mind when she let herself into the property. Her sister was a chronic asthmatic; the fear was that she'd suffered a severe attack. She'd done that all right.

Flashing ID at security and reception, Bev headed for A&E, boots squeaking on shiny lino as she power-walked the corridor. If the medicos had failed to stabilise Mrs Redwood, Bev knew it was unlikely she'd get a look in let alone an interview, but the sister was here too. Powell was desperately hoping she could give them a heads-up. The inspector had no doubt the break-in was down to the Sandman. It had the hallmarks: the sand, the pillow, the pound sign carved in the flesh.

The DI was overseeing ops at Knightlow Road where a full forensic team was finger-tipping the place seeing if any evidence could be salvaged. The fact that Kate Darby had contaminated a crime scene was neither here nor there given the state of her sister. According to the DI, Ms Darby had found the victim tethered to the bed, gasping for breath, an inhaler inches from her bound hands. Kate had administered medication, called an ambulance and alerted the cops. In that order. Even so, it was touch and go whether Libby Redwood would make it. Bastard Sandman? Sadistic monster.

Bev neatly sidestepped an orderly's mop, nearly collided with an empty trolley being wheeled by a heavyset porter with industrial acne. Palm raised in apology she stepped up the pace, registered inconsequential detail in passing: fingermarks on pea green paintwork, flu jab poster, picture of the Christmas raffle winners. Lucky for some.

It struck her again how hospitals were like cop shops: open all hours. Current action wasn't Saturday night fever level, though nowadays any night could be binge-fuelled febrile. The buzz was low but building as she approached the department: beeps and hums, rustling curtains, swishing screens, toast and coffee smells detectable among cleansers and TCP.

The scene as she turned the corner brought Bev up sharp. It was too late. She knew it the second she caught sight of the dignified though distraught woman clutching a hand-bag on her lap as if her life depended on it. Kate Darby was seated in an orange plastic chair over by the far wall, silent tears streamed down her ashen face as a doctor sitting beside her spoke in hushed tones. Bev heard the odd phrase: oxygen levels, respiratory failure, everything we could. And sorry.

Even from here, Bev could see the woman's knuckles were white, the bones looked as if they'd split the skin any time soon, a foot tapped a jerky beat. She halted, reluctant to intrude on the raw emotion, felt a flash of anger. What planet was the doctor on? This was no place to deliver a death message. Private grief. Public arena. Glancing round, she registered that wasn't quite the case. A couple of nurses stroked computer keyboards but there were no punters in sight or earshot.

She took a calming breath and swallowed. Realistically when it came down to it, the location was immaterial. Libby Redwood was dead and nothing, let alone mourning etiquette, was going to bring her back. Bev balled her fists. It was show time. She'd have to butt in, probe, push, trot out trite words. She hated this aspect, loathed it to buggery. Like most cops she was sick to death of telling herself it was a shit job but someone had to do it. Shit didn't even come close. So? Put up or shut up. Heat. Out. Kitchen. Make that hospital.

And it was time to enter; the uneasy dialogue over the way was clearly coming to an end. Wishing she had a speech writer, even an idea of her lines, Bev braced herself, plastered on a well-rehearsed face. "Ms Darby?" The woman lifted her head, the doctor whipped round in his seat. Bev didn't offer a hand, it didn't seem appropriate somehow. "I'm sorry for your loss. I know this is a bad time. I'm Detective Sergeant…"

"No way, officer." Glaring through horn-rimmed glasses

that didn't fit, the doctor jumped up and tried doing the human barrier act. The name badge on the open-necked shirt read Alistair Munro. Big Al came up to Bev's shoulder and was several years junior. "How about showing a bit of respect here?"

One thing Bev appreciated was being lectured at by a condescending speccy short-arse. Lip curled, she drew herself up to her full height. Then looked closer and backed off. She clocked the signs of exhaustion on his face: lilac shadows under bloodshot eyes, flaky skin, not-so-designer stubble. The man was missing more than a few hours' sleep, he'd just lost a patient and was trying to protect a woman who'd undergone what was probably the worst night of her life. She could empathise with him. Up to a point.

She raised both palms. "You got it, doc. If Ms Darby doesn't…"

"Don't 'doc' me, detective." He took a step closer, jabbed a superior finger. "Can't you see you're out of order?" Officious little prat.

Bev felt the blush rise, her palms tingle. And not with embarrassment. He was pushing his luck. She arched an eyebrow, nodded at the horseshoe work station a few metres away. "A word, Doctor Munro." Something in the tone? A darkening of those blue eyes? The guy hesitated but only a heartbeat or three. "Please excuse us, Ms Darby." Soft, solicitous request from Bev.

She heard his footsteps behind, turned deliberately sharply just before they reached the destination. She wanted him up close but not personal: the mouthwash didn't mask the baccy breath. Voice low, matter of fact, using a little licence, she said: "The man who killed Libby Redwood is out there." It was pre-dawn but he cut a wary glance to dark, rain-lashed windows. "He's killed before. Got a taste for it now. Odds are he'll kill again. The other victims are so traumatised they'll probably never lead a normal life."

Pale grey eyes widened as he pushed the glasses up his nose. "Other victims?"

"Four women scared of shadows. Including their own." Casual delivery, deadpan features. "See, Doctor Munro, I'm trying to help. I want to give those women closure and stop the bastard getting to anyone else. Cos you know what?" She cocked her head. "He doesn't scare me. Fact is I'd like to beat the shit out of him. I don't like men intimidating women." She stepped in, couldn't get any nearer. "Do I make myself clear?"

For a second she thought he'd try and save face by telling her to piss off, but he was only a baby bully. "I take your point, detective." He backed away, glancing over his shoulder where Kate Darby sat, still clutching the bag. "But look at her." The victim's sister stared into the distance, lips moving almost imperceptibly, foot still drumming the floor. "She's in shock."

"No. I'm not." She cut him a glare, made eye contact with Bev. "I'm trying to remember exactly what Libby said."

Bev's jaw hit the tiles. "Said?"

"Before the ambulance arrived." The woman rose, self-assured, graceful. "Is there a coffee bar? Caffeine helps me think. And it's important I get it right. Whoever did this needs locking up. And that's where you come in, isn't it, sergeant?"

Byford's bulky outline blocked the doorway. He clutched a sodden Fedora in both hands, his black trench coat slick with rain. The kitchen at Knightlow Road had been given the forensic all-clear or he'd be in whites. If worth it he'd slip into kit anyway, put back the brief if need be. It was still early yet. Wall clock showed the time coming up to seven. "What have we got, Mike?"

A startled Powell whipped round, mug in hand. "Guv? What you doing here?" Byford smelt coffee, the DI must have been helping himself. He let it go: Powell wouldn't get away for hours, everyone needed a break. As to why Byford was at the crime scene – he was sick of sitting on his backside, seemingly twiddling his thumbs.

"Relax. I'm only taking a look." He masked a smile at Powell's vain attempt to conceal his unease. He probably thought the big man was checking up or muscling in. And to an extent, he'd be right. Mike was a decent cop, more plodder than high flier, but he'd only been back in harness a couple of days, it would be easy to miss something. Byford raised an eyebrow: like everyone else hadn't. It wasn't just that, though. The senior detective had felt more than the normal urge for action. The higher the rank, the bigger the desk, the more difficult to get away. Much of his job was strategy, admin, shuffling papers, not dealing with people. Give him hands-on any day, however dirty the work.

Powell rinsed the mug under a tap. "As to what we've got, being honest, not a lot. There are prints on the tethers, but Chris reckons they'll be the sister's when she released the vic."

Byford nodded. "I'd heard." He'd bumped into the FSI manager on the way in, also learned that the sand and tethers would almost certainly be untraceable. And that the point of entry – french windows at the back of the house – was clean as a bleached whistle. No useful treads either; the over-sock technique had been employed again. Fact the house hadn't been trailed with mud gave them a pointer towards the timeline: according to the Met people, the rain hadn't started until around five a m. Big deal.

Top line was this: given the perp's past record they had little hope of coming up with the forensic goods.

Byford glanced round. The kitchen was what he supposed they called farmhouse chic: brass pans hanging from cream walls, pine dresser full of blue and white striped crockery, bowl of dried lavender on a washstand, frilly curtains, feminine touches. He shook his head, wondered if Mrs Redwood would ever want to return after what the intruder had put her through. "Why her, Mike?" He narrowed troubled grey eyes. Something had to connect the victims, sometimes seemed the more he looked the less he saw.

"If we knew that, guv…"

He raised a hand, didn't need telling. "So what are we doing?" Powell leaned against the sink as he ticked tasks on fingers. House-to-house was underway, area search would kick off at first light, CCTV would be pulled in and pored over. Byford's jaw ached with the clenching. As Bev would say, Same old, same old. The big man's frustration and anger had grown exponentially during Operation Magpie. Not that he'd admit it, but this morning, hearing the latest reports from the crime scene he'd felt a tinge of despair, depression. The Sandman wasn't just a step ahead, he was out of sight.

The big man sighed, twirled the hat in his fingers. "Get through to Bev?"

"She's at the General." He frowned, lifted a finger then fumbled for the ringing phone in his pocket. "Good timing or what?" The ironic half-smile faded fast. Byford didn't need to hear to know the news wasn't good.

Biting his lip, Powell ended the call. "The vic didn't make it. Bev's hanging on. There's a chance the sister's got something for us."

23

Bev ended the rushed call to Powell, shoved the mobile in her bag. She was at a corner table in the hospital's coffee shop waiting for Kate Darby to finish in the loo. Apart from a bored looking barista with a sub-Amy Winehouse beehive, they had the place to themselves. Bev didn't do patience, and in this case it was hard to hide the signs. Playing a plastic spoon through her fingers, she was on the edge of her seat physically and mentally. Was it possible the Darby woman held a key – if not the key – to the case?

Stilettos clacked across fake parquet. Bev turned her head, watched closely as the tall and enviably slender Kate Darby weaved an elegant path through empty Formica-topped tables. The previously mussed blonde chignon had been smoothed into place and she'd applied running repairs to her face, only removing smudged make-up not adding a layer. With classic bone structure and even skin tone, Bev wondered why the woman bothered in the first place. Maybe the supreme confidence came from her looks; the posh accent, just shy of Celia Johnson's in *Brief Encounter*, probably helped. Given Kate Darby hadn't long taken final leave of her sister, tough cookie was a phrase that sprang to mind. Not that Bev was complaining. Sooner tough than crumbling.

"Thank you, sergeant." She tilted her head to indicate the cappuccino and sank into the seat opposite. Slipping her shoulders out of a costly looking camel cashmere coat, she let it hang over the back of the chair. "Right now I could kill for a cigarette." Fag hag with an asthmatic sister? She must have intuited Bev's mild surprise, dismissed it with

an airy hand. "I gave up years ago, but there are times…"
Pain briefly pinched her regular features. It was there, just
not paraded.

Fingers laced, Bev leaned forward. "I'm so sorry for your
loss, Ms Darby." But let's get on with it, lady.

Intelligent hazel eyes assessed her for five, six seconds.
"Yes, sergeant. I think you probably are." She took a sip of
coffee. "But I'm not here for tea and sympathy. I want the
thug who did this rotting in jail. I want to sit in court and
hiss and scream abuse. And if I didn't value my life and
liberty too much I'd take a gun along and shoot him in
both eyes." Bev's widened. Tough cookie? Steel-wrapped
reinforced concrete. "Surely you deal with cases when you
ache to dispense instant justice, sergeant? Lash out? Bend
the rules?"

Yep. Yeah, You bet. But this sure ain't the time for an eth-
ics debate. "Ms Darby, think we can…?"

"Libby may have seen her attacker before." Open-
mouthed, Bev watched as the woman drank more coffee.
"She was sure someone followed her home from work one
day last week. A thin, dark-haired man."

Uh? Bev frowned. "Your sister told you this last
night?" When she was barely conscious? Was Kate Darby
enjoying the spotlight a tad too much, was she inventing
the entertainment as she went along? Drama queen as well
as galvanised Garibaldi?

"No, no." She cut a 'keep up' glance as if Bev was being
dense. "On the phone over the weekend. I told her to talk
to the police, to take care when she went out. Libby could
be a little nervy from time to time. But maybe I should
have taken it more seriously." The bottom lip was getting a
pensive chew. "I'm now thinking the incidents could be
related."

"No way of knowing that yet, Ms Darby." It was obviously what the woman wanted to hear and Bev wasn't convinced there was a link. Surely the Sandman was too smart to show himself? He'd probably never broken sweat let alone cover. She made more soothing noises then took out a notebook, recorded what detail Kate Darby could remember: time and day, the route her sister would normally take. The stranger's scrappy description was less than useless but it may be that Libby Redwood and her putative tail were on CCTV. It could give them an inquiry line but whether it would lead to the Sandman was up for debate. Best check with Kings Heath cops as well, see if Libby had reported the incident. It was close but not the cigar Bev had been hoping for or been led to believe.

"There's more, sergeant. Something Libby said." Darby narrowed her eyes. Aid to recall? Concentration?

Bev's heart skipped a beat, mental feet stayed on the floor. "Go on."

"You have to appreciate she was fighting for breath. I was trying to save her life, not listening as carefully as I might. And I don't see how it fits with a stranger following her…" There was an unspoken 'but' in there. Bev waited a few seconds before voicing it.

"I think she said the name Dan… maybe Stan. But I may be wrong and it may not even be relevant." She sighed her frustration, reached for her bag on the next seat. Bev clocked the distinctive G: a Gucci-cost-a-bomb job. No wonder she'd been clutching it. "I don't know if this will help, but I brought it any way." A dog-eared address book, loose scraps of paper stuffed in the pages. "Libby kept all her friends' and contacts' details in there. It was her social bible."

Bev took the book from Kate's hand. "Good thinking.

It'll help a lot." Known associates on a plate. No guarantee the perp was a KA of course, and if he was it knocked the stranger theory on the head. Either way the info was useful, they'd need to talk to anyone who could shed light on Libby Redwood's life.

"This you and your sister?" A creased colour photograph had fallen from the pages. Bev picked it up, took a closer look. They had to be related. The woman on the left was a younger version of Kate Darby. Beaming smiles, champagne flutes: happy times.

Darby gave a sad nod. "Libby's birthday. Her first night out since losing Paddy."

"Paddy?"

"Her husband. He had a brain tumour." Another widow. Bev made a mental note. "It was all so sudden." Darby licked froth from the teaspoon. "Diagnosed in the June. Dead in the November. Poor Libby. She'd only just got round to sorting his clothes, personal items. I offered to do it for her, but…"

"Where was this taken, Ms Darby?" She held the print closer, squinted at the background.

"Please, sergeant, call me Kate. We were in The Hamptons. It had only just opened, Libby…"

The Hamptons. Bev's antenna twitched again. It was the bar where Charlotte Masters worked. Coincidence? Significance? Her mental notebook needed more pages.

The interview lasted a further twenty minutes, turned into more general conversation as they made their way to the car park. The rain had stopped, thank God, but they had to skirt swimming pool size puddles. There were more people around, car park beginning to fill up. Place was coming to life. Though not for everyone.

"This is me." Kate halted at a gleaming black Audi. "Know

something, sergeant? Libby and I should be landing in Paris now." Her eyes were unnaturally bright but the voice brisk as well as clipped. "If there's any more I can do, you know where I am." Sutton Coldfield. Private estate. Kate was a career woman, had her own interior design company.

"Appreciate it." Bev raised a palm. Had no doubt they'd be in touch. Pensive, she carried on walking towards her wheels. A church clock somewhere was striking the hour. She counted eight, stepped up the pace. If not a break-through, at least the inquiry had a few more lines to work on. And if she hit the gas she could throw them out at the brief. Shit. She pulled up sharp. The Polo's windscreen had taken a direct hit from what had to be a flock of sodding seagulls. Adding injury to insult, some fascist traffic warden had slapped on a ticket as well.

God, she wished she'd kept her mouth shut. Mac was humming *Always Look on the Bright Side.* For the zillionth time. Life's a piece of doo-doo. Yeah right.

"Not funny, mate." She tapped fingers on thigh. They were waiting for the big man to show. Squad room was packed to the gills, windows running with condensation, eau de after shaves and canteen bacon. Bev gave a surreptitious sniff to her own outfit: faintly medicinal. That day's shower was still on hold.

"S'posed to be lucky you know, boss." Mac was slumped back in a hard chair, podgy hands nestling on paunch cushion. "Bird poop."

Not for the birds. If she got hold of them she'd be wring-ing a few necks. "Give it a rest, eh?"

"Think they were from Special Branch, sarge?" Darren New – all feigned innocence – was getting in on the act now.

"Wise up, Daz." Mac again. "It'd be the Flying Squad."

"When you on stage next, Tyler?" Bev studied her nails, knew he had a comedy gig coming up in Digbeth. Standing in for Eddie Izzard. Not.

"End of the month. Want a ticket?" He shifted a buttock, reached into a back pocket.

"Going cheap, are they?" Daz tittered. Mac pulled a cheeky sod face.

"Not cheap enough," Bev drawled. "I'd rather eat…" Mental eye roll. She swallowed the s-word, but they pissed themselves laughing anyway. Byford staunched the flow when he bustled in file under elbow, mug of something in hand. Bev caught a whiff as he passed. He was on the mint tea.

There was a synchronised straightening of spines and ties, everyone's focus on the guv. Without so much as a "morning troops" Byford perched on the edge of the desk, opened fire. "I hoped we'd catch the bastard before he struck again." Expletive not deleted. That bad. "I've just come from the latest crime scene." Bev lifted a curious glance from her notes. He'd not mentioned it when she'd phoned him the gist of her Kate Darby interview.

The pause was deliberate as the superintendent ran his steady gaze over every officer present. "This one has to be the last." Yeah right, guv. If personal conviction led to collars, the Sandman would've been banged up weeks back. Then there was the real world…

"DI Powell's still at Kings Heath," Byford said. "As of when I pulled out there was nothing significant." She listened as he filled in forensics, detailed actions going on in and around Knightlow Road, and responded to lacklustre questions that didn't amount to a bean, singular. "Closest we've got to a decent lead is what Bev's brought back from the General."

He pointed to the front, asked her to run the latest past the squad. Gathering her notes and the victim's address book, she took centre stage.

Not everyone knew how Libby Redwood had died. That the life-saving inhaler had been just inches away. When Bev disclosed what the Sandman had done – and failed to do – heads shook, mouths tightened, a few muttered, "Callous bastard." Most officers glanced at the photograph she'd blu-tacked to the latest murder board. The image had only been there five or ten minutes and wasn't the best shot. It was the happy snap taken in The Hamptons. Kate Darby would be looking out a better pic in the next day or so. Bev talked them through Kate's concerns and contributions: the stranger who'd allegedly followed Libby home, the name whispered in what turned out to be the last traumatic moments of the victim's life. Bev had already checked for a Dan or Stan among the woman's contacts. Nothing doing.

"Known associates of the dead woman." Bev waved the dog-eared book in the air. "Anyone volunteering?"

"I'll have a look, sarge," Carol Pemberton offered. "It's quiet on the jewellery front. Do we know if anything was stolen last night?"

Bev cocked her head at the guv who shrugged a don't know. "Should get a heads-up on that later today, Caz," Bev said. She'd arranged for Kate to visit the house that afternoon, an FSI guy would hold her hand while she looked round. She'd not know everything but was sure to have more idea about missing items than anyone else around, and spot anything alien. Bev tossed Carol the book on the way back to her seat, knew it was in a safe pair of hands.

Byford tasked Daz with rounding up CCTV of Libby Redwood's route home from work. She'd had a part-time job at a Kings Heath florist, more to get out the house than

174

cash flow problems. Paddy Redwood hadn't left her short. The guv asked Sumi to talk to the dead woman's work-mates, find out if she'd mentioned her concerns. Even if – long odds – they'd seen anyone hanging round outside the shop?

Byford pulled a face when he slurped the tea. "Thoughts, anyone?"

Yeah, why drink the stuff? Bev kept that one to herself, nodded at the victims' portrait gallery; "Another widow, guv. Is that the link we're after?"

"Beth Fowler's divorced. Sheila Isaac's single. Diana Masters was married." Byford retained facts, rarely needed to check.

"Yeah, I know." Her gaze was still on the line-up. "But three of them are. Maybe something there…?"

"Let me know when you come up with it." Was he being sarky? "Anyone else?"

"We have another dark-haired guy," Mac said. "Young. Thin."

"Narrows it down then. Only a few million of them around." The pop was from Jack Hainsworth; the information officer was tapping a keyboard. He'd turned sneering into an art form. Art. Picasso. The little girl's cat thief. Another dark-haired mystery man. And Bev was with Mac. When there wasn't a shed-load of evidence around, you built on what you had.

"You gonna release the kid's visual, guv?" The media were already milling round Highgate. At Byford's instigation, Bernie had called a news conference for nine. The press pack was hungry; it'd need feeding a scrap or two.

"I'll issue it this morning. With caveats." He rubbed both hands over his face. "I'm meeting the *Crimewatch* people after lunch. We need all the help we can get." She raised a

175

sceptical eyebrow. "What've you got on today, Bev?"

"I've pencilled in a follow-up visit to Alex Masters's chambers." A couple of DCs had already talked to some of the barrister's associates. But not everyone had been around; a few names were still outstanding. More background they could gather the better.

Byford nodded. "Mention it to Mike first." Powell was SIO on the murder inquiry. "He may have something more pressing." Fair dos. "Don't get despondent, guys. The perp's luck will run out." The guv rose, gathered his belongings, issued a late rally. "Stay focused. Keep sharp. Be positive."

Mac waited till the guv was out the door, nudged Bev's elbow. "There y'go boss. What'd I tell you?" He leaned in close, started crooning, *Always Look On The Bright Side…*

Bev curled a lip. Tyler was a crap comic. And he couldn't sing to save his life.

24

Masters and Burns's chambers were in Newtown Row: Victorian, redbrick, shiny brass name plaque on matt black front door. Indoors was bronze marbled pillars and Minton tiles, dark panelling and dusty parlour palms. It was all a bit Victorian: definitely more Dickens than *Damages*. Bev was a tad disappointed, had expected a sharper set-up from the legal eagle they called The Raptor.

She was in reception sitting cross-legged on a cracked leather corner sofa flicking desultorily through a well-thumbed copy of the *Law Gazette*. Why couldn't they have *Heat* or *Hello!* lying round like the hairdressers? She'd had a word with a couple of juniors and a legal secretary, now hoped for useful ones with the elusive Evie Jamieson: Alex Masters's PA was in work after two days' sick leave.

"If you'd like to follow me?" A short dumpy woman beckoned from a side door. Bev pegged her as the tea lady, probably down to the polyester frock being the shade of weak PG. Thick tan tights, scuffed lace-ups and tight beige perm furthered the impression. Dumpy didn't say a word as she led the way up a wide staircase then along a dimly-lit corridor. Tobacco-coloured walls were dotted with framed facsimiles of newspaper front pages: Masters's most celebrated cases as covered in *The Times* and *Telegraph*. Dumpy held open a heavy oak door on the right, waited for Bev to finish nosing. "Please go through."

Bev's quick scan registered more panelling, dark wood floorboards, heavy shelving, half-drawn blinds. Stale air smelt of ink and cheap scent. It was difficult to hide her surprise when Dumpy took up pole position behind a desk that was a cop's dream: empty in-tray, nothing pending.

"Do sit down, sergeant."

Bev's nascent inquiries about the PA's health were dismissed with a flap of the hand and a tight smile. Jamieson launched straight in. "You're investigating my former employer's murder. How may I help?"

Aware she was under sharp scrutiny, Bev shifted slightly in her seat. "We're trying to build a picture of Mr Masters. Learn a little background." Encouraging smile. "You must've known him well, Ms Jamieson?"

"Miss." The single word said a lot. Bev watched closely as the PA steepled fingers displaying ugly bitten nails. She'd put the woman's age at fifty, fifty-five. "I worked for Alex Masters for nineteen years. He was a consummate professional, a highly intelligent man with one of the sharpest legal brains in the country. A great raconteur, cultured, sensitive…" Yada. Yada. Yada.

"Did you like him?" The question appeared to take the woman by surprise. There was a fractional widening of dishwater eyes, a tightening of already thin lips.

"He was my employer…"

"You said."

"I had enormous respect for Mr Masters." Car horn blasted in the street. No reaction. The ticking clock in the silence that Bev again let stand had more leverage. "No one could wish for a better… employer."

And employee? Evie Jamieson personified efficiency. She reeled off names, dates, small detail with almost total recall, only once did she wander over to a filing cabinet to check a fact. It was enough for Bev to lean across, sneak a look at the framed pictures on her desk. As the PA waxed lyrical about one of her boss's greatest hits, the animation enlivened her plain features. Bev shaved ten years off the original guesstimate of her age. Even so, Diana Masters wouldn't have lost any sleep. If Alex had ever felt the itch, Bev couldn't see him asking Evie to scratch it.

When Bev moved on to ask about possibly disgruntled clients, threatening defendants, Jamieson was adamant there'd been none, her shock at the line of questioning seemed genuine. "I can't see why you're asking these questions, sergeant. If the press is to be believed, surely the murder was a burglary that went horribly tragically wrong?" Bev spouted the usual police-speak about exploring avenues, unturned stones and face values. The last phrase gave her pause for thought. Taking Jamieson at face value had been a big no-no.

Recognising the cliché-spiel, the PA raised a hand. "Are you saying there's a possibility Alex was the intended target that night?" Alex? First time she'd used his Christian name. As to the question, it was one Bev had asked herself. The Sandman hadn't put a foot wrong until he entered the Masters property. So was that debacle down to a copycat clown who wanted the barrister dead? Or was it – as Powell and most of the squad thought – a case of Masters being in the wrong place at the wrong time? "We can't rule anything out of court, Miss Jamieson." She winced inwardly at the unintended pun.

Evie Jamieson crimped her lips. "If there's nothing else…"

"Did you ever meet the boss's wife?" Bev asked, hoisting her bag as she rose from the chair. The throwaway line appeared to cast a flicker in the woman's eyes.

"Once or twice. Why?" Her stare was unwavering, but Bev heard a foot tapping under the table.

"Just wondered what you made of her?"

Slight pause, then: "It's not my job to make anything of Diana Masters, sergeant." Why the dry ice? Disapproval?

Resentment? Diana had everything Jamieson didn't: style, beauty, bank balance and until recently, Alex Masters as bed partner. "If that's all..." The hands she placed palm down on the desk trembled slightly; sweat beads were visible in the fine hair over her top lip.

"That's all." Bev held the PA's gaze for several seconds. "For now." She turned at the door. "Tell me, were you surprised to learn Mr Masters was home that night?"

Zero hesitation. "No. He phoned from the Old Bailey. The case had collapsed. He rang to say he was coming back."

He'd called his PA but not the wife. What did that say? If anything? "Were they happily married, Miss Jamieson?"

"How should I know, sergeant? Shouldn't you be asking her?"

Bev couldn't read the glint in the woman's eye, but knew this: whatever Dickens thought about the law, and despite Jamieson's professed ignorance – the PA was no ass.

Perched on a high stool in the window of Caffè Nero, Bev stared out into lunchtime New Street. The steamed-up glass was still bordered by fake snow and fairy lights. Motley crews streamed past: shoppers laden with Primark bags, city suits, loud school kids, wannabe WAGs, chavs pushing buggies. On the pavement opposite, a bedraggled busker in a Sergeant Pepper jacket was mangling *Flowers In Your Hair*.

Unseeing, distracted, Bev had been stirring an Americano for a minute and a half. The espresso she'd stumped up for was getting cold. Mac was running late or she'd be hitting him with a few ideas; her thoughts were eddying, too. Adding more sugar, she stirred again, picturing the dowdy Evie Jamieson. The PA certainly seemed to hold no brief for the wife. Was that down to jealousy? Jamieson's feelings for the barrister clearly went beyond the professional. Why else keep his picture on her desk? OK, it was in with a bunch of others, but was that normal? Seeing your boss's mug every time you glanced up from your key strokes? And why had the woman bent over backwards to stress the professional nature of their relationship? Except for the one time she'd let slip his Christian name, it had been Mr Masters this, Mr Masters that. Mr Masters bit-of-the-other? In Jamieson's dreams maybe; Bev couldn't see any monkey business going on there. She gave a lopsided smile. Imagine if she kept a picture of Byford on her desk: Highgate's funny looks brigade would go into overdrive.

Grotesque features were suddenly pressed into the glass inches from her face. Some street nutter was gurning, swinging his arms like a demented windmill. She mouthed *Fuck off*, pointedly turned her back. Why'd she always attract the fruitcake? Same on buses. The loony latched on to her every time.

"No way for a lady to talk, boss." Mac approached with an innocent grin. Shame about the tell-tale grime on his nose.

"Stick to the day job, eh?" Lips tightened, she pointed to his coffee. "How'd it go?"

She saw him cast a greedy glance at the counter before answering. "On a scale of one to ten? Minus two." He'd been lending a hand with house-to-house at Kings Heath. Two major incident teams were actually covering six ongoing inquiries. Uniform and the squad were stretched thin, thinner than they ought to be. Straining at the bit, he asked if she was eating. Mac sure wasn't in danger of fading away. Her lip twitched. "Just coffee, ta mate." She'd already downed a BLT. He came back with a ham croissant, two wraps and a slice of apple pie.

"Glad to see you're still on the fruit." The pie was apparently a treat to go with her coffee. He stuffed his face while she gave him the gist of the Jamieson interview. They finished about the same time. Pushing his plates away, he said: "So where you coming from on this, boss? Are you saying there's more than meets the eye to the merry widow?"

"Wish I knew, mate." They'd known since the get-go Diana stood to inherit, but that alone was no reason to view her as a suspect. She shrugged. "Know where we're going though." She had a copy of Libby Redwood's photograph in her bag. It needed showing to the Sandman's other victims: Diana was first on the list. And given where the pic had been taken, Charlotte Masters came pretty high. "You got wheels, mate?" He told her he'd cadged a lift into town. "Come on, then. The Polo's in Temple Street." Mac wrapped the apple pie in a couple of napkins, shoved it in his donkey jacket pocket. "Waste not, want not."

As they walked to the car, a shop window full of TVs showing the news brought them to a halt. "The guv released the e-fit then?" Mac stating the bleeding obvious. A man's face was plastered over a bank of monitors: dark hair, deep-set eyes, wide mouth. Bev bit her lip. Getting Picasso to work with the little girl had seemed like a good idea at the time, seeing the result she wasn't too sure. Every time a visual was given airtime there was risk of duff info overload. The phones at Highgate would soon be red hot again. Byford looked none too happy either. The guv's grim face now filled every screen.

"I hear he got a mauling at the press conference," Mac said. "Concerted attack. Media want to know why more officers haven't been drafted in."

Don't we all? "Come on, mate. Places to go, people to

grill." She stalked off, hoiking her bag, spotted a familiar-looking guy walking towards them. A quick flick through her memory bank came up with Jagger lips, Fighting Cocks. "Hi, Laura. Great to see you again. How you doing?"

Struggling. Sweating. Skin crawling. Laura! Mac was never going to let her live this down. "I'm good." Apart from the hot flush. "You?" The guy was well fit, younger than she remembered. But what the hell was his name? Christ, it was only Sunday they'd spent the night together.

"I'm cool. It's my lunch break. I work just across the way." He jabbed a thumb over his suited shoulder; silk tie needed tightening a notch. He flicked Mac a polite face, probably thought she was with her dad. "Hey, I'm just about to grab a coffee...?" Seriously tasty or not, she wasn't about to join him. A drug user was a bad habit for a cop to get into.

"Sorry, mate." She forced a smile. "Another time?"

"Any time. Give me a bell." He gave a mock salute.

Mac didn't utter a word, just hummed all the way to the motor. *Tell Laura I Love Her.* Bev stood with the key in the door, one foot tapping. "Come on, Tyler. Spit it out."

"Me?"

"Now."

"Nothing to do with me, boss. You want to lie about your name, play around with toy boys. That's your shout." He dropped his voice. "Long as you..." *Don't let it get in the way of the job?*

"Don't go there, constable." Her voice was dangerously low. She had the motor running before he'd fastened the seat belt; her knuckles were white round the wheel. Tyler hadn't intended taking the piss, he wanted to dish out a lecture.

Arms folded, Mac stared through the windscreen. "What

I was going to say is, long as you don't get hurt."

She hit the gas; soft words and shit advice she could live without. "Back off, fatso."

The twenty-minute drive to the Masters place took fifteen, the silence punctuated by occasional gasps as Bev cut corners and Mac hit imaginary brakes. Her insouciant sniffs suggested he should thank God the infinitely nippier Midget was still in dock.

Locking the motor, she scanned the street, expanded her lungs. Even the air round here was clean. Three days after Alex Masters's murder and Park View Road was restored to cosy affluent suburbia: *The Good Life* without the sanctimonious neighbours and smelly pigs. Looked as if the cops had pulled out too. She creased her eyes: not quite. A strip of dirty police tape flapped listlessly in the gutter. Kneeling, she picked it up, shoved it in her coat pocket. Shame it wasn't so easy to pick up the pieces after the crime as well. The impact of Masters's death would affect some people for the rest of their life. As for picking up the crim? By the neck preferably.

The door was opened by the gormless skinny girl. Marie, was it? Bev flashed her ID. "Mrs Masters in, sweetheart?" She'd not phoned ahead, forewarned and all that, but it'd be a surprise if the woman was out socialising or shopping given she was in the early stages of grief.

The girl leaned a scrawny arm on the doorframe. "She's having her hair done."

Hair done? Bev rubbed her chin. Not sure a cut and blow dry would be a priority if her old man had just been butchered. Still, who was she to judge? One man's meat... "When you expecting her back?"

Beetle brows formed a wavy line. "She's not out." Like

184

they should know. "She's in the kitchen."

"Come in then shall we?" Bev didn't barge, but the girl had to step back swiftly. Mac tried stifling a sigh and tailed her. Whatever was kicking off in there sounded like a bundle of fun; the laughter died when Bev tapped the door, popped her head round.

"Sergeant Morrison. Was I expecting you?" Not angry or put out. The widow's frown seemed concerned more than tetchy as if she might've forgotten an arrangement. She certainly didn't appear ill-at-ease or embarrassed, but clearly wasn't expecting callers let alone cops. Hair plastered to the skull, she was caped to the neck and some guy with a pony-tail was prancing round like Edward Scissor-hands. Bev did a covert second-take. The face was seriously gorgeous, though she had her doubts about the get-up. The pink string T-shirt and tight leather strides could go either way.

"Just popped in on the off-chance, Mrs Masters." She cleared her throat, sensed Scissors giving her the glad eye. "We can always come back if it's not... convenient." The stress on the last word bordered on snide.

"No, of course not, come in. I'm happy to help." Looked it, sounded it, too. "Is there any news?"

Gaze still fixed on Bev, Scissors moved behind his client. "I'm here for you, Diana." Bev's mouth dropped when he laid a solicitous hand on the widow's shoulder. "But I'd best make myself scarce hadn't I, sweetie?" It was a joke, the voice teasing, playful; close your eyes and Glamour Boy was Graham Norton with a dash of Dick Emery. No wonder Mrs M didn't mind the cops butting in – it was hardly coitus interruptus.

"Would you?" Diana smiled. "We shouldn't be too long?"

"Your wish is my command." The elaborate bow from the waist showcased a neat bum. "I'll be in the sitting room." He winked as he sauntered past Bev then seemingly on second thoughts spun round, headed back, stood in her face. "Don't take this the wrong way." She flinched when he lifted her fringe. "If you ever fancy a decent cut give me a call." He was a gnat's eyelash from a knee in the groin. Fists balled, she backed off. His focus was still on her hair. "Seriously, sweetie."

Sweetie! Vidal was on another planet. "Look, mate…"

"But it hides your eyes." The smile was breathtaking. "And they're so beautiful. Drop in and see me sometime. I'll give you a good price." Another wink. "Ciao." He took off whistling. Cheeky git. So why did her lips have the ghost of a smile?

"Samuel has that effect, sergeant." Diana gestured to a couple of chairs. "I'm sure you think me shallow and vain but he's more than just a nice young man who looks after my hair."

"Come here often, does he?"

"Once or twice. When he heard about Alex, he rang to see if I was all right. He's one of those rare creatures who know how to make people feel good, a giver not a taker. He's like a breath of fresh air." She leaned forward conspiratorially. "And he's camper than a marquee. His words not mine."

"Sergeant Morriss has a picture we'd like you to look at, Mrs Masters." Mac's words. His face was like a constipated gargoyle. Point taken. Bev cut him a glance as she handed a copy of Libby Redwood's photograph to the widow. "We think the woman on the left was the latest victim of the man who murdered your husband, Mrs Masters. Reckon you've seen her before?"

"Was?" She'd picked up the tense. Fine lines appeared round her eyes as she looked to Bev for elaboration.

Bev gave a tight nod. "'Fraid she didn't make it."

"Oh my God." A hand went to her jaw. "How…? What…?"

"Have you seen her before, Mrs Masters?" Mac clearly wanted to cut to the chase. Squinting she held the picture closer. "She does look slightly familiar." Bev shifted on the seat. Come on. How? "I just can't recall where." She sighed, shook her head. "Maybe it'll come back to me?"

Bev pushed, got nowhere, went down a different track. "Is your daughter around, Mrs Masters?" She was fishing. If Charlotte was on the level, it'd be the last place she'd be. Bev was curious whether Diana would be so candid over the family set-up.

Thin smile. "Not right now."

"Expecting her soon?"

"I'm not sure, sergeant. Charlotte's a law unto herself." Not a lie, probably not the whole truth, though the pained look on the face seemed genuine. Bev had only heard Charlotte's take on the mother/daughter relationship. Diana's could be totally different. And utterly irrelevant. She'd leave it for now. "I could give her a message?" Mrs Masters offered.

"We'll catch up with her later. No worries." She spent a few minutes talking the widow through the inquiry's current state of play: officer numbers, statements taken, some of the inquiry lines. It was public relations as much as anything. The woman had a right to know and Bev wanted to keep her on board.

"I'm sure the police are doing everything they can, sergeant. And if anything comes back to me, I'll surely get in touch." The glance she flicked at the door told them – unwittingly perhaps – she wanted them out. It was a wrap anyway. Almost.

Halfway there, Bev turned, threw in an apparent after-thought. "Miss Jamieson? Your husband's secretary?"

"PA." A finely plucked eyebrow arched. "She wouldn't thank you for calling her a secretary, sergeant." Cool. Catty?

"She knew he was coming back to Birmingham that night. He rang to tell her."

"He would." Faint smile. "It was business, and she'd need to know."

"And you definitely had no idea?" Bev prompted.

She shook her head. "If I had, I'd never have gone to bed. And if I'd been up... who knows...?" Lip quivering, she dropped her face in her hands, visible across the knuckles were the thin red lines left by the Sandman's knife.

Waiting for a gap in the traffic, Bev gunned the motor in front of an elderly Volvo. Mac eased the apple pie from his pocket. Her sideways glance registered pureed puke. "There's tasty." They exchanged matey grins, the earlier spat forgotten. It was one of the reasons they made a good team, she couldn't stay spiky with him for long.

"Reckon the widow's on the level, boss?"

"S'pose." What did they have to go on? A phone call that wasn't made? A PA with a spiteful gleam in her eye? Not exactly prima facie, was it? Diana Masters didn't strike Bev as a Judi Dench. Only the Dame could pull a grieving widow act like that, surely? Unless Diana was up for an Oscar. "Can't see what she'd have to lie about."

"Never saw her as a serious contender myself." Mac was licking crumbs from his fingers.

She did a double-take. "You never ate that?"

He shrugged. "Shame to see it go to waste."

Shaking her head, she hiked the volume on the radio. It was just coming up to three and she was keen to hear whether the Sandman latest would hit the headlines.

Glancing at Mac, she toyed with telling him about the break-in at Baldwin Street, the timer left as a present. Not that anything since had sparked her personal safety alarm and, boy, had she been on alert. She opened her mouth, thought better of it. Best wait a while, see how things panned out.

The story wasn't the lead. That was some Westminster sleaze-fest, then some drivel about heavy snow and dangerous driving conditions in the north. At last. The newsreader linked into a clip from Byford. Bev could just imagine his face given how strained the voice sounded. After listening to the same old same old witness appeal, Mac lowered the sound.

"The gay with the scissors?" he dropped in casually. "You gonna let him loose on your hair… sweetie?"

Diana Masters ran her fingers through Sam's hair. He'd played a blinder; she should never have doubted him. Last night's glitch had been a temporary blip. "You were absolutely brilliant, darling." The police turning up out of the blue could've been a disaster. Sitting on the edge of the bed, negligee draped round her naked shoulders, she shuddered at the very thought.

"Are you cold, Dee?"

As he reached for a bottle on the floor, she traced his spine with her nails. Behind them, ivory satin sheets were stained, crumpled, by rights steam should be rising. Patting them, she raised a coy eyebrow: "I don't think so, Sammy."

Candlelight glinted on glass as they clinked. Veuve Clicquot. Her favourite. He leaned across, kissed her, tasted the champagne on her tongue. "Couldn't have done it without you, babe." He launched into an impersonation of Diana that by now was faultless. "He's a giver not a taker."

"I'll be here for you." Diana's of him was uncanny.

189

"I could've died when you told her she had beautiful eyes."

"I rather liked: 'If you ever fancy a decent cut.'"

They laughed again. They'd re-run the afternoon scenario several times in the hours since the police left.

Suddenly serious if not quite sober, Sam dropped the act. "Really think we can do it, Dee?"

"You saw the cops." She licked her lips. "What do you think?"

"Don't think I overdid the gay thing?"

She slipped a hand between his naked thighs. "Let's find out shall we?" They fell back on the bed, giggling. Diana had no qualms about the cops. It was the greedy bastard who was trying to screw them both who cast a shadow on the future. If she could get her hands on him... No, scrub that. Her cat eyes glinted in the soft light. When she got her hands on him.

25

After three hours at the paper mill the desk wasn't quite as new-pin neat as Evie Jamieson's empire, but then Bev's boss unlike Alex Masters was alive and kicking. Kicking ass come to that. Well, OK, ear-bashing. The guv had laid into just about everybody at the late brief. Or maybe it just seemed that way. It was probably more a socks-up-and-fingers-out dressing down than serious bollocking. Let's face it: the squad was well capable of giving itself a hard time. Four weeks since the first Sandman attack; four days since Alex Masters's murder. And where were they? Oh, look, was that square one flying past the window?

Blowing out her fringe on a sigh, Bev reached for a bottle of J2O; after Red Bull overload, the apple and mango was going down a treat. Including the juice trickling down her chin; a judicious sleeve caught it. At least they were ticking the no boxes. In any inquiry, eliminating the negative was up there with pursuing the positive. Just didn't get the adrenalin flowing the same way.

After Bev and Mac's fruitless troll round south Birmingham that afternoon, they could virtually rule out a connection between Libby Redwood and the Sandman's other victims. Neither Faith Winters nor Sheila Isaac knew the woman from Adam or Eve. Unless Diana Masters suddenly saw the light or Beth Fowler on return from Brighton came up with a link, it was dead-end avenue. Or maybe not. They'd still to run the image past Charlotte Masters. The girl hadn't been at home when they'd dropped by and a call to the wine bar where she worked failed to shed light on where she might be.

A definite cul de sac was Libby Redwood's known associates. Carol Pemberton had scratched a metaphorical red line through the names in the address book. Dazza had scoured every inch of relevant CCTV, Libby's alleged tail had failed to materialise. That had not been the brief's high spot. Had there been one? Bev held the cool bottle to her brow. Confirmation of more troops, she supposed; fifteen uniforms from West Mercia were being drafted in plus four pairs of extra admin hands assigned to the phone lines.

Kate Darby had come up with a list of jewellery she thought had been stolen from her sister's property. No way of knowing if any cash had been lifted. As in the other cases, descriptions of the items would be circulated to shops and other outlets less upfront let alone legit.

Edgy, antsy, Bev rose, strolled to the window, breathed in the cool night air; heard the buzz of city traffic, the odd blaring horn, watched skimpy blue-black clouds scud across full-cream moon. She narrowed her eyes. Why not even a chink of light in the case? By now in an inquiry, they'd expect to have the wisp of an idea, a piece or two of the puzzle to go on. The Sandman was untouchable, invisible. Leaning out she called lightly. "Where are you, you bastard?"

"Morriss! Don't do it! Don't jump!" High octane mock alarm from Mick Powell, the smirk was a mile high. Startled, eyes blazing, she spun round. "Enough clowns in this place without you getting in on the act."

Maybe it was down to the word clown. But when the DI's face fell, she knew what image was in his head. After witnessing the student take off from Selfridges' roof without a chute, he'd been as cut up as Bev had ever seen him.

"Crap line even for me, eh, Morriss?" His laugh was humourless. Hands shoved in pockets he cast a sheepish gaze at the carpet.

"Crap line for Russell Brand that." Arms crossed, she perched on the window sill, caught the twitch of his lip.

"What the hell were you doing anyway?" Moving in fast, he gave an over-the-top shiver. "It's boracic out there."

"Communing with nature."

He snorted. "Having a fag?"

"You should try it some time."

"Smoking?" Like she'd suggested eating shit.

"Communing with nature."

Mouth down, he made a budge up gesture with his thumb, joined her at the window, elbows on sill, they both gazed out at the stars, the night sky. Bev pictured little Daisy Towbridge with her telescope. Had she spotted the Sandman?

"Why'd she do it, Bev?"

She had to think for a second who he meant. Still didn't know why he asked. By now the cops knew: Jessica Harvey had been bipolar, high on crack, and off her face on absinthe. "Out of it, wasn't she? Tripped off to Planet La-la."

"Yeah," Powell sighed. "But death. It's so sodding final, isn't it?"

She bit back a Star Trek line about frontiers. Powell was dead serious and though he was stating the bleeding obvious, the haunted delivery held hidden depths. Lines on his face seemed more pronounced, too, the skin round his tired eyes like old bruises. The DI had been up with the insomniac larks. And it was what? His second day back? Talk about being chucked in the deep end. Even so Bev didn't want to get into a philosophical discussion. She shrugged it off with a less than profound: "Life's a bitch."

"Yeah. And then you die. You don't top yourself. She had her life ahead of her. Crikey, Bev, look what you went through..." Bev's spine stiffened, space invader senses on full alert. "Bet it never crossed your mind once, did it? Killing yourself?"

"Not myself." She sniffed.

"'Xactly. While there's life, there's…"

Cliché. "Mike. What you trying to say?"

"It's always worth hanging on? Never give up? Life's beautiful? Things can only get better?"

"Bet Tony Blair regretted that last one."

"Nah. Shame that kid wasn't more like you, Morriss."

"Oh yeah?"

"Tough as old boots." He gave her a shoulder a playful punch, headed for the door. "Catch you in the morning."

She shook her head, ghost of a smile on her lips. A minute or so later, she watched Powell stride across the car park, tie over his shoulder, raincoat flapping in the breeze. Glancing up he must've caught her silhouette in the window. "Not got a home to go to, Morriss?" Joshing, not harsh. She returned his salute with a wave, pulled the window to and slumped at her desk. Course she had a home to go to – but Fareeda was there. She'd yet to tackle her about the predictor kit. And if Bev was honest, she didn't feel like facing yet more of the girl's stonewalling.

Like she had a choice.

"Bev?" Byford called from behind as she was leaving the nick five minutes later. Midway down the backstairs, she glanced over her shoulder.

"Wotcha." She waited for him to catch up, noted a lack of spring in his step, deep lines, dark planes on his face. Was the guv starting to slow down, show his age? She hoped it was just the temporary pressure. Nothing a few early nights wouldn't see off. Not that this was an early night. "Bit late for you isn't it, guv?"

"You're not the only one puts in the hours." Snippy.

"Well slap my wrist." She bristled. "I meant you were out at Kings Heath first thing – so you've been on the go for ages." So'd she but who was counting?

"So've you." He smiled as he held the door. "Don't mind me." Close up and in this light he still had the George Clooney thing going. Even the Fedora was at a jaunty angle.

"Long day. Short fuse. Happens to us all, guv." Falling into step across the car park, she realised uneasily how comfortable it felt: just like old times. Perish that thought, Beverley.

"It was good getting away from the desk," Byford said. Chit-chat or something more?

"Come out with me any time, guv." Mental head slap. Sounded like she was hitting on him.

"How does Sumitra Gosh strike you lately, Bev?" He'd probably not heard, clearly had weightier matters on his mind. Her step barely faltered. "How'd you mean?"

"She seems quieter to me. Not contributing like she used to at the briefs." They'd reached Bev's motor. "I wonder whether CID's too much for her, maybe she's not quite ready for it. Last thing I want is a potentially good detective losing heart or feeling they're not up to the challenge."

Caring, perceptive, astute, three of the reasons he was the best boss she'd had. "Nah, guv. Sumi's fine." Worried sick about her cousin, in bits over what action to take, paranoid about the Saleems, apart from that... "Smack on." The crossed fingers behind her back had a mammoth task on their hands. "I can keep an eye on her if you like, gee her up a gnat's need be."

"Maybe." Noncommittal. "By the way, good work at the hospital this morning. You got some useful info from Libby

Redwood's sister."

She shuffled her feet; he'd have her blushing in a minute. "Ta, guv." Reason number four in the Byford Good Book: he didn't stint on a bit of praise-due now and again.

"So where you taking me?" He jangled keys in his coat pocket, raised an expectant eyebrow.

"Eh?" Her cheeks would be a fetching shade of beetroot.

"Come out with you any time, you said." Old bat ears had heard all right. Was he winding her up or angling for a night out?

"I was talking on the job." Cringe. It had come out harsher than she'd intended. She closed her eyes. Why hadn't she done the same with her mouth? She'd probably talked herself out of a date.

"And I'm not?" Dead serious. "Enough said." He tapped the side of his hat. "Night, Bev."

Mr Enigmatic. Torn, she watched the big man walk towards his motor, dithered over whether to dash across or let him go. "Guv?"

He didn't turn back. Maybe she'd not shouted loud enough, maybe he'd not heard, maybe he had. Whatever. Racked off, she took aim and kicked a stone across the tarmac. It crashed as it hit the wall. Smacked to Bev of an own goal.

Mac's new pad in Stirchley was a step up from his former grotty bed-sit in Balsall Heath: it boasted stairs for one thing. Home-bittersweet-home was now an Edwardian redbrick terrace complete with trellis. Though that would get the elbow soon as he got round to it. Currently he was standing in front of the wardrobe peering into the mirror, trying yet again to tie a half-decent knot in his tie. Well out of practice, he was beginning to wish he'd bought one of those clip-on jobs. He gave the damn thing a last twist and final tug then stepped back. He reckoned the grey silk went fine with the blue shirt, but then he'd never had a cool finger on the fashion pulse. And boy was he out of touch with this dating lark.

Lindy was going through a divorce as well. Early forties, three kids, she was something in NHS admin. They'd bumped into each other in Sainsbury, trolleys at dawn down the chiller aisle. It was early days – this would be their third date. Mac still had first night nerves. He glanced round for his tumbler, took a sip of scotch courage. Turning side on, he cast a critical gaze in the mottled glass. He was pretty sure he'd lost a few pounds, whatever motor mouth said. *Back off, fatso.* Charming.

Then he breathed out.

Maybe she had a point. Yeah, well, Mac had one, too. He'd meant what he'd said, the words she'd jumped down his throat to try to stop him saying: he didn't want her to get hurt, make that more damaged. He gave a wry smile: even when she needed a good slapping. *Fatso,* indeed. Picking up his glass, he wandered downstairs. There was still half an hour to kill. Not that he was nervous or anything.

Fareeda had the front door open while Bev was still fumbling in her bag. Lucky that, cos new locks had been fitted – the key had no chance. The arrangement had slipped Bev's over-worked mind, like a bunch of other stuff probably. Stepping inside, she forced a bright smile as she brandished a fish supper fresh from the Oceania chip shop. "We're frying tonight, kid. Warm some plates while I pop to the loo?"

The girl glanced down playing with the bangles round her tiny wrist. "I've eaten, Bev. To be honest, I'm so tired I just want an early night."

Every cloud. Least they wouldn't have to go through the

brick-wall-banged-head routine this evening. "No sweat. Sleep tight. See you in the morning."

Fareeda paused at the foot of the stairs, hand on the banister. "Your mum rang. You should call her back, Bev. She sounds so sad."

Motes, beams and eyeballs sprang to mind. Bev could do without what sounded like a lecture from a kid. "How d'you think yours feels, Fareeda?" No answer to that. Seething, foot tapping, Bev watched until the girl disappeared round the landing corner.

The air in the kitchen was blue. Bev had chipped a plate and stubbed a toe before sitting at a table with a solitary dinner-for-two laid out in front of her. Sighing she toyed with the fork, forced down a few chips. Come back Frankie, all is forgiven, at least La Perlagio could sing, make her laugh, and cook pasta to diet for. Not that Bev felt like eating right now. The nasty taste in her mouth wasn't because of the spat with Fareeda. The banging about and F-words were down to guilt. Emmy Morriss didn't deserve the arctic shoulder. Irony was, since losing the babies, Bev had neglected her mum. Fact was Emmy cared too much. Bev was no good with soft words, meaningful looks, unspoken pity.

"Sod it." Jettisoning the fish and chips in the bin, she opened a bottle of Pinot, took a glass through to the sitting room and hit the flashing red light on the answering machine.

Hi sweetheart. Just me. How are you doing? Been up to anything... exciting? Hope all's... OK. Me and your gran are... OK. Give us a call... if you have a minute. Love you... Bye, Bevy.

All those pregnant pauses.

Bev sat in the dark, twin tear trails running down her cheeks, dripping from her chin. Fareeda was spot on. Bev had just refused to acknowledge it before. The message was similar to a shed-load of others her mum had left over the months: beneath the superficial upbeat tone there was pain, Emmy was worried to bits.

She swallowed hard, took a few calming breaths. Then a few more. Wiping tears with her sleeve, she made a grab for the phone. It rang before she reached it. Startled, she snapped her name.

"Bev?" Oz, sounding unsure.

Bolt upright now, she licked her lips, finger-combed her hair. "Who else? Madonna?" Cool it, girl.

"You OK?" he asked.

"Natch." Curt. Over-compensation for a voice she couldn't trust not to break. The wallow in deep emotional waters had exacerbated raw wounds.

"Sure?"

"You a doctor now?" She closed her eyes. Not so much at the crass line more the caustic delivery. What the hell was wrong with her? Three, four second pause suggested Oz was wondering the same.

"Call me when you've snapped out of it, eh?"

"Peachy me, mate." Cheeky sod. Hearing his voice had thrown her – just a tad.

"Could've fooled me."

She bit back a cheap jibe. Had he got a point? Was stroppy her second nature these days? And she wasn't seeing it – like she refused to acknowledge her mum's hurt? "Sorry, Oz. How you doing?"

"You wanted to pick my brain?" She gave a wry smile, imagining anatomical features she'd rather poke around. Either way, the conversational opening was missed – Oz was all business.

"Yeah." Feet tucked under, she reached for her glass.

Keeping her voice down, she told him about Fareeda. How she'd turned up on the doorstep bruised and battered refusing to say who'd inflicted the injuries, how the Saleem family had no idea where she was and how Fareeda had no intention of returning home. "Found a predictor kit in her bedroom drawer as well."

"Found?"

She sniffed. "Sumi and me thought she was missing one night."

"And you thought you'd find her in a drawer?"

Bev sniffed. "Yeah, well. If I hadn't had a nose round we'd be none the wiser, would we?" If the girl wouldn't reveal who'd beaten her up she wasn't going to say who'd knocked her up.

Sounded like he was scratching his eyebrow. "And you can't get her to name names?"

"Can't get her to do diddly, mate." She talked him through some of the tacks tried and failed.

"Want me to have a go?"

"Nah. I'm of a mind to pay the Saleems a visit, have a quiet word with her dad. Say the college has reported her missing or something? What you reckon?" She'd no problem with treading on people's toes, she needed Oz to point a way through the cultural minefield.

"You fancy the father for this?" he asked.

"Wouldn't be surprised." Car door slammed in the street, next door's dog was having a fit.

"Where's the evidence?"

"Got me there." Intuition, bad vibes, fear in a girl's eyes when her father's mentioned? Not enough to convince a custody sergeant let alone the Crown Prosecution Service.

"'Kay, here's how I see it." She pictured those beautiful eyes, stunning cheek bones, perfect mouth. Concentrate, dumbo. "She's old enough to leave home." Oz's first vision. "She's not pointing the finger, she's not even made a police report. Go in there on gut instinct and your feet won't touch the floor."

"The girl's face is broken, Oz!" Loud. Accusatory. She strained her ears, thought he'd cut the connection, though that was normally her forte. When she'd called time on the relationship, Oz had tossed the emotional ball into her court – that's why there'd been no play.

"I'll try and come up in the next day or so." How wrong could a girl be? He'd been working on ways to get here not keep his distance. She'd question later why there was a shiver in her spine. Even so, it could be a wasted journey.

"She'll not talk to you, mate." Sodding dog was still going ballistic.

"No. And the Saleems won't talk to you." White, female, cop – ticked all the wrong boxes. Bev narrowed her eyes; was Oz…? "Saying you'll go round there?"

"Yeah. Cos if I don't you'll go barging in anyway. All guns blazing knowing you."

"I'll come with you, then." There was a smile in her voice. "Always fancied riding shotgun."

"Thought it was me who always played Tonto?"

And what did that make her?

"I'll hang fire till I see you." It wasn't her best line – and the smile had faded anyway. Blinking, she bit her lip. "Catch you later."

Yapping dog. Shut the fuck up. Bloody animal was worse than a burglar alarm. Hands jammed in coat pockets, the dark-haired man walked straight past the house. He knew she was in there; itched to take her out now. Patience, man. When he acted she'd get no warning – not even a neighbour's mad mutt. She'd lied through her teeth, used him, made him look a complete retard. No one treated him like that. No one. Bitch wouldn't even give him her number. He'd had to nick her mobile. And he'd been so generous with his gifts. A sly smile tugged his lips. He hoped he hadn't hidden the timer too well.

Timing – as they say – is all.

FRIDAY

26

Highgate, first thing, place was buzzing. Rumours of a break were running round like petrol-fuelled wildfire. Bev had picked up a whisper in the corridor when she'd bumped into Powell on the way to her office. The DI wasn't privy to the detail, only Byford and the operator who'd first listened to the recording knew the full story. She'd just had time to fit in a quick call to Interflora. The biggest bunch of flowers this side of Kew Gardens should soon be winging its way to her mum. The card would read: Down payment for lunch. See you Sunday.

Now, Bev and the rest of the squad waited breath-bated to be brought up to speed. Air in the briefing room was electric, not a spare edge-of-seat in the house. Rife speculation ended abruptly when Byford flung open the door, he started shooting soon as he walked in.

"We may have a witness." Reaching the front, he turned hand held high to silence the whoops. "A caller claims he saw the perp leaving Libby Redwood's house." May? Claims? Clearly the jury was still out. Bev sat back, crossed her legs: she'd spotted a tape in the guv's other hand. Maybe the best was yet to come. Readying the player, Byford told the squad the message had been left less than an hour ago on a confidential police hotline. "Listen up." Like a pin dropping on velvet wouldn't be deafening.

The killer you lot are after? Male voice. Scottish accent? Nasal as if he had a heavy cold.

I seen him last night coming out of that posh gaff in Kings

203

Heath. He was wearing that clown mask like on the telly, at first any road. At first? Bev leaned forward, elbows on knees, chin in hands.

Here's the thing: I wanna know if there's a reward like, or anything? Or anything: barbed wire round the grasping bastard's bollocks for a start.

Grassing ain't safe is it? I reckon I deserve a bit o' danger money, like."

Sotto voce snort from Bev. Stony glare from the guv.

Think it over. When I see something about a reward on the news – I'll get back.

"Guy's a joker," Bev spouted before Byford hit pause. "The accent's all over the shop. The cold's prob'ly faked. There's not a word on there he couldn't have picked up from the press. No name, no number, nothing."

"Finished?" The guv traced an eyebrow with a finger. "Obviously, there are holes."

"Holes? It's a moth eaten sieve." She sat back, foot circling. "Traced the call yet?"

"Phone box. City centre."

She hooted. "Quelle surprise."

Mac interrupted the exchange. "What we doing about it, guv?"

"Bernie's working on a news release."

"There is no reward though?" Carol Pemberton seeking confirmation.

"A carefully-worded news release." Byford gave a thin smile. "We'll hint there's money on the table without going into details."

"Have that in common with the loser, then," Bev sneered. "Big fat fact deficit."

"Do you have a better idea, sergeant?"

Surly, she folded her arms. "Working on it."

"Well, until you do, stop the pops. I'm not a complete idiot. If it's a hoax, I'll do everything I can to make damn sure he's done for wasting police time." Glancing round, he spotted the DI leaning against the wall. "Take over here, will you, Mike. I need to see what Bernie's come up with." Byford paused in front of her on the way out. "The guy could be on the level, Bev. Ignoring the call's a risk I'm not prepared to take. And I'm the one calling the shots."

Bang bleeding bang.

"The bastard's gone to the cops, Dee." A panicky Sam not exactly beating about the bush on the pay-as-you-go. He sounded more gutted than when they'd heard the Redwood woman had choked. The death was a mistake, unfortunate; Diana hoped it would be the last. She flicked the TV remote. "I know. I've just watched the news." Regional lunchtime bulletin, full of street crime and traffic jams, the Sandman had been top story.

"God, Dee, how can you stay so calm?" She pictured him flushed, sweating, tearing at his hair.

"One of us has to, Sammy." Languidly, she unfolded herself from the settee, crossed the drawing room to the sideboard where Alex kept his booze. "And anyway what exactly have they got?"

"Only a fucking witness." He'd not listened carefully, not read between the lines.

"Our friend has given them jack-shit." Pouring Smirnoff into a tall glass, she was a touch smug to see the hand was steady. "That's why they need him to come forward again."

"You can't know that, Dee." There'd be that tiny frown between his eyes. Shame he wasn't alongside so she could stroke it away.

205

"Think about it." She sipped the vodka. "If the police had a name, Sammy, would we be having this conversation?" That was a great comfort, he was virtually whimpering. "Cool it, Sam."

"But he was there, Dee! He saw me. It's all right for you."

"Can't you see he's tightening the screw?" Maybe she'd thought about it longer or Sam was nowhere near sharp as she'd thought. She hoped that wasn't going to become a problem. As to the broadcast, far as Diana was concerned the plod had been duped into delivering a subtle personal message from the blackmailer. "That crap on the news was a veiled threat."

"Veiled? Thank God it wasn't pointed."

She rolled her eyes. "There wasn't even a vague description, Sam. Our friend's on a power trip. He wants us running scared. He's saying he'll shoot his mouth off so we pay up."

"Is the cash ready?"

"Sure, I went to the hole-in-the-wall this morning." She stifled a sigh. "What do you think, Sam? I can't just whistle up half a million. Getting hold of that sort of money takes time."

"We haven't got time, Dee. He wants it within forty-eight hours."

"What?" Chipped ice. Why had Sam kept her out of the loop? The glass was empty, she topped it up, took a slug. A shaft of weak sunlight fell across Alex's portrait on the wall. Diana raised a mock toast, turned her back.

"He called just before I rang you." There was more, she heard it in the voice. "He still wants you to make the drop." She swallowed. Thank God for that. Less chance of it being cocked up.

"No problem."

"There is. He's tightening the screw all right – he claims he's holding Charlotte."

The glass almost slipped from her fingers; grabbing it she tightened her grip, took swing and hurled it at the wall. Shattered fragments glistened where they lay like a sprinkling of ice.

Evie Jamieson's Arran cardigan was buttoned to the neck, the ancient radiator blasted out heat, still the PA shivered. Someone walking over her grave, she told herself. Picking up Alex's photograph from her desk, she gazed at the face of the man she'd loved for nineteen years. "Is someone trampling over yours, darling?" The murmur emerged through barely parted thin dry lips. The endearment wouldn't have escaped when Masters still drew breath.

It wasn't the first time Evie had asked the question in the last day or so. The young detective's visit had unsettled her in more ways than one. DS Morriss had raised – however obliquely – the spectre of foul play. Like everyone else, Evie had believed that Alex died when a burglary went wrong, a simple though tragic case of being in the worst place at the worst time. That could still be so, of course. But what if it was premeditated? Evie had posed the question directly, but Morriss hadn't given a straight answer. She tapped a thigh with testy fingers. What did 'exploring every avenue' mean exactly?

Sighing, she took a key from a Snoopy penholder, walked across the office to a grey metal filing cabinet. Knees creaked as she squatted, then fumbling with clumsy fingers released a brown envelope taped to the underside of a drawer. Only she, Alex and one other person knew its contents. Evie fancied she could almost hear the bomb ticking.

Rising unsteadily, she had to lean against the wall for support, clutching the package to her breast. What should she do? Alex had sworn her to secrecy. She could still hear his wonderful voice in her head: not until the time's right, Evie, not until the time's right. Now he was dead and the time would never be right. And she could be so wrong. She screwed her eyes tight. Releasing the contents would destroy reputations, sully memories. But would Alex rest in peace if she let sleeping dogs lie? Sleeping dogs? One such sprang to mind immediately: Diana Masters. Evie barked a mirthless laugh, mouth twisted in contempt. She loathed the woman. Diana had never been good enough for Alex, and, who knew… if the bitch hadn't come along?

Torn, fighting tears, she carried the package to her desk. Once more her hand went to Alex's photograph. Her lips had kissed his a thousand times – through the glass. Life and death separated them now, and she didn't know what to do. Her glance fell on a card near the phone. DS Morriss had left it, telling her to call if anything came to mind. Narrowing her eyes, Evie reached for it now, ran it between her fingers, tapped it against her teeth, then tore it into tiny pieces.

Hands behind her head, eyes closed, Bev was as horizontal as it gets when you're in a swivel chair using a desk as a footstool. KitKat wrappers and empty coke cans littered the surface, a handful of M&Ms had escaped to the floor. The caffeine and sugar kick had fuelled a marathon afternoon session: she'd phone-bashed for China, written a stack of reports, reviewed about a third of the inquiry's statements, re-examined every Magpie item in the exhibits office. Evening now and wheat and chaff whirled in her brain, grey cells trying to sift and sort a cerebral dust storm.

The missing link was in there somewhere.

"This you 'working on it', boss?" Actually, it sounded like the missing link had just lumbered in. She'd been waiting for Mac to show. At the late brief, Powell had tasked them with following a tip-off. Hopefully it would be a piece of piss. The first weekend off in a while beckoned; Oz just might put in an appearance and on Sunday her mum was getting out the fatted calf – well, pig. Still reclining, Bev opened a mock resigned eye. "Don't you ever…?" Sod it, no point. She knew he never knocked. "This is me thinking, mate. It's heady stuff."

"Thoughts racing, eh?"

"Flat out. You should try it sometime." Stifling a yawn, she swung her legs down, cut him a glance as she shucked into her coat. "Won the pools or something?"

He spread empty palms, industrial strength beam still in place. "A guy can't smile round here these days?"

"'Gainst the law, mate." She grinned. "Come on, Mr Happy, give."

"You'll take the piss." His bottom lip jutted.

"Prob'ly."

"I've met this woman." Gazing down, he toed the carpet with a desert boot. "She makes me feel like a kid again."

"Shoot, mate, how old is she?" Her lip twitched as Mac's mouth tightened.

"I knew it…"

"Genuinely happy for you, Mac." She grabbed her bag, headed for the door. "You'll make someone a wonderful wife."

"So'd you."

She froze, spun round hackles rising. "See that, mate." Pointing to the floor. "That's a line. And you've just crossed it." Diva or what? Even to her ears it sounded OTT.

"Get over it, Bev." Casual, matter of fact, but his eyes were intense. She knew the Morriss ring fence wasn't what he had in mind. He'd been there the night of the stabbing, seen the Black Widow's fatal lunge. Mac was telling her to move on from that. Like she didn't want to? Blue eyes blazing she was about to give him a mouthful then paused. The pram was currently out of toys. "I'm trying, Mac." Her lips attempted a smile.

"Very." He winked as he passed her to get the door. "Come on, boss."

"Be a waste of time, mate." They fell into step as they walked the corridor. An anonymous caller had left a name and address on one of the squad room's hotlines. Liam Small from Newtown was allegedly a dead ringer for the e-fit released yesterday. Anonymous caller said it all: probably some loser trying to stitch up a guy who'd nicked his girlfriend. "Trouble with this job," Bev moaned. "Most of the punters who ring in haven't got a clue."

Diana Masters was slightly tipsy. A liquid diet was all she could face at the moment. Frantic and furious, her gut was churning, mind racing. The nausea would pass, she was sure of that. In the same way she knew she'd stop drinking before losing control. Diana had never been drunk in her life. Sipping the vodka, she rolled it round her tongue. If ever she needed a clear head, now was it.

Slipping off her coat, she chucked it over the arm of a chair, smoothed her hair, then stood in front of the mirror. She was surprisingly pleased – and relieved – to note the inner turmoil wasn't evident, the immaculate mask was intact. Diana had just returned from a fact finding tour: Charlotte definitely wasn't in any of her usual haunts. The discovery had dashed Diana's faint hope that their friend's

CV had 'lying bastard' writ large, as well as blackmailer. She realised now he almost certainly wasn't bluffing.

Swaying slightly, she dimmed the lights, drifted to the CD player, decided she could do without musical distraction. Charlotte's abduction complicated matters. Diana was hardly in a position to go to the police. Her lip curved at the understatements. Hugging herself she paced the faded carpet, the pay-as-you-go clutched in her fingers. Think, woman, think. There had to be a way round it. Could her original plan still work? Sam shadowing her on the drop, pulling a knife at the handover, only this time forcing the bastard to reveal Charlotte's whereabouts before he was taken out. Taken out? Such a civilised euphemism. The thin smile turned skeletal. Call it what the hell you like, the idea was the best she could come up with.

Yet so much could go wrong. She ran her fingers through her hair. Maybe the cops were the only option? No. She was a damn sight smarter than the slime-ball who was holding her daughter. Scowling, she threw a log on the fire, curled up in Alex's armchair, willed the phone to ring. Pay-as-you-go? Oh, yes. The bastard would pay all right. Before being permanently despatched. For several minutes, deep in thought, she watched the flicker of flames and curl of smoke as the fire took hold. Charlotte would be fine. Diana closed her eyes, told herself again: Charlotte would be just fine. Failure was not an option.

Bev awarded herself ten out of ten for prescience, perfectionism and all round good-eggism. As she predicted, Liam Small had emerged squeaky clean from his grilling. The anonymous caller's stitches had come adrift: Small's alibi was tighter than a cat's rectum not to mention he had the colouring of an anaemic albino. By way of a slap on the back, she'd treated herself to a cheeky little Pinot which even now lay winking from the passenger seat. She'd swung by Oddbins after dropping Mac at the nick. Hopefully it'd be the last she'd see of him until Monday. Unless there was a major break, she'd not be called in. And if there was – she'd want to be there anyway. Win-win situation.

She slapped in a Kinks CD to celebrate, sang along to *Sunny Afternoon*. Moseley was gearing up for Friday night, flash motors were parked bumper-to-bumper either side of the main drag, music spilled out of wine bars and pubs, boobs spilled out of lace and lurex. Bev's goose bumps were rising in sympathy: it was minus five on the street. She lowered the window a tad just to take in the smells of pizza and curry: oregano, cardamom, cinnamon, coriander. She'd already decided on an Indian, fancied Rogan Josh tonight but it was early yet, she'd ring later. It'd be a bit coals to Newcastle for Fareeda but the girl could always fend for herself. Maybe she wouldn't even bother coming down if the migraine was as stonking as she'd made out on the phone.

"Thanks, Raymondo." Smiling, Bev cut the Kinks, grabbed bottle and bag and fished out the new key. House felt warm, even though no one was on hand with the nibbles and red carpet. She guessed Fareeda was still nursing a sore head. Coat and bag ditched, Bev nipped upstairs, peeked into the spare room. Ten out of ten again. Give that girl a gold star. She dithered on the landing but only momentarily. Her mum suffered migraines, reckoned the only cure – apart from death – was silence and a darkened room. She'd leave the kid to it. And being brutally honest, she fancied having the place to herself for a night.

Five minutes later, she was curled up with Johnny Depp. Well, Depp was on the DVD, swashbuckling and timber-shivering, Bev was supine on the sofa, glass in hand, bowl of Quavers balanced mid-trunk. Would she walk his plank? Any time, matey. Her lascivious leer morphed into a testy frown. Was that the bloody door? Using elbow as prop, she listened out for the bell. Knowing the erratic hours she put in, the few mates she had outside the job never turned up on spec, cold and casual callers could go get stuffed; on past experience it was probably Jehovah's Witnesses trying to save her soul. Her lopsided smile suggested they'd have their work cut out.

The bell rang again, a persistent finger on the buzzer. Her eyes widened. What if…? Heart skipping a beat, the Quavers took a tumble as she shot up, swung down her legs. She had a mad idea it was Oz. Wouldn't be the first time he'd turned up unannounced, Khanie had a habit of springing surprises.

It was that all right. Confusion reigned. For a split second she thought she'd phoned Spice Avenue. But she hadn't called for an Indian and the grey-haired guy wasn't delivering a takeaway. He wouldn't need two henchmen for that.

Two seconds later the rupee dropped. It had to be a Saleem family outing. Had they come packing? If so, what were they carrying? Heart pumping, bowel on ice, she aimed for a disarming smile, made damn sure it didn't reach her eyes, detected not so much as a lip twitch in return.

The old boy could've been carved from fissured rock; the hooded eyes were expressionless, certainly illegible. Quick scan showed the brothers had inherited the father's genes with time on their side: dark-haired, early twenties, tasty except they so knew it. Part of her wanted to slam their faces into a wall; part of her was bricking it.

"My name is Malik Saleem. I think you know why I'm here." He was in off-white shalwar kameez and a zipped blue nylon jacket. The brothers-in-arms wore street uniform: baggy denims, loose fitting hoodies, Nike trainers. Calculating the odds went like this: she despised bullies, was well able to look out for herself but if push came to shove it was three against one. Could be asking for trouble inviting them in?

"Best come in." Standing to one side, she fought not to flinch when the old man raised a gnarled hand. It was only to turn down her offer.

"I want you to tell Fareeda she must come home." He who must be obeyed or what?

"No." Not even if he said please. How'd they found out where she was though? Had they put a tail on Sumi?

"I am not looking for trouble."

Arms folded, she held his gaze. "You ain't getting any."

"Evening, Bev." A loud yell from across the road. The old man who lived opposite was standing outside his house. "Everything all right, girl?"

"Hunky, thanks, Mr Yates." Alfie looking out for her improved the odds; the Saleems wouldn't do anything stupid in front of a witness.

"I want my daughter back." Like there'd been no interruption. "Tell Fareeda we can work it out. It will be better for her if she comes home."

"Better than what? Getting beat?"

That stepped up the heat. She watched him cool it with a couple of jaw clenches. "You should not interfere. You don't understand."

Her turn to see red bullshit. "Damn right I don't." She was sick of hearing it. "I don't understand how anyone can pummel a girl's face till it breaks. I don't understand why a girl's scared shitless to open her mouth. I don't understand why sadistic pieces of work get away with it time after time."

"You are a police officer. Do you really think I would be here if I had done this terrible thing to my own flesh and blood?" She didn't know. He could be on the level or lying through those stained teeth. Unless Fareeda testified the old man was home and dry. He must know she hadn't spoken out or the police would be knocking on his door, not vice versa. If the girl returned home, Saleem could make sure she kept her mouth shut. Maybe permanently.

"Who did then?"

His eyes darkened. "I will make it my job to find out."

"Think you'll find that's my job." Sunshine. "And when I do, he's going down."

"If that's an accusation…?" He didn't elaborate and she let it hang. Oz was right: she'd not a thread of evidence. On the other hand it looked to Bev as if the old man was having a hard time keeping a lid on it. He clearly didn't take to being challenged let alone contradicted. "Fareeda does not belong here. Her mother misses her. She cries herself to sleep every night."

"And your daughter doesn't?" She glanced over his shoulder. Alfie was sweeping the pavement. In the dark. Whistling. *You'll Never Walk Alone.*

"May I speak with her please?" Saleem senior was doing all the talking. The brothers knew their place: on the sidelines cracking the occasional knuckle.

"She's not up to visitors. Got a migraine."

"You are lying to me."

Cheeky sod. She'd had enough. "G'night." She made to close the door. They could be there till the cows came home then left on a world cruise. Unless Fareeda had a change of heart, it wasn't going to happen.

"My daughter does not belong here." She recoiled at his garlic breath as he took a step closer, tried to put a foot in the door. "Send her home. Soon." The voice was low but had a sharper edge. "Then we can forget about it."

You might. "Are you threatening me, Mr Saleem?"

"Good night, officer." Bouncing on the balls of their feet the sons moved aside so he could leave first. "I hope it won't be necessary to trouble you again."

Diana Masters stroked Sam's brow, ran her fingers through his damp tousled hair. His cheeks were flushed, he felt fevered. They stood face to face in the kitchen. She suspected his heightened emotion was down to fear. That he was running scared. More than ever they needed to stand strong, to stand together. A weak Sam was ornamental but no use, dangerous in fact. "Sam, Sam, it will be OK."

"How can you say that, Diana?" His eyes pleaded with her before he turned to cup his hands under the cold tap to take a drink. Observing, calculating, she waited until his focus was again on her.

"He won't kill Charlotte, Sam. It's just big talk."

"And that's what?" The package he'd brought was on the table. Gone midnight, but he'd driven straight over when he found it pushed through the door of his flat.

"It's hair, Sam. It might not even be Charlotte's." Stupid. Of course it was.

"You're in denial, Diana. It's her in the photograph."

That was more… disconcerting. It was definitely her daughter gagged, blindfolded and bound to a chair. "At least we know she's alive."

"For how long?" He threw his hands into the air. "There's no option now. You have to go to the police."

Diana fought to conceal her contempt. It was vital not to lose him but he was acting like a lily-livered wimp. "Get real. You're the Sandman for God's sake. If it comes out you'll go down for the rest of your life."

"If he keeps his mouth shut it won't come out." God. How could he be so dense? There was only one way to make sure the blackmailer kept his mouth shut. And she had every intention of taking it.

"You're not thinking straight, Sam. Watch my lips. There can be no police involvement. *We* get her back. We do what he says."

She watched as he pulled at his bottom lip, working out where she was coming from. "Pay the ransom you mean?"

"If that's what it takes." Over Diana's dead body. She needed time to get Sam on track.

"It's too risky, Dee." He ran both hands through his hair. "He could take the cash and still kill her."

"But we won't let him, will we?" She'd rather die than go down as Sam's accessory. Scrub that. She'd prefer to kill. Anyone who got in her way. He wasn't completely convinced. But there were lots of ways to make him come round. She held her arms open. "Come on, Sammy. Let's go to bed."

Bev slammed the door on the Saleems' departing backs, but not before hearing the old man hawk then spit on the ground. She leaned against the wood, slamming fist into palm. *I hope it won't be necessary to trouble you again.* Sounded like a veiled threat without the veil. Bring it on, gobshite.

But was it a warning? Realistically, how'd she know? Maybe he genuinely wanted his daughter back with no hassle. Drifting back to the sitting room, she took a few pensive sips of wine. It was just conceivable Saleem hadn't laid a finger on Fareeda. It was the girl's word against… Hold on? She frowned. Fareeda still hadn't uttered a syllable of any import on the subject. Fact was Bev knew no more now than the night she'd found Fareeda and Sumi huddled outside. Correction. The predictor kit was pretty telling. Not that there'd been opportunity to tackle the girl about it. Lips pursed, she glanced at the ceiling then mental sleeves rolled headed for the stairs. Migraine or not – it was time to take issue. And there'd be no standing on ceremony.

"Need a word, kid." Bev stood at the bedside, tapping a foot. She'd done the decent thing leaving off the light, but even in the shadows she saw Fareeda had pulled the duvet over her head. Natch. More comfortable than burying it in the sand. "Sooner we talk – sooner I'll be out of your hair." Big brush off. Feigning sleep was child's play: Fareeda was a big girl now. Mouth tight, arms crossed, Bev pushed a toe against the mattress. "I ain't going nowhere, kid." Not a murmur. Bev pushed again, harder this time. Nothing. She narrowed her eyes, hair rising on the back of her neck. No one slept that deep. Suddenly alert, scalp crawling, she took a step closer, looked for the gentle rise and fall of shoulder under duvet. Holy Mary. It wasn't.

Dear sweet Christ. Not dead, please, not dead. Heart pounding, hand shaking Bev flung off the cover, muttered obscenities under her breath. Fareeda wasn't dead. Fareeda wasn't there. Just well-placed towels, pillows and a few lines on a post card.

Please don't try and find me. It's better no one knows where I am. I have a friend and we'll be fine. Thank you for being there, Bev.
Xxx

Weak with relief, eyes brimming with tears she dropped to her knees. "You stupid, stupid girl." It wasn't only Fareeda she had in mind.

MONDAY
27

Seven a m. Highgate. A business-suited Bev had the squad room almost to herself, ploughing through a backlog of printouts and police reports, catching up on detail that might have slipped her net. She'd monitored news bulletins over the weekend, knew nothing major had kicked off in the Sandman inquiry or Powell would've called her in like a shot. Blowing on a cup of steaming canteen coffee, she reckoned a summons would have been welcome given how much downtime she'd spent on domestic stuff. House was cleaner than an operating theatre now: not difficult. Mind, it had needed a seeing to, she'd had to dust the board before doing the ironing.

Shuffling the paperwork into a neat pile, she knew the chores-fest had been displacement activity. It had stopped her obsessing over Fareeda, and a bunch of other stuff. Sumi had been as much in the dark over her cousin's whereabouts; Bev had called Goshie the minute she found the girl gone. Later – much later – she'd left voicemail telling Oz not to bother coming up. Hadn't realised till then how much she'd been looking forward to seeing the guy. What with that and low-level all round antsy-ness it had been a pretty shite weekend. Anticipation greater than the event? Got that right. Nipping a tin of ta-very-much Roses across to Alfie and whizzing round Sainsbury hardly qualified as social whirls. She pursed her lips: what did it say about her life when her mum's roast pork and crackling had been the highlight?

She needed reminding what it was all about. Rising, she drifted cup in hand to the victims' picture gallery, keen blue eyes lingered on each face in turn: Faith Winters, Beth Fowler, Sheila Isaac, women terrorised and terrified by the Sandman; Donna Kennedy and Libby Redwood, dead; odd man out Alex Masters, killed. Taking a sip of coffee, it occurred to her that if the timing of previous attacks was anything to go by, another strike was overdue.

Moving across to one of the whiteboards, she stood in front of the e-fit, stared into what could be the perp's dark deep set eyes. Maybe the Sandman had been too busy of late making silent phone calls? After receiving another half-dozen silent hang-ups, she'd asked BT to check the line.

"You're early." How long had the guv been watching her? He was in the doorway Fedora and attaché case in hand. She spotted a shaving nick on his neck. "Good break, Bev?"

"Brill." Bright smile. "The best." Like she'd admit Boot Hill had more life.

His finger traced a quizzical eyebrow. "What'd you get up to?"

"Y'know how it is, guv." Mouth turned down, she made a wave of her hand. "Bit o' this, bit o' that."

"That quiet, uh?" Deadpan delivery, voluble gaze. The big man could read her better than anyone she knew.

"Rubbish." She sniffed. "Glad to get back to work." Lesser of two evils. Saturday night was the first in a long time she'd not gone on the pull, the very thought had turned her stomach. Least here there was company she didn't have to get rat-arsed to keep.

He paused a beat or two then: "Always glad to have you back, Bev." Ambiguous smile, mock salute and he was gone. Had she read something deeper in those eyes, the way he'd said the words? Or had she just wanted to? Miles away, she tapped a pen against her teeth.

"Earth to Morriss. Come in please." The moment had passed. Mike Powell bemused grin, arms folded, leaned against the doorframe.

"DI Powell." Eager smile. "How may I help?"

"You taking the piss?"

"Would I?"

He rolled his eyes, jammed a hand in his pocket. "You didn't miss much, Morriss." He'd been in all weekend. She listened as he talked her through a couple of ticked boxes: the house to house in Kings Heath had finally been completed, checks on whether there was a property link between the victims had drawn a blank. There'd been no further contact from the grasping bastard after a non-existent reward.

"That it?" she asked.

"Have to sharpen our spades, won't we? See you at the brief." He turned at the door. "Oh yeah, a woman phoned here for you a couple of times."

"Oh?" Not likely to be anyone she'd already spoken to, she always gave out a bunch of numbers she could be reached on.

"Wouldn't leave a name. Said it wasn't urgent. She'd try again."

She shrugged. "Get a number?"

"I'm not your sodding secretary." He disappeared then popped his head back. "Course I did. It's on your desk."

Bag and coat dumped, Bev dug out the number from under a pile of files and post-its. It didn't ring a bell, frowning she reached for the receiver, tried it twice, would've left a message but no answerphone kicked in. She glanced up, some joker was playing a drum solo on the door. Not hard to guess who. She gave a resigned sigh. "Come in, mate."

Mac ambled in humming *Knock, knock, knocking on heaven's door.* Subtle. The song choice was no surprise compared with the shock on clocking his new look. He'd ditched the lumberjack gear for blue shirt and charcoal chinos.

"My God." She lifted an imaginary jaw from the floor. "Give us a twirl."

"No more barging in, boss. Turning over a new leaf, me."

New woman more like. "Hold you to it, mate."

"Not just that. I've bagged up a load of old clothes. Splashed out on a new wardrobe. Nothing like a fresh start."

Mental eye roll. Must be part of Mac's one-man move-Morriss-on campaign. She let it go; his heart was in the right place somewhere under the paunch. And maybe he had a point.

One eye closed, Byford took aim and launched the Fedora at the hat stand. His muted *Yes* was accompanied by a triumphant air punch. Hitting the target didn't necessarily mean a good day ahead, but success gave the big man a childish thrill. It wasn't part of the morning routine he shared with anyone. Sighing he sat at the desk, tugged his bottom lip. Like the weekend – that had been pretty solitary too: long solo walk in the Malverns, dinner alone in a restaurant, single bed in a soulless hotel. Throughout, Bev hadn't been far from his thoughts. Why the hell couldn't they get their act together?

If he'd decided nothing else over the last two days, he'd decided this: when Operation Magpie was concluded he'd ask if she wanted to give it another go. Find out once and for all if they had a joint future. He reached for his briefing notes. All they had to do now was nail the Sandman.

222

Sam's hand shook as he passed the phone to Diana. "He wants to speak to you."

Thank God for that. There'd been little contact for two days. Edgy herself, she'd kept Sam with her most of the time trying to convince him the blackmailer was playing mind games. It hadn't worked. Her lover was pale, sweaty, barely eating. He'd not touched breakfast, just pushed scrambled egg round with a fork. Diana shoved away her empty plate, any nausea she felt stemmed from having to be the strong one all the time. Taking a deep breath she held the phone to her ear. "Diana Mast…"

"I know who you are, lady. I've been pissed around enough. Where's the cash?" The voice was metallic, distorted, not as menacing as Sam described it. Maybe she was better prepared, or less easily intimidated.

"It's not been easy…"

"I don't give a flying fuck. I want it tonight or the deal's off."

A flash of fury lit her eyes. "You don't get a cent until I know my daughter's alive." What little colour there was drained from Sam's cheeks. It wasn't how they'd decided to play it. Her role was supposed to be desperate mother, willing to do anything the blackmailer asked. Fact was, she hated being jerked round by scum.

"Sure about that, lady?"

"Perfectly."

"You have two minutes to change your mind."

"Or?" She curled a lip. Bastard had hung up.

Eyes wide and staring, Sam ran both hands through his hair. "You're out of your tiny. You may as well ring the cops yourself."

"Shut the fuck up. I'm trying to think." She closed her

223

eyes, index fingers pressed against temples. The current predicament was down to her. She should've stuck to the role. Much as she resented the whole sorry mess, until they saw the whites of the blackmailer's eyes, they were over a fucking big barrel. Cocking her head, she tried to locate the source of a strange sound. Sam was kneeling on the floor, sobbing, tears running down his face.

"I can't take any more, Dee."

She grabbed the phone before its second ring. "OK. Tell me what you want. I'll do anything you say."

"OK, we re-interview everyone we've spoken to since day one." It was Byford's response after an increasingly uneasy silence to a request for input at a brief that had been both uninspired and uninspiring. He'd held centre stage for the better part of half an hour, but it was more up-sum of where the inquiries had been than where they were going: review rather than foresight. Bev had cast the odd covert glance at the team, heads were generally held down, fingers flicked through notebooks. Sumi Gosh wasn't the only officer taking a metaphorical back seat keeping her mouth clamped. Bev had never known it before, not so much as a naff suggestion being thrown into the pot let alone a bright idea. The squad's slumped body language said more than anyone was prepared to voice: most officers were as exhausted as the lines of inquiry. Eroded spirits rather than physically knackered. Cops were human, too. There were only so many brick walls the communal head could bang, an inquiry team needed a break, and she wasn't talking bacon roll and cup of tea.

Break. Brighton. Mental light bulb. "Beth Fowler should be back this morning." Blank look from Byford. "She was the first victim. Been away for a few days?" Bev had called last week, left a message on the answerphone. Byford nodded. Not exactly overwhelmed but at least it broke the silence.

"What about a reconstruction, guv?" DC New's puppy-dog eyes shone. Bev masked a smile of wry amusement. When all else failed, Dazza always came up with that one. He'd clocked himself on the regional news once.

"Of what, Darren?" Byford sounding more patient than he looked. "With five crime scenes, it'd be like re-making *Ben Hur*. We'll leave it to the professionals, eh?" *Crimewatch* presumably.

"Ben who?" Dazza looking hangdog.

The guv flapped a hand. "Next?"

Not that a bacon roll and cup of tea weren't a welcome break too. Mid-morning and Bev was in her favourite seat in the canteen halfway through both. The way the interviews she'd been lining up were spaced there'd be no chance of grabbing a bite later. Munching reflectively, she glanced through the window, reckoned the forecast was right. The sky had that pearly sheen which presaged snow. Good excuse for buying the new coat she had her eye on, she was going off the leather look. Her lip curved. Maybe it was new man Mac's sartorial example. She glanced round at the sound of footsteps; Sumi was approaching with the glimmer of a smile on her face.

"Hey, sarge, I got a postcard this morning." And it looked as if she was about to share.

Mouth full Bev pointed the roll to usher DC Gosh into the seat opposite. Even if Bev had been able to get out the words, there was no need to ask who'd sent the card. From where could be useful though. "It's postmarked Manchester." Sumi perched, off-loading apple juice and a banana on the table.

Bev licked greasy fingers, wiped them on a napkin, took

the offering.

Everything is fine. I am with a friend. Please don't try and find me. It is better you don't know where I am. Love, Fareeda xx

It was very near verbatim to the lines left on the pillow. Lack of imagination – or had the girl been taking dictation? Assuming she'd had a hand in it. Bev drew her lips together. However casually posed, she suspected her question would have the same effect. "Definitely her writing, is it?" It did. Sumi's smile faded.

"Yes." She didn't sound too sure. "I think so."

Bev shrugged. "Got any old cards or letters from her?"

Sumi nodded, not stupid. "I'll check when I get home." She was probably on the same page as Bev now: why, when it was so much easier, hadn't the girl texted or phoned? It could just be that Fareeda didn't want two-way communication. Or the card could be a signpost shrouded in fog pointing them down a blind alley. Fact was, even if had been written by the girl, anyone could've posted it.

Bev aimed for casual again. "She been in touch with her parents?"

Sumi held Bev's keen gaze. "She hadn't when I saw them on Saturday." She'd offered to speak to her uncle, put him in the picture. That had been fine by Bev, she wasn't the old man's biggest fan and he'd definitely crossed her name off his Eid card list.

"Best have another word, eh?" Catching the time, she drained the tea, wrapped what was left of the roll and scraped back the chair. "What did he say when you told him Fareeda had gone?"

"Nothing," Sumi said. "Not a word. But I don't think he believed me."

Bev didn't know what to believe either.

28

Beth Fowler's house had a For Sale sign outside. No. Make that three. As Bev locked the motor she spotted two other upmarket estate agents' boards in the grounds. The mock Tudor's splendid isolation in Moseley had turned into lonely desolation the night the Sandman broke in and subjected its owner to a nightmare ordeal. As they walked up the drive, Mac voiced Bev's thoughts: "Is she keen to get out or what?"

Not going by the number of locks and bolts that had to be released before Mrs Fowler opened the door on a chain. Bev hadn't seen the victim since interviewing her in hospital the day after the attack. If they'd passed in the street now, Bev doubted she'd have recognised her. Grey roots showed in unkempt mousy hair, the face was a gaunt make-up free zone though no amount of slap could have hidden the stress lines. The divorcee was forty-four going on sixty. It was only after she let them in then went through the Fort Knox routine in reverse that Bev could see the woman's weight loss. The sludge-coloured two-piece suit was hanging off a frame that must have dropped a stone or more.

"Have you caught him yet?" She threw the question back as she traipsed down a tiled passageway to a stone-flagged kitchen. Bev supplied the same answer she'd given on the phone earlier that morning. "Doing our best, Mrs Fowler."

"I'll take that as a no. Still. Sit down." Peremptory. They perched on one of the bench seats at a dusty trestle table; a cut glass vase in the centre held dead flowers, the water had a greenish tinge and was probably the source of one of the

227

less than fragrant odours pervading the house. There was no preamble or social nicety, the woman launched into brusque monologue. "I could've stayed in Brighton. My son was happy me being there." She was wringing her hands oblivious to the pressure marks it left in the skin. "But he's got his wife and kids and I'm not what you'd call good company right now." She gave a brittle laugh. "Useless in company, useless on my own. They say I'll get over it but…"

"Mrs Fowler," Bev intervened gently. "Why don't you sit down a minute?"

Haunted amber eyes seemed suddenly to register she wasn't alone. She slumped on the bench opposite, bony fingers reaching for a pack of B&H. After watching the woman's feeble attempts to spark up, Bev took the box from her, held a flame to her cigarette. "There y'go." Warm smile.

"Thanks, sergeant."

"Bev, please." She was working out how to play the scene; interviewing trauma victims was par for the course but several weeks after the attack this woman hadn't moved an inch. Mac came up with an opening quicker. "How many grandchildren d'you have, Mrs Fowler?"

"Three." She stubbed out the baccy even though it was barely touched.

"Hey! And me." An enthused Mac edged forward on the seat. "Smashing, isn't it? Like having your own all over again but without the hassle." The severe thin line of Beth Fowler's mouth softened fractionally. Bev masked incredulity at Mac's whopper. His kids hadn't reached puberty never mind parenthood. She listened as the doting pair swapped stories for a couple of minutes. Mac's fairy tale hadn't waved an emotional magic wand over Beth Fowler – transformation like that took years in therapy – but at least the woman wasn't wound so tight she was in danger of snapping.

"D'you have children, Bev?" The question threw her momentarily. She stiffened as the automatic internal barrier came down, knew displaying it here would get them nowhere.

"No, Mrs Fowler." Forced smile. "Not yet." Hell's still hot isn't it?

"You really…"

Bench scraped slate as Mac jumped to his feet. "Can I get a drink of water, Mrs Fowler?"

The woman waved him down told him to stay where he was. "I'll see to it. Or perhaps you'd both like coffee?"

Coffee was good, and it gave Mrs Fowler something to do as Bev led her gently through the steps the police were taking. Going by the occasional nod and right noise while she fixed then poured the drinks, the woman was obviously taking it in. She sat opposite now, cup clutched in both hands. "So what do you want from me?"

A tap dripped as Bev took a couple of seconds to find the words. She wanted the victim to try to dredge up a forgotten detail. Aye, there's the rub. To do that, she had to ask Mrs Fowler to relive mentally the experience she was desperate to forget. Bev didn't have to open her mouth, the woman knew what was needed.

"I've gone over it again and again in my mind." A hand went to her neck, the brittle laugh echoed again in the cavernous kitchen. "I wish I could get it *out* of my mind. I see his eyes, that gross smile everywhere I go." Reaching for a cigarette she had second thoughts, angrily pushed away the pack. "I wish it weren't so, but there's nothing, absolutely nothing I haven't already told you."

Further gentle probing proved futile. Going through the motions, Bev took out the envelope of victims' photographs from her bag asked Mrs Fowler to take another look. Libby

Redwood and Alex Masters were the only new faces. "He's the barrister, isn't he?"

"Yeah." Bev exchanged keen glances with Mac. "D'you know him?"

Still gazing at the pic, she shook her head. "I've never met him. But if you see Diana, pass on my condolences."

"Diana Masters knows Beth Fowler." Bev slammed her palm against the steering wheel. "Why'd she lie about it?" They were still parked outside the Fowler property, Bev more fired up than Mac. First snowflakes were drifting on to the windscreen, she flicked on the wipers.

"Maybe she didn't recognise her. It's not a brilliant picture. And it doesn't sound like they're bosom pals." Mac gazed at the photograph while Bev tried thinking through the implications. During follow-up questioning, Mrs Fowler had told them she'd met Diana twice, on both occasions when the divorcee had dropped items at Oxfam. The relationship was hardly intimate but why had Diana denied it? "Even if she's seen her before – what does it prove anyway, boss? Could've just slipped her mind. You don't think you're making too much of it?"

"Yeah, cos we've got so much to go on." She sighed. OK, it wasn't a sworn confession signed in blood. But it was a lie, a discrepancy. "Makes you wonder what else she's lying about though, mate." Bev turned the engine.

"If she's lying, boss."

"Everybody lies."

"Yeah, well." He shoved the pictures back in the envelope. "We heading out there, now?"

"What you think?" She checked the mirror; saw the twinkle in her eye. "Granddad."

29

Diana Masters answered the door wearing a black funnel neck coat, a classy brooch added a bit of light relief; Bev could see her reflection in the silver. Unlike the widow's, the Morriss bob could have done with a comb. Every shiny strand on Masters's head appeared in perfect place, the expression seemed a tad strained. "What is it, Sergeant Morrison? I was just on the way out."

"It's Morriss, Mrs Masters." Patient smile; either she got the name wrong on purpose or the widow had the memory of a goldfish with Alzheimer's. "Just a few questions."

"Of course." The glance at her Rolex was intended to be noticed.

"Won't take a minute," Bev said. "Cold out here though." Her shiver was as subtle as the widow's time check. They were allowed in, but no further than the hall. The roses were just beginning to shed a few petals, still stunning though.

"Off to Oxfam are you?" Bev asked, smile still in position.

"I beg your pardon?"

"Oxfam. Must meet quite a few people there."

"Is there a point to this?" The question was addressed to Mac.

"Beth Fowler," Bev replied.

"Who?"

"One of the Sandman's victims? You were shown her picture? Said you didn't know her?"

"As you say, sergeant, I meet a lot people through my work. I don't see where you're going with this."

Mac had the photo ready. "Take another look if you wouldn't mind, Mrs Masters." The snap had been taken

231

before the Sandman's attack, it bore little resemblance to the wreck she'd turned into. "Have you met her before?"

Masters traced a finger along her jaw line as she studied the likeness. "I could have... I'm not sure."

"She knows you," Bev prompted.

"She may well, sergeant." The cat eyes narrowed. "I'm out back a lot. I don't notice everyone who comes in."

"She says you passed the time of day a couple of times."

"Then I'm sure she's right." The smile seemed fake and revealed lipstick on a front tooth. Hallelujah, the widow's grooming wasn't perfect. "Is there a problem with that? Is it a crime to speak with someone and not be able to recall it months later?"

"See, here's the thing: I'm wondering if there's anyone else you haven't been able to recall? Cos that could really help us with our inquiries." One slip-up from the widow would be understandable, but what if the other victims used the shop? What if Diana Masters had lied about not knowing those women, too? Was that the link the inquiry had been looking for? And what the hell would it mean? Bev kicked herself for coming here half-cocked. She should have checked with the other victims first, thought it through better.

"I'm under a lot of strain, sergeant. I can't be expected to remember every little thing. And quite frankly I can't see that it matters. Not when I have so many other... matters on my mind. I wasn't on the way to work." She took a handkerchief from her coat pocket, dabbed her eyes. "If you must know, I was on the way to choose a headstone for Alex."

Best conversation stopper Bev had heard in a while. "Sorry to hold you up." She hoisted her bag. It was time to hit the road anyway, see what light the other women might be able to shed, before coming back better prepared.

Bev was at the door when she turned. "Almost forgot... I need a word with your daughter. Any idea where she is?"

"She fucking knows, Diana. That cop knows something." Sam stood in the kitchen doorway, arms spread-eagled against the frame for support. The word crucified came to Diana's mind. His face had an unhealthy sheen, sweat beads oozed above his top lip. The police visit had spooked Diana Masters too, not that she'd show it. She shucked off the coat, draped it over the banister. "Get me a drink."

He threw his hands up. "Perfect. Get plastered. Why not?"

"Water." Face screwed in contempt she spun on her heel. "I'll be in the drawing room."

"What did your last servant die of?"

God. So original. "Stab wounds," she muttered. No mileage debating finer points with Sam until he'd calmed down. The room was cold, she hadn't bothered to light a fire. She crossed to close the heavy velvet curtains, gazed at the falling snow for a few seconds. It wasn't settling yet, please God it stayed that way. She couldn't afford to mess up timings tonight. She pressed her head against the glass. How much longer could she keep her cool? It had been mere luck spotting the cops' car from an upstairs window. She'd warned Sam, slipped on a coat and at least semi-psyched herself for the stand-off. Looking on the bright side, it had probably been more useful to her than the cops.

She felt Sam's touch on her shoulder, turned and took the glass from his trembling fingers. "Thank you." Hers were steady as she drained it.

Hands on hips, he slowly shook his head. "How do you do it, Dee?"

She shrugged. "The cops know nothing, Sam." Or very little. "Obviously they haven't got a clue about Charlotte. Or we'd hardly be standing here, would we?" She led him by the hand to the chesterfield.

"I know that." He pouted. "I'm not stupid. But that other stuff, the Fowler bitch…" She stroked his hair as he laid his head in her lap.

"So? What does it prove? I've got a shit memory? The cops were on a fishing trip is all." Diana had kept well out of sight in the shop while making her assessments, was ninety-nine per cent certain none of the other women had spotted her. Morriss might, just might, work out how the victims were selected. But none of that was going to unmask the Sandman or link him to Diana. She looked at him now. Shivering, smelling faintly of sweat it was difficult to believe he'd put the fear of God into a string of rich bitches. Her smiling face masked complex emotions, harsh judgements: her fate was with this man. At least for the foreseeable.

"Aren't you scared they're closing in, Dee?" She couldn't meet his desperate gaze. "Not even a little?"

No. Sherlock in a skirt could dig as deep as she liked, it wasn't the great detective that bothered Diana. It was a faceless voice on a phone. "It won't be long now, Sam. We just have to keep our nerve." At least, I need to keep mine, she thought; yours is shot to shit.

"It's in there somewhere, guv." Slightly flushed, Bev pointed at the report that Byford was now scrutinising for the second time. It was a hastily cobbled resumé of the visits she and Mac had made that afternoon. For Bev, the realisation had struck home even before the checks were complete, which was why she was hitting Byford with it before the brief. Seemed to her time was running short. As he read, she wore out his carpet, slowly shaking her head. "I so should have seen it sooner."

Oxfam. Dead men's clothes. It was what widows did. Shit. In what seemed another life, Bev had even dropped the Black Widow's bin bags at some fundraising do. Talk about irony. The crazy who'd nearly killed her had unwittingly helped lift the eye-scales. "The pointers were there all along, guv." She re-ran them in her head: Kate Darby saying Libby Redwood had only recently got round to sorting her husband's clothes, bin liners Bev had actually stepped over at Faith Winters's house. Jesus wept. Donna Kennedy had actually used an Oxfam pen to write the sodding suicide note. Even Mac had mentioned bagging his old gear and still she'd not put two and two together.

"Don't beat yourself up, Bev. It's not exactly in-your-face, is it? Beth Fowler and Sheila Isaac aren't widows." No, but she now knew they'd both been regular visitors to the Oxfam shop where Diana Masters worked as a volunteer.

"Still should've spotted it sooner, guv."

"The Oxfam link's here. That's a given." The big man traced an eyebrow with a finger. "But I'm not sure where it gets us." Frowning he glanced up. "Sit down, will you, Bev." She perched, foot still tapping. "I'm not disagreeing," Byford continued. "I can see how the shop fits with the victim selection process. Question is who was doing the selecting? You say none of the other victims could ID Diana Masters?"

She shrugged. "Said herself she spends a lot of time out back. They may not have seen her, but she was well placed to clock callers."

"The shop has surveillance?"

"Betcha." Mac had sussed it, called in from the premises not ten minutes ago.

Byford rose, walked to the window, perched on the sill. "What about other staff? Could anyone else be in the frame?"

"Mac reckons there's no one under sixty in the place. My money's on Masters, guv. We ought to pull her in."

"On what?"

A sodding skateboard. She unclenched her fists. Why couldn't he see it as well? "Come on, guv. She had to be feeding this information to the Sandman. You said yourself he didn't just flick through yellow pages."

"Where's the proof? And there's no point rolling your eyes. If she's involved, you ran the risk of tipping her off today."

"Yeah, well. She wasn't exactly shaking in her boots." She pictured Masters in her widow's weeds, dabbing that refined little nose. Off to select a headstone. Course she was.

"She'd hardly show she was rattled, would she?" He tapped a finger against his lip. "If you're right Bev, it makes her an accomplice."

"More than that, guv." She held his gaze. "Makes her accessory to murder." Through the window snow was falling, Bev thought of covered tracks, sands of time. "She needs bringing in."

"We still need evidence, Bev. We can't hold her without that. And while she's out there, she could lead us to the Sandman."

"You thinking a tail?"

He nodded. "I'll run it past Phil soon as I can get in to see him." Phil Masters. ACC Operations. Even if he gave it the green light, it wouldn't happen until first thing. "What we need now is intelligence; talk again to the people who know her."

236

The sitting still was getting to her, she jumped to her feet. "D'you need me at the brief, guv?"

"Why?" He glanced at his watch: 5.05. "Where are you...?"

By 5.06, she'd gone.

Bev slipped half a bitter in front of Mac, slumped in the seat opposite then tilted her head at his glass. "Not much call for that stuff round here." Here was The Hamptons, poncey bar on the canal-side down Brindley Place. The wall-to-wall monochrome including furnishings and fixtures gave it the feel of a set for a black and white movie. Not that there was much action. Charlotte Masters hadn't shown since before her father's murder. Bev hadn't really expected to find her there, the girl was grieving for God's sake, but she'd wanted a word with the boss, a tall lanky guy in dark suit and designer sun glasses. Pretentious prat. She'd discovered that Charlotte's attendance had been patchy for weeks. More to the point, none of the staff could suggest where the girl might hang out. Certainly wasn't Selly Oak; her pad had been their first port of call.

"Cheers, boss." Mac slurped half the contents then pulled a gnome-having-stroke face. "No nuts?"

"Empty calories, mate. Think of the figure." She winked, slung him a pack from her pocket. "Don't eat 'em all at once."

Just the one palmful, then: "I can see why you want to talk to her – but what d'you want out of it?"

Bev sipped Pinot, wiped her mouth with the back of her hand. "Come on, mate, you sat in on the interview at her place. We weren't even prompting when she came out with how she feels about her ma."

"Get the thumbscrews out next time, eh?" Mac waggled his eyebrows.

237

"We need someone to dish the dirt." She sighed. With the exception of Charlotte, no one had uttered a bad word against Diana Masters. During the inquiry the widow had emerged from interview after interview smelling of chocolate roses. Bev had also wanted to lean on Evie Jamieson. The PA hadn't actually badmouthed the boss's wife, but she'd sure not joined the chorus of effusion. Mind, it was academic at the moment, getting hold of Jamieson had proved as difficult as the daughter, the PA hadn't shown at the chambers today.

Bev took another sip, glanced round as a blast of cold air entered bringing in a stream of what looked like office workers. The drinkers headed for the bar, snow dandruff glistened briefly on coat shoulders, people shook flakes from their hair, stamped wet footwear, cracked feeble one-liners about the weather. Mac was about to open his mouth when Bev's mobile chirped. She read the text, smiled, shoved the phone back on the table. "You were saying…?"

"I was wondering if the girl's OK." He brushed salt off his shirt front. "She was pretty cut up about her dad."

"Hopefully she'll see the note we left, get back soon as." Bev turned her mouth down. "Prob'ly staying with a mate. Blood's not always thicker than water."

"Talking of which." He lifted the glass. "This is gnat's piss. Fancy a big boy's drink at the Prince?"

"Nah. I'm thinking of swinging round Evie Jamieson's place when we're done here."

Judging by the falling face, she bet he had a hot date. She shook her head, wry smile curving her lip. "Where'd you want dropping, Romeo?" The old girl probably wouldn't be in. Even if she was Mac didn't need to be there.

"Sure?" Bless. He was like a bloodhound after a facelift.

"Come on, lover boy." She drained the glass. "Let's make tracks."

Literally as it happened: they left a trail of footprints on pavements slick with snow. The Polo's windscreen had a light smattering, too. She chucked him the scraper, patted the top of the motor. "Make the most of it, mate." The garage was dropping the Midget back in the morning, thank God. "This'll be your last outing in this thing."

"That why you look so chirpy?"

That and the text from Oz. Not so much hot date as old flame. Engine running, she switched the heater on full. "Yeah. You could say that."

Outwardly calm, Diana Masters was seething. Cold sweat trickled down her spine when she leaned forward to peer through the Merc's windscreen. Swirling snow didn't help. She was on the lookout for what would be the third phone box on a not-so-fucking-merry dance the blackmailer had been leading since a call to the house less than an hour ago. *No cops. No clown.* The bastard had actually sniggered at that point. *Or you'll never see the bitch again.* The creepy Dalek voice had gone on to issue directions to a sprawling sink estate where Diana had found instructions in a phone box that stank of vinegar, cat piss and God knew what else. The stench in the next box had been worse. The instructions there had led her here. Alum Rock. And a hard place. Dear God let this be the end of the road.

The call box was on the corner near a row of cheap shops, two were boarded up one looked bombed out, the rest had rusting iron grilles. She pulled the motor over, sat for a few seconds, hands clutched tight round the wheel. What the hell was the blackmailer playing at? Where was he? He had to show his face if he wanted the cash. And Charlotte's. She cut a glance to the passenger seat. Cases full of money. Not that the creep would get a cent of it. Payback was behind:

Sam in a white transit tailing her. She patted the knife in her coat pocket. A little life insurance. Just in case.

Before leaving the safety of the motor she scoped out the surroundings. Street scum thrived like vermin round here. Her mouth curved in wry amusement. A woman with murder in mind wary of feral kids. Better safe than screwed. Stepping out of the car, she pulled her coat tighter. Cold out here. As the grave.

Before going in, she held a hankie to her face, the fabric lavishly sprayed with Chanel. Opening the door, she screamed, shot back in horror when a liberated rat darted through the gap. Calm down for God's sake. Where were the instructions? Faint stir of panic. What if…? Her glance spotted the paper on the floor in the far corner. Like the others it was composed from words cut out of newspapers Gingerly she knelt, used only her fingertips to retrieve it from wet concrete.

Her head told her to wait until she was back in the car. But the game had gone on long enough. She didn't do Tom and Jerry. Her hand shook with rage, furious tears pricked her eyes as she read the words again – she'd already got the message.

TONIGHT WAS A DRY RUN.
UNTIL TOMORROW, BITCH.

Bev clocked the place through the passenger window as she finished her baccy. PAs clearly weren't on the same whack as their bosses. Evie Jamieson's modest pebbledash semi in Kings Norton needed tarting up. Bit like the owner in that respect, a lick of paint would make the world of difference. Stubbing the butt, Bev shook her head. Blimey, girl, what is this? A makeover show? *Location, Location* meets *Ten Years Younger*. Made her think about the telly though. She couldn't believe the guv had bought a new tie for tomorrow's *Crimewatch* recording. She twitched a lip. Nah. He must've been joshing. Sounded almost like his old self when she'd called to fill him in, not that there'd been a bunch to contribute. Glancing again at the house, it didn't look likely there'd be much to pick up here either. There were no lights on; no signs of life. Could she really be arsed?

Sighing she locked the motor, picked her way through snow that was rapidly turning into grimy slush. Her knock on the front door dislodged a few flakes of peeling maroon paint. Same story round the back: even a cobweb in the kitchen window-frame was unoccupied – apart from a dead spider and desiccated fly. Stamping frozen feet, she scribbled a line on another card, shoved it through the letterbox, headed back to the car. Trouble with this job, there were times she felt like a sodding postman.

30

"Read that." Lip curled in contempt, Diana Masters thrust the note over her shoulder towards Sam. Arriving back at Park View slightly later than Diana, Sam had hurtled into the drawing room found her sitting cross-legged in front of the fire, staring into the flames. Frantic, his darting glance had taken in the carnage: broken glasses, shattered bottles, smashed picture frames, a sea of books swept from the shelves. He took faltering steps towards her. "What happened here?"

"Read the fucking note!"

Kneeling now he took it from her trembling fingers. "Dry run?" He glanced up, registered her flushed face, shallow breathing, dried tears on her cheeks. Bollocks. If she cracked now they were under shit creek, they wouldn't need a paddle. "The guy's a scumbag, Dee."

"Bastard. Bastard. Bastard." She beat the carpet with her fist.

"Come on, babe." Gently he pulled her into an embrace. "It'll be OK."

Angry she shook him off. "Easy for you to say, Sammy." Saliva glistened in the corner of her mouth. "You're not the sucker who's been jerked round all night."

"Yeah, but I was right behind you, babe."

"You won't be tomorrow." She rose, wrapped her arms around her waist.

"But, Dee…"

"For God's sake. Tonight's charade was a little test. Remember what he said? No cops? No clown? The bastard's been on the phone. He saw you, Sam. We have one last chance

242

to get it right."

Bev clocked Oz first. No surprise given she'd been watching for him from the sitting room window. For the nth time she told herself he was here on biz. Whether Fareeda Saleem's exile was voluntary or not, Oz had thought it worth pursuing a chat with the father. The Small Heath visit was pencilled in for tomorrow, Oz was dropping by Baldwin Street to say hi. Given they'd barely exchanged two words since the break-up, how come she felt like Bridget Jones on a v v bad day? No time to explore that one, he was locking the motor.

Play it cool, girl. She took a deep breath, twitched the curtains to, licked her lips, smoothed her hair, pinched her cheeks, hitched the skirt, tugged the T-shirt, glugged on a glass of Pinot, fell off a three inch heel in the dash to the door. Miss Cool-io opened it before the bell rang.

"Wotcha, Khanie." Hand against jamb, heart racing, she gave a lazy smile.

"Hello, stranger." Oz brushed her cheek with his lips before stepping inside. "How've you been?" God, she'd missed that smell.

"Tickety. You?" Hardly worth asking. He looked tastier than ever. Four Michelin stars just for starters.

"I'm good." The small talk wasn't doing a bunch to hike the word count. Standing around in the hall shuffling their feet didn't help either, especially with a snapped heel. After a few seconds' silence they kicked off together.

"Fancy a…?"

"How 'bout…"

"You first…"

"Nah, you…"

The laugh was only a tad forced as she led the way to the

kitchen praying the limp wasn't too obvious. "Have you eaten?"

"Have you cooked?" Like she could've been performing open heart surgery with a spatula.

"Guinea fowl slow-roasted on a bed of squash served with pomegranate and rhubarb jus. How's that sound?"

"Like a wind up."

She sniffed. Was a time he'd have fallen for it. "Or beans on toast." She peered into the bread bin. "Without the toast." A smiled tugged at his lips. She'd forgotten how it did that. "Fancy a takeaway?"

"I'm fine, Bev, honest." She stared as he straddled a chair. Lucky chair. "Wouldn't say no to a coke though. What's wrong with your foot?"

"New shoes, mate." She tottered to the fridge found him a can, helped herself to a top-up. She chilled as the chat flowed: his new flat in Fulham, films they'd caught, books they'd read. He asked after her mum and gran. Social wheel-oiling; surface stuff.

"So how's Byford these days?"

She almost choked on the wine. Even without dodgy foot-wear, the personal question had caught her on the hop. She gave a casual shrug hoping to restore equilibrium. "Up against it. We all are with the Sandman out there." Oz wasn't talking work pressures. She was aware of that. He knew they'd had a thing going, held the guv partly responsible for her inability to commit.

He gave her time to elaborate then arched an eyebrow. "Back off, shall I?"

Head down, she sensed his gaze on her. "We're not together if that's what you mean." Was he weighing up his chances? And what the hell would she say if he came on to her?

"Who you with now, Bev?" Briefly she closed her eyes,

244

recalled the male tails she'd chased of late: fucking waste of time.

"Brad Pitt's getting pushy." She studied her nails. "Thinking I might need an injunction."

"Footloose then?"

"Yeah."

"Was a time I thought you and the guv would tie the knot." So had she, and the thought it had passed still hurt like shit.

"'Nother coke?"

"Sure."

"The Saleem stuff?" She handed him a second can. "How'd you want to play it? I'll need a bit of notice, got shed-loads on tomorrow." His turn now to avoid eye contact.

"Yeah right. Thing is, Bev… I've just come from the house." The hum of the fridge had never sounded so loud.

"What?" Sinking back into the chair, she lowered the volume. "Why?"

He pulled the ring can, swallowed several mouthfuls before answering. "Being completely upfront, Bev – having you there wouldn't've helped."

"Don't hold back, mate." Scowling, she folded her arms.

"I'm only telling it like it is." Saleem, as he'd told her before, was unlikely to open up in the presence of any woman, especially a young white cop. "Plus I have to get back to London earlier than I thought. It was kind of now or never."

She didn't return his smile. His reasoning had logic, it didn't stop her feeling cheated; riding shotgun to Oz had definitely held appeal. "So what happened?"

Saleem had been hostile initially but Oz spoke the same language: literally and culturally. "I couldn't go in casting allegations. I made it clear we knew about his daughter's injuries, and that she was no longer around."

"And?"

"He claims not to know why she left home in the first place or have any idea where she is now."

"There's a surprise."

"I think he was telling the truth, but if he's a better liar than I give him credit for, at least he knows his card's marked."

"Great. No worries then." Remind me to mention it when Fareeda turns up as fertiliser.

"Bev." He leaned forward elbows on table. "Girls do run away. If they're escaping abuse, violence, forced marriage, whatever, they don't want to be found. Fareeda could well be staying with friends some place."

"And if she's not?"

"We may never find out. It's not an episode of *The Bill*. Life has loose ends."

"Do me a favour, Oz." Patronising git.

"Sorry, Bev. I just don't see there's much more to be done at this stage. I left Saleem in no doubt we'd looking out for Fareeda and keeping an eye on him."

Tight smile. She'd asked for his help, his expertise, she could hardly throw it back in his face. "Appreciate it." And maybe he was right. If Fareeda was pregnant she'd have even more reason to make herself scarce. Crikey, she could even be with the father. Lost in thought, she missed the spectacle of Oz dismounting, only got to see the chair being pushed back in place. "You off?"

"Yeah. Thought I'd head back tonight."

What was that sudden lurch? Oh yeah, her sinking heart. Seeing him standing there, smiling down at her, she so didn't want him to go. "Don't have to." It was the closest she could get to asking him to stay. She held her breath, couldn't look at him any more. He reached out gently pulled her to him, wrapped her in his arms. It felt so good: listening to the steady beat of his heart, her cheek against his chest.

He kissed the top of her head. "Walk me to the door, then?"

What? Eyes stinging, she pulled back, held his gaze. Maybe getting closer wasn't out of the question. "Stay tonight, Oz… please." He'd never know how much that cost her.

"I can't, Bev." He reached to touch her face. She'd hurt him too often, that was all, she could talk him round.

"Come on, Ozzie." She smiled, tried making light of it. "You spoken for or something?"

She was twenty-five, PC Ayeesha something-or-other. They'd been seeing each other three months, thinking of shacking up together. At the doorstep, he held her briefly. "Stay in touch, eh?"

What like some bloody pen pal? As if. She gave her brightest smile as he drove away; the tears came when he'd gone.

The car was parked a few doors down Baldwin Street; a figure wearing a hoodie slumped behind the wheel, dark gaze fixed on the mirror. The observer hadn't intended pulling over – not tonight – but then he'd clocked the Asian. Very fucking touching. Not content with jerking him around, the bitch was now screwing someone else. Lips bared, his trembling fingers left damp trails as he stroked the baseball bat. Filthy slut had brought it on herself, but the shakes and sweats were too bad tonight. When it happened, he'd be the one in control. He could wait… the timing had to be right.

TUESDAY

31

"Hey, Morriss." Bev glanced over her shoulder, saw Powell looking particularly suave striding along a Highgate corridor towards her. "Ready for your close-up? As Norma might say?" She masked a smile; the guy was so transparent, even without waving the imaginary fat cigar.

"Major or Desmond?" If he'd hoped to catch her out – no chance. *Sunset Boulevard* was one of her favourite movies. *Crimewatch* taking a few shots hardly qualified as a remake.

"La Desmond," he said. "though looking at you…."

She cut him off with a raised palm. Knew what he was getting at. If a close-up was called for, she'd need a damn sight more time in make-up. The bags under her eyes needed straps. After several hours tossing and turning, she'd very nearly overslept. Her wake-up call had been a knock on the door from Carl at Easy Rider. Seeing the Midget parked outside Baldwin Street had brought the first smile to her face since Oz drove off into the metaphorical sunset. It hadn't lasted long given the journey in had been through thick slush with the promise of more snow later. Oh joy!

"They're only after a bit of wallpaper, y'know, mate."

Like the guv had made clear in an e-mail, expect a TV crew in the incident room mid-morning, the producer needed general shots of the squad; blink-and-miss bland gvs for the presenter to voice over. Only officers who were on IR duty anyway would be involved, and the crew had been told to film round people not get in the way. The big man would be the star, he'd be interviewed at his desk and on location.

"I'm only putting in a guest appearance, Morriss. Making sure everyone knows what's what."

"Course you are." The DI was a media tart. Give him his due though, he'd run an exemplary brief first thing. Took skill to galvanise troops into going over old ground, he'd deployed most of them back on to the streets round the crime scenes canvassing passers-by in the hope of striking witness gold. The rest were phone-bashing, checking statements, following up calls. He'd asked her to pursue the Oxfam link – like she needed asking.

As Powell held the door she walked straight past, caught a glimpse of lights, camera and Dazza hunched over a desk. "Where you going?"

"Looking for the action, mate."

Bev found the note on her keyboard after lunch.

Call Evie Jamieson on…

Hoo-flipping-rah. Dumping her bag, she grabbed pen and paper, punched in the number. Come on, come on… "Miss Jamieson? Bev Morriss here."

"I got your note."

"Thanks for getting back. I need to speak to you."

Few seconds pause then: "I need to speak to you, too." Even better.

"Fire away."

"Not on the phone… It's rather delicate." Better and better. Wasn't snowing yet, rush hour hadn't started. Bev glanced at her watch. "Be with you in…"

"Not right now. There's someone else you need to see. He can't get away until later."

The PA was adamant. She set a time and that was it. Pensive, Bev ended the call.

"Four o'clock before she'll see me, guv." Bev had nipped into Byford's office to bring him up to speed. The lights had only just been de-rigged after the TV interview, place was like a sauna. She'd watched him shuck out of the jacket, now the tie was coming off.

"Any idea what Jamieson's got?" he asked.

Apart from a crush on her dearly departed boss? Bev turned her mouth down. "Hard to call, guv. Cards. Close. Chest. She wouldn't even tell me who the guy is she wants me to see. Only thing I'd say is she doesn't seem to have a lot of time for Diana Masters."

"You taking Tyler along?" The sleeves were getting the treatment now.

"Probably not. He's over in Moseley knocking doors." And not looking for overtime today, he'd told Bev.

"Keep me posted then." Jesus. He was undoing the top button on the shirt now.

"You got it." Shame she couldn't stick around for more revelations.

Just gone four, formal greetings over, Bev sat opposite Evie Jamieson. Apparently snow on the M6 had delayed the mystery man's arrival from Manchester. He was a private investigator – that was as far as the PA would go. God knows why she was being so cagey about the guy; she seemed dead keen to get down to other matters. She looked wired, jumpy, her sepia cheeks blotched pink. Bev reckoned the woman was relishing the limelight after years in the wings. The hand pressed to the side of her face failed to hide a tic in the crepe layers of her right eyelid. Bev sat back hoping her relaxed stance would help the woman chill.

"Before we start, sergeant, I want you to answer me one

question." Twitchy fingers fiddled now with the cuff of a beige cardi.

"Sure, if I can." The tic was burrowing maggot-like.

"Is there any possibility that the murder was planned?" No clarification needed. Jamieson was interested in only one victim. And she'd only ask if she had suspicions.

"We've no evidence pointing that way." Clearly not what the PA wanted to hear. Bev added a judicious, "Yet."

"So it's not been ruled out?" The gleam was back in her eye.

"Nothing's ruled out, Miss Jamieson. But we have a problem, see, there's no…"

"Motive." She didn't work in the law for nothing. "I don't know if this constitutes motive, sergeant." Lips like serrated blades, she pulled a brown envelope from a drawer, pushed it against the desk. "It certainly provides grounds for action."

Opening the flap, Bev's scalp tingled. The contents merited a mental wolf whistle: six grainy black and white pics obviously taken by telephoto lens, but then the loving couple was hardly likely to pose willingly. The grieving widow in steamy clinches with another bloke, and with a body like that it had to be a toy boy. Bev ran her gaze over each incriminating image. Diana Masters obscured his face in every shot.

"Who's the guy?"

The PA raised a hand. It was her big scene and she'd play it her way. Again, it seemed to Bev she revelled in the attention. "I agonised over divulging this matter, sergeant. Twice I tried to get hold of you over the weekend. In a way I was relieved you weren't available. It seemed like fate playing a hand." Bev clenched a fist; she wanted to slap the smug simper off the stupid woman's face, certainly hit her with a withholding charge. Timing is all. She forced a smile instead. "Glad you changed your mind, Miss Jamieson."

"I'd hoped it wouldn't be necessary. But it was clear the police investigation was going nowhere. I couldn't stand the thought that... that... woman might be involved in Alex's death. He swore me to secrecy you see. But he planned to divorce her. The adultery would have cost her a pretty packet."

Questions milled, one jumped the queue. "Did she know?" Bev leaned forward. The PA was taking her time.

"Alex was sure she didn't." Jamieson swallowed, eyes bright. "He was going to present her with the pictures as a fait accompli. Even Diana Masters couldn't have talked her way out of that one." Bev glanced at the top pic. Given where the mouth was, she couldn't have talked, period.

"This is important, Miss Jamieson – could she have found out the marriage was on borrowed time?"

"I thought not." Jamieson lifted her gaze from her boss's photo. "Until Alex's murder."

"He says he'll kill me... do what he says, please, please do..." Phone pressed to her ear, Diana's perfect face crumpled. Sam had taken the call, passed it to her on the blackmailer's orders. She'd been expecting the Dalek tone issuing instructions not the anguished terrified voice of her daughter. "Charlotte, Charlotte, listen..."

For several seconds, all Diana heard was static; it was almost a relief when the familiar tinny distortion came on the line. "There y'go, lady. Proof she's alive."

Sam stood behind, his arms around her waist. She saw their reflection in the mirror on the drawing room wall. It was like watching characters in a play except she didn't have a script. "How do I know it wasn't a recording?"

"You don't. Trust me, lady – the slut's alive. It's down to you to keep it that way."

Diana met Sam's gaze in the glass. "What do you want me to do?" She scowled as the blackmailer dictated directions. God, the creep was going to pay for this.

"Any tricks and she vanishes. If you're a good girl, you'll have her home safe tonight. Make a mistake and believe me, lady, it'll be fatal."

"They got careless, see, sarge." The PI was certainly making himself at home. Lounging back in his chair, ankle crossed on knee, he slurped tea noisily. Bev forgave him; she'd forgive him most things. He'd arrived more than an hour late at Jamieson's office but Dougie Tempest had brought in more than snow and cold air. He'd just handed Bev a second set of snatched shots. The widow and her lover weren't the only ones who'd been careless. The instant Bev saw the guy's face she clocked it; cringed inwardly. How could she have been so dense? Scissor-hands, she'd blithely mocked. Camper than a marquee, Diana had giggled. Gonna let him loose on your hair, Mac had joshed. Even the man himself had said he'd give her a good price if she ever fancied a decent cut. Oh yes, you bastard: rusty blade to your slimy balls.

"You all right, sarge?" Tempest asked, dunking a Rich Tea. She nodded; it was easier than talking through a mouthful of feathers. "Well, as I say, when I first started tailing them it was a soddin' nightmare." The barrister, she'd learned, had hired Tempest two months back. "They'd turn up separately, never leave together. Different bleedin' hotel every time." Jamieson visibly bristled at the language, maybe the estuary accent. As he spoke, Bev took in the wiry little man's cheap navy suit, shiny lace-ups, boot-polished

253

short-back-and-sides. He looked like a dodgy rep; mind, hotels were full of travelling salesmen – not canny ex-cops trained in surveillance and covert filming. She'd marked Tempest down as an eighties throwback when to most cops PACE meant running to the bar. Ten out of ten for his results though. "Tell you what, sarge, it made my life a damn sight easier when they fixed on a regular love nest."

"They definitely didn't cotton on?" Bev asked, leafing through the images again.

"Do me a favour, darlin'."

Fair enough. "What's the guy's name?"

"Tate. Sam Tate. Ring a bell?"

Oh, yes. *Samuel has that effect on women, sergeant. Someone called Tate on the phone, Mrs Masters.* Christ on a skateboard; she stiffened. Libby Redwood's last words... Not Dan. Not Stan. Had she been trying to say Sam? Was Tate the Sandman? The double-act with Diana had been flawless. If Tate was gay – Bev was teetotal. Did his repertoire include masked sadist?

"Is it enough to charge them, sergeant?" Jamieson was on the edge of the seat, her whole face flushed.

Bev ignored her, carried on looking through the pics. "When was this lot taken, Dougie?"

"Day before he got topped. I'd not even sent them." He reached into a breast pocket, handed her an envelope. "Bit more intelligence here: addresses, dates, that kind of thing."

"Ta, mate."

"Sergeant Morriss, I said..." Frowning, Bev raised a hand, desperately trying to work out the implications. "Sergeant..."

She scraped back the chair, grabbed her bag. The PA was getting on her tits. "It's evidence of adultery, Miss Jamieson." Irrefutable proof Diana Masters and Sam Tate were passionate lovers – but cold-blooded killers? "As to murder?" She shrugged. "Don't know yet. Shame you didn't open your mouth a bit sooner."

32

"It's enough to bring them in for questioning."

Like she didn't know that. She'd caught Byford on the phone just as he was leaving for the late brief. He was up to speed now on the Masters-Tate adulterous liaison. Whether it was a criminal alliance still needed nailing. But if the duo were behind the Sandman burglaries, the magnitude of the conspiracy was breathtaking. "Where are you, now, Bev?"

"In the motor. Outside the chambers." She wiped the steamy windscreen with her sleeve, had already scraped three inches of snow off the bodywork.

"Mac with you?"

She cut a glance to the empty passenger seat. "On his way."

"I'll get a team to Tate's flat." Tempest's intelligence had provided the address plus the salon's where Tate worked. "You pair head out to the Masters place."

"Nothing'd give me greater pleasure."

"Rein it in, Bev. We need proof there's a Sandman connection. Plenty of missing pieces still."

"Sure thing, guv." Way she felt she'd rein it in all right – with a lasso round the bloody woman's neck.

"And, Bev. Bear this is mind… if Diana Masters is the Sandman's sidekick, she stands to go down for life. She'll have nothing to lose."

Stay cool. Stay cool. The words were Diana Masters's mantra as she drove the Merc through heavy snow to the handover – assuming the blackmailer wasn't lying. The creep had said last night was a dry run. He'd got that right. She'd already collected directions from two scuzzy phone boxes: another not-so-merry dance. A sly smirk curved her painted lips. This time she'd lead the last waltz.

Her gloved hands gripped the wheel. For the millionth time she checked the mirror. Melted snow glistened in her fur hat from the last frigging foray into the cold. Deep breath. Stay cool. She imagined Sam warming her up, licked her lips. He was lying low back at his flat; she'd call when this was all over. She'd wanted him out of harm's way. He'd promised not to follow, but she'd not been sure he'd stick to it. And if the blackmailer spotted a tail...

Or the knives: one in the pocket of her coat, another in her sleeve, a third in her clutch bag. Overkill? She hoped so. Cold steel, iron nerve. She had one big advantage: she wasn't scared. If it went pear-shaped, she'd die rather than go to jail. She'd nothing to lose, apart from half a million pounds and her daughter's life. And that was so not going to happen.

Next left the Satnav squawked. The call box was on the corner. She checked the mirror, scoped the street. At least the snow meant there was no lowlife around. Pavement was white-over, virginal. She picked her way carefully, wouldn't do to sprain an ankle. She gave a thin smile – not on the final leg of the journey.

Except there was no note. Where were the frigging directions? Stay cool. Stay cool. Think. Think. She was bang on time. What the hell had gone wrong? Sinking to her knees, she scrabbled on the dank foul-smelling concrete. Nothing. Not a word. It felt like a body-blow. Still kneeling, head in hands, hot tears coursed between her fingers. She'd followed instructions to the letter, done everything the bastard asked...

The phone rang when she was almost back at the car. Spinning on her heel, she lost her footing in the snow, slipped, struggled to stay upright. It was only a few steps to the call box but she was gasping for breath when she picked up the phone.

"Good girl. No tail. The drop details are at your place."

Bev had sent Christmas cards that looked like Park View. Six inches of snow – and falling – was giving it that festive feel: all fir trees and holly bushes, rosy glows from mullioned windows. Very merry-gentlemen-and-deck-the-halls. Except for what went on behind closed doors, or at least Diana Masters's door. Not that action was ongoing. The property appeared empty, just hall lights left on. Bev was keeping a watching brief from the Midget parked opposite. Mac was on his way, hopefully he'd get here before the widow showed. She'd told him to bring vests, anti-stab not woolly.

Killing time, she lit a Silk Cut, inched down the window. Despite the falling mercury, she was fired up. She'd had a while to think. If Tate and Masters had masterminded the Sandman burglaries to mask the prime motive of the barrister's murder, the level of duplicity, depravity, were off the scale. It would mean vulnerable women had been clinically selected and subjected to unimaginable terror so Alex Masters's killing would look like a Sandman cock up. Tate had certainly had his cock up. Even if there was no Sandman link, Masters had taken mendacity to a new level. Oh yes. She was up there with Uranus. Bev took a deep drag, recalling the doo-doo the widow had spouted: *Alex and I were very much in love. This room is where I most feel his presence. I was on the way to choose a headstone.* Lying twat.

But was she accessory to murder? She was accessory all right. Arm candy to Alex Masters and groomed within an inch of her life. Eyes creased against the smoke, Bev pictured

258

the widow the last time they'd met. Masters had worn that black funnel neck coat, didn't have a hair out of...

Bollocks. Spine tingling, she bolted upright, thoughts swirling. Suddenly, she saw the light, and not just the full beam of an approaching motor. It was a vision of the widow's silver brooch that day. Bev had glimpsed her reflection in its shiny surface, but failed to see the full picture, until now. The item wasn't Diana's. It had belonged to Donna Kennedy: a one-off designer piece, photo and details in exhibits at Highgate. Gotcha.

The guv had to know; she grabbed the phone, hit fast dial. They'd need full back-up now, preferably armed. Diana Masters made the Black Widow look benign.

Headlights dazzling, the oncoming car was almost upon her. Bev shielded her eyes as it slewed wildly in the snow, almost missed the turning into Masters's drive. The bitch was back – and cutting it fine.

33

Fury and revenge fuelled Diana Masters. Slamming the Merc's door, she stormed to the house careless of the snow. Silhouetted in the doorway she stood for several seconds, staring open-mouthed at the scene in the hall. Her slanted eyes saw the noose suspended from the banister, the scotch, the paper, the pen – her sluggish brain couldn't compute. Taking faltering steps towards the console table, her thoughts dragged, too. "What the hell?"

"Details of the drop." Startled, she swirled round. More incomputable data. Sam lunged from behind, smiling as he slipped the knife from her coat pocket. "Do exactly as I say and you won't get hurt." Still with that perfect smile, he pressed his own blade against her cheek. "Well, not by me."

Wary, uncertain, her eyes searched his face. "Is this some kind of joke?"

With a tap of the blade, he set the noose swinging. "Call it gallows humour if you like."

Stay cool. She had to regain the control here. Taking off the hat she nodded at the writing gear on the console. "What's that all about?"

"Let's see…" He waved the knife, raised his glance to the ceiling, ostensibly seeking inspiration. "It's about a woman driven mad by grief. A woman so devastated by her husband's murder, she can't face life without him. Sadly, she sees only one way out." He set the rope swinging again.

"You're mad."

"You're fucked." He cocked his head at the pen and paper. "Take a letter."

"Come on, Sam," she wheedled. "We can work this out."

Like hell, you double-crossing shit. Her brain was back in action. Whatever was going on here, he'd pick up the bill. She knew the clutch bag was out of reach; could she retract the knife from her sleeve?

"Pick up the pen, Diana. Now."

"Sam, please, this is ridiculous. Let's just…"

"Shut the fuck up," he yelled. "I'm done with you ordering me around. I'm sick to death of hearing your prattle. Let's just get this over."

Eyes smarting, she nodded meekly. "If I've lost you, Sam… I've lost everything." And she'd say it with flowers… Turning to reach for the pen, she grabbed the vase with both hands, swung it over her head, hurled it with every ounce of pent up fury. Glass whacked bone, blood streamed from nostrils and split lips as he dropped to the floor, clutching his face. Diana was oblivious to water dripping from her chin, wilted rose petals caught in her hair. She focused exclusively on her target, kicked Tate as hard as she could in the head. He fell to the side, unconscious, no longer groaning. Eyes like slits, she carefully slid the knife from her sleeve.

"I really wouldn't do that if I were you."

Diana whipped her head round. Coming down the stairs was a slight figure dressed in black wearing a clown mask.

"I'm pretty sure they're both in there, guv." Gaze fixed on the property, Bev still kept a low profile in the Midget, soft voice on the phone.

"Could be," Byford said. "I've just heard from Mike Powell – Tate's flat's empty."

Bev had witnessed the widow's dash from the car, the long pause silhouetted in the doorway. It was enough to twitch the antenna. "We've got the bastards, guv." She'd filled him in on the stolen brooch, the missing link.

"Not yet." She heard a rustle, reckoned he was checking his watch. "Back-up'll be with you any time. Bev, don't…"

"What you take me for, guv?" She'd no intention of playing hero. Last time she'd crossed a widow she'd lost two-nil.

"I mean it, Bev." Slight pause. "I don't want to lose you."

I not we? She put that one on the back burner. "Later, guv."

Later like Mac. At least he'd called. The snow was slowing traffic – and blood flow. God it was cold. She leaned across, scrabbled in the glove compartment. Scowled. Everything in it but bloody gloves. Eyes narrowed she spotted the edge of a nylon scarf jutting out from under the passenger seat. She frowned then remembered the old dear outside the chippie last week. The scarf had been in the Midget ever since. She tugged it free, heard a clink as the knife still wrapped in its folds fell out. A voice in her head said: don't even think about it. So she didn't. She shoved it in her bag instinctively – because she felt like it.

Like she felt like standing outside the car and having another smoke. If she hadn't she probably wouldn't have heard the scream.

Diana Masters was rigid with rage, her face almost ugly in contempt. "Take the fucking mask off." It hadn't taken long to work out. Since Sam had staged the whole pathetic show, only one person could be hiding behind it. Predictably, her daughter was going for the dramatic effect.

Charlotte ripped off the mask, hatred in her eyes, a knife clutched in her hand. "You think you're so clever, don't you?"

Diana cut a glance at her former lover. "Clearly not." She swung a vicious kick at his kidneys. No response. Charlotte screamed to leave him alone. Screamed again when Diana lashed out with the other boot. The third kick drew Charlotte closer. Within harm's reach now, the girl looked puny, stick thin, a pushover.

"You and him." Diana ran the blade between her fingers. "How long's it been going on?" The rage had given way to an unnatural calm. Sam had shafted her. Now she'd cut her losses.

"Way back." Smug triumph. "Did you actually think he loved you? Get real. You're old enough to be his mother. You were just in the right place at the right time, blithely imagining it was your idea. We were stringing you along from the get-go. You and the old man were a means to the end." Diana's keen glance flitted between hand, rope, stairs; brain coldly calculating.

"The end being?" Like she didn't know: love of money was the only thing they'd ever had in common.

"My inheritance of course." Charlotte gave a brittle laugh. "That's when the hard graft pays off. Sam had a hell of a job playing the gibbering wreck, y'know. As for me, the Dalek voice was a real stretch. Mind, we had a ball planning your trips. Hope you enjoyed them – cos you're a long time dead. And when the dust settles, me and Sam will take off."

Diana snorted. "He's not going anywhere, is he?" She nudged his head with her toe. "Prat can't do anything right. Couldn't even kill Alex. I had to finish the old boy off."

"You?"

"What's the problem? You were happy to take his money, weren't you?"

"Not happy." She glanced down for a second. "It was collateral damage." And didn't see it coming. Diana grabbed the girl's wrist, slammed it against the banister. A crack rang out, Charlotte screamed, the knife fell. Tears of pain coursed down her sallow cheeks as she held the shattered arm protectively close. Diana grabbed the noose, forced it over the girl's head, started dragging her towards the stairs.

Charlotte knew what was coming, kicked, struggled, screamed. Diana barely noticed; she was calculating the drop. Roughly. Suicide wasn't a bad idea – there'd just be a change of personnel: her daughter could take the swing.

The scream was loud enough to wake the dead. Bev tensed, instantly alert, heard the hiss when her baccy hit the snow. Then another scream. Hell's teeth. Sounded like blue murder kicking off in there. She scanned both sides of the street, dashed across. No blue lights but the third scream was enough to drown distant sirens.

Sneaking past the Merc, she clocked a bunch of keys in the ignition, reached in and pocketed them. The widow wouldn't be leaving in a hurry. The door's fanlight was too high to be any use; she pressed an ear to the wood instead. Made out the odd word. Who was the widow having a go at? The other voice was younger, shriller. Another woman's. So where was Tate?

More to the point, where was back-up? Sod it. Curiosity killed cats – said nothing about cops. She could always leg it if they clocked her. Slowly, soundlessly, she raised the letter box. Her scalp prickled, heart pounded. It was a stand-off. The widow and her daughter. Both carrying knives. Almost subliminally Bev took in the vase on the floor, pools of water, rose petals. Her focus was on the rope and the dialogue.

… I had to finish the old boy off.

You?

What's the problem? You were happy to take his money, weren't you?

Not happy. It was collateral damage.

264

Breathtaking cynicism followed by heart-stopping action. Eyes wide, Bev watched the drama unfold: the widow whacking her daughter's arm, forcing the noose over her head. Events were spiralling. If she didn't go in, people were going to die. Last thing they'd do was open the door for her. The car keys? She scrabbled in her pocket. If one was for the house, she'd... What?

Intervene to save the lives of a couple of devious shits? Last time she stepped between mother and daughter, she'd taken a blade in the belly. Blade. Subconsciously had she had an inkling all along? Was that why she'd stowed the knife in her bag? Palms tingling, she reached for it now. Another scream. Another look through the box. Shit. The girl'd be on the banister any time soon. All it would take was one shove from the widow.

There was only one Yale. It fitted. Still Bev hesitated. Protect life. That was every cop's first, second, third priority. But what if the sick twisted crazies deserved to die? Ears pricked, she caught sirens in the distant. Back-up was imminent – except time was running out. If she did nothing, she'd be little better than the mad bastards inside and might as well jack in the job. Yeah. And? Still, she dithered. The next scream turned her insides to ice. And forced a decision.

Only seconds to take it in: Tate was out of it on the floor; Diana glared down from the landing. Bev had to get to the girl. The drop hadn't been fatal but she'd choke if she didn't stop struggling. Still clutching the knife, Bev chucked her bag down, raced over, took the girl's weight on her back. In her peripheral vision she glimpsed the widow sneaking downstairs. "I swear, lady, come near me, I'll kill you."

Diana Masters glowered from a safe distance. For a second or two it could've gone either way. The police sirens probably tipped the balance. She settled for a final kick at lover boy, fled without a backward glance, presumably trying to save her own neck.

Sweating hard, breathing fast, Bev eased the rope over Charlotte's head, lowered her to the floor, laid her in the recovery position. The only life the little cow deserved was behind bars. Bev didn't hear Tate, first she knew was when he grabbed her, swung her round. "Interfering bitch."

Eyes flashing, hackles rising, she hissed: "Picked the wrong one this time, babe." It was almost too easy. Tate was in a weakened state, Bev so fired up she'd have taken him anyway. Every kick and punch she landed was for the victims, mental pictures of the women a spur to beat the shit out of him.

Back-up was outside now; she became aware of blue lights, sirens, car doors slamming, muffled footsteps running through the snow. Self-defence until they were in here though. Not that Tate was up for it. Arms protecting his head, he surrendered, dropped to his knees, snivelling, the pretty boy face now a mess of tears, blood, snot. Not a whole bunch different from the mask.

"Fucking clown." Scowling, Bev slapped on the cuffs. Without a blade, the Sandman was a walk-over.

34

The Prince was packed with jubilant cops, dimpled table tops were strewn with glasses, empty crisp packets. Last orders had been called, the guv was at the bar getting them in. Mac was relating to another rapt audience how the fleeing widow ran slap bang into his arms; Powell was cosying up to Sumi Gosh in the corner – no surprise there, nor a snowflake in hell's chance. Bev raised her glass, gave a lopsided smile, thought fleetingly of Fareeda, hoped the girl was safe. Everywhere she looked there was camaraderie, familiar faces; cops were like one big happy family. The Masters sprang to mind. Maybe not.

Glancing along the scuffed leather bench, she spotted Danny Rees bending Dazza's ear. Danny boy had been chatting her up earlier, telling her she was his role model. Yeah right. She sipped her wine, not so pissed she didn't know he was angling for a CID opening. Wasn't just detectives celebrating though, when news of the arrests broke almost everyone at the nick had piled over to the pub. They'd crowded round the telly at ten, cheering when the BBC led on the story, some of the footage nabbed from the *Crimewatch* shoot.

The back-slaps and bonhomie had actually started back at the Masters place. Byford had shown just after the cavalry. Far from giving Bev a hard time for going in, the guv had hinted at a commendation. Made a change from disciplinaries. Back then, she couldn't share the general euphoria. Draining a third, no, fourth glass she was feeling a tad mellower.

She cocked her head. Some joker had put REM on the

juke box: *Everybody Hurts*. Yeah, and cries. She snorted. No, make that lies. The widow had excelled. Not just her – everyone in the inquiry. It was the widow's face she couldn't get out of her head though, staring from the back of a police motor, rose petals still clinging to her hair, make-up a wreck. The cuffs had made a nice touch. Accessories were so important. Bev scowled. How could a woman sink so low? Like mother like daughter... last Bev had seen of Charlotte was in the back of an ambulance. Ditto the Sandman. Bad riddance. They'd all be going down. A forensic team was at Park View, a second at Tate's flat. Job done. Yeah, course it was. Pensive, she tugged her lip, mulling over how differently that final scene could have played out.

"There y'go." Byford shuffled up next to her, shoved another Pinot across the table.

"Ta, guv."

"Sure you're OK, Bev?" He was on scotch; his concerned gaze was on her.

"Dandy." Another drink maybe she would be; maybe she'd forget the victims' faces, the pain and terror the Sandman had put them through, her own reluctance to intervene. Maybe she wouldn't.

"You ever done the right thing for the wrong reasons, guv?" She circled a finger round the rim of the glass, still not sure whether she'd have stepped in to save the scumbags if she hadn't heard the sirens. She counted six, seven seconds before he answered.

"Isn't the result what matters, Bev?"

Was it? "Got me there, guv." The question was deep and she was drunk, dog-tired. People were drifting off, Mac had just blown her a kiss, must be off his face as well. She stifled a yawn, reckoned it was time to hit the road. The

MG'd be OK in the car park. She could just about stagger home, truth be told she fancied a trudge through the snow. She drained the glass, slipped into her coat, gave a mock salute. "I'm off. Catch you later."

"Fancy a nightcap, Bev?" Those grey eyes held more than an invite for cocoa and that George Clooney smile could melt dry ice. God it was so tempting. But boy was she whacked, knew she looked rougher than a rough thing from rough land. On the other hand...

"Yeah." Mischievous wink. "How 'bout tomorrow? Eight o'clock?"

Byford was still smiling when he unlocked his motor. Glancing up the road he could just make out Bev's retreating figure in the distance: black against the snow; shoulder bag like a Santa sack. Despite a reasonably clean end to the case, something was clearly bugging her. He toyed with the idea of catching her up, decided against. No point rushing it. Maybe she'd open up tomorrow. About to get in the car, he spotted another figure that looked to be gaining on her. Byford narrowed his eyes; something about the body language hit his radar. His copper's instinct told him something was wrong. A scream confirmed it.

No warning. The first blow took Bev's breath away, knocked her off her feet. The snow had muffled the attacker's approach. He had some sort of weapon. Baseball bat, she thought. Explosions were going off in her brain. She felt herself being dragged off the street, then a weight on her back. Pinned to the ground, she took another blow to the head. Screaming, she struggled, desperate to throw him off. Fighting back was her only chance. It wasn't an option: she could barely move. Silverfish thoughts. Who was it?

One of the Saleem brothers? Dorkboy? Twisting slightly she glimpsed hoodie and scarf. Got whacked in the face for her effort. A mugging? Was she the victim of street scum? Teeth gritted. Sod that. She was nobody's victim.

Every muscle flexed, she writhed and bucked. Couldn't budge the bastard. Waves of nausea washed over her; she felt dizzy, her eyelids fluttered, heart pounded ribs. The booze, the fight with Tate must've taken it out of her. What strength she had was seeping away. Dear God, don't let me die like this. The attacker grabbed a handful of hair, yanked her head back.

"You didn't return my calls. You didn't even thank me for your lovely presents. What an ungrateful girl you are." Presents? The heart? The timer? Who the fuck…? A chunk of hair came out by the roots with the next yank. "Open your eyes." She tried, but the pain was too bad. "Open your fucking eyes. You have such pretty eyes… Laura." She stiffened. One of her pick-ups. Tentatively she opened an eye, glimpsed the guy she'd dubbed Jagger lips. Jesus Christ, was he stoned or crazy? Either way he sounded amazingly sane.

"Lissen… I'm a cop." Lisping, she barely recognised her own voice.

"I know what you are. You're a slut. You hit on me – then treat me like shit. I don't like being dissed, Bevie." Spit trickled down her face. "You lied to me." Everybody lies. "If I hadn't nicked your mobile I wouldn't even know your name. I hate liars. And I hate cops." She felt a slight draught, sensed he was lifting the bat for another blow. "Two birds with one stone time."

Drowsy, beginning to drift, Bev wondered vaguely who'd painted the snow red. The sudden release of pressure on her spine made her catch her breath. "Police. Drop it."

Minuscule tug of split lips. She'd know the guv's voice anywhere. Eyes still closed, it hurt to move. She heard the fight: fists on flesh, rasping breaths, gasps, groans. Then silence. Slowly, gingerly she turned her head. Her attacker lay motionless, stared sightlessly at the night sky. Breathing heavily, Byford knelt in the snow, felt for a pulse. She didn't need to ask. The jagged rock close by was stained with blood. Big question was whether he'd hit his head going down, or Byford had lent a hand?

"Nasty fall that, guv." Through her pain she gave a weak smile. "Ask me – it could've happened to anyone."

Everybody lies.

CRÈME DE LA CRIME

More witty, gritty Bev Morriss mysteries
from Maureen Carter:

WORKING GIRLS

Fifteen years old, brutalised and dumped, schoolgirl prostitute Michelle Lucas died in agony and terror. The sight breaks the heart of Detective Sergeant Bev Morriss of West Midlands Police, and she struggles to infiltrate the deadly jungle of hookers, pimps and johns who inhabit Birmingham's vice-land. When a second victim dies, she has to take the most dangerous gamble of her life – out on the streets.

ISBN: 978-0-9547634-0-4   **£7.99**

Dark and gritty... an exciting debut novel...
– Sharon Wheeler, Reviewing the Evidence

DEAD OLD

Elderly women are being attacked by a gang of thugs. When retired doctor Sophia Carrington is murdered, it's assumed she is the gang's latest victim. But Detective Sergeant Bev Morriss is sure the victim's past holds the key to her violent death.

Her new boss won't listen, but when the killer moves uncomfortably close to home, it's time for Bev to rebel.

ISBN: 978-0-9547634-6-6   **£7.99**

Complex, chilling and absorbing... confirms her place among the new generation of British crime writers.
– Julia Wallis Martin, author of *The Bird Yard* and *A Likeness in Stone*

BABY LOVE

Rape, baby-snatching, murder: all in a day's work for Birmingham's finest. But she's just moved house, her lover's attention is elsewhere and her last case left her unpopular in the squad room; it's sure to end in tears. Bev Morriss meets trouble when she takes her eye off the ball.

ISBN: 978-0-9551589-0-2   £7.99

Carter writes like a longtime veteran, with snappy patter and stark narrative.
– David Pitt, Booklist (USA)

HARD TIME

An abandoned baby…
A kidnapped five-year-old…
A dead police officer…

And Detective Sergeant Bev Morriss thinks she's having a hard time!

Bev doesn't do fragile and vulnerable, but she's struggling to cope with the aftermath of a vicious attack.

Her lover has decided it's time to move on, the guv is losing patience, and her new partner has the empathy of a house brick. If she can't trust her own judgement, what's left to rely on?

Just when things can't get any worse, another police officer dies.

And the ransom note arrives.

And hard doesn't begin to cover it.

ISBN: 978-0-9551589-6-4   £7.99

British hard-boiled crime at its best.
– Deadly Pleasures Year's Best Mysteries (USA)

BAD PRESS

Detective Sergeant Bev Morris tangles with the media.

Is the reporter breaking the news – or making it?

A killer's targeting Birmingham's paedophiles: a big story, and ace crime reporter Matt Snow's always there first - ahead of the pack and the police.

Detective Sergeant Bev Morriss has crossed words with Snow countless times. Though his hang-'em-and-flog-'em views are notorious, Bev still sees him as journo not psycho.

But a case against the newsman builds. Maybe Snow's sword is mightier than his pen?

Through it all, Bev has an exclusive of her own…a news item she'd rather didn't get round the nick. DS Byford knows, but the guv's on sick leave. As for sharing it with new partner DC Mac Tyler – no, probably best keep mum…

ISBN: 978-0-9557078-3-4   **£7.99**

If there was any justice in this world, she'd be as famous as Ian Rankin!
– Sharon Wheeler, Reviewing the Evidence

You can also meet Bev Morriss again in

CRIMINAL TENDENCIES

a diverse and wholly engrossing collection of short stories from some of the best of the UK's crime writers.

**£1 from every copy sold of this first-rate
collection will go to support the
NATIONAL HEREDITARY
BREAST CANCER HELPLINE**

*She lay on her face, as if asleep. I turned her over
and saw the deep wound on her brow...*

– Reginald Hill, John Brown's Body

*Her mouth was dry and she was shaking badly. Terror was gripping
her; the same terror she previously experienced only in her dreams...*

– Peter James, 12 Bolinbroke Avenue

*His lips were thin and pale. "She must be following us.
She's some sort of stalker."*

– Sophie Hannah, The Octopus Nest

*When he thought he was alone, he squatted down and opened the
briefcase. I was interested to see that it contained an automatic pistol
and piles and piles of banknotes.*

– Andrew Taylor, Waiting for Mr Right

Published by Crème de la Crime
ISBN: 978-0-9557078-5-8   **£7.99**

MORE GRIPPING TITLES FROM CRÈME DE LA CRIME

SECRET LAMENT   **Roz Southey**
18th century musician Charles Patterson investigates when an intruder and a murder endanger the woman he loves.

Who is the man masquerading under a false name? Are there really spies in Newcastle? Why is a psalm-teacher keeping vigil over a house?

And can Patterson find the murderer before he strikes again?

ISBN: 978-0-9557078-6-5   **£7.99**

DEAD LIKE HER   **Linda Regan**
It seems like a straightforward case for newly promoted DCI Paul Banham and DI Alison Grainger: the victims all bore an uncanny resemblance to Marilyn Monroe. But they soon unearth connections with drug-running and people-trafficking.

ISBN: 978-09557078-8-9   **£7.99**

THE FALL GIRL   **Kaye C Hill**
Accidental P I Lexy Lomax is investigating a suspicious death in a decidedly spooky cottage. Kinky, her truculent chihuahua, hates the place, but he seems to be in a minority.

She's hindered by her obnoxious ex, and a mysterious beast dogs her footsteps. And dark forces are running amok...

ISBN: 978-0-9557078-9-6   **£7.99**

LOVE NOT POISON   **Mary Andrea Clarke**
The death of ill-natured Lord Wickerston in a fire leads Georgiana Grey to ask questions.

Who would want Lord Wickerston dead? Does her brother Edward know more than he is willing to say? And how is the notorious highwayman known as the Crimson Cavalier involved?

ISBN: 978-0-9560566-0-3   **£7.99**

Jan 2010
14.95